D1274848

The Chain of Kindness

PAUL TUDOR JONES

August House Publishers, Inc.

LITTLE ROCK

Printed in the United States of America

10 9 8 7 6 5 4 3 2 1

LIBRARY OF CONGRESS CATALOGING-IN-PUBLICATION DATA
Jones, Paul Tudor, 1909–
The chain of kindness / Paul Tudor Jones. — 1st ed.
p.   cm.
ISBN 0-87483-197-0 (hb : alk. paper) : $21.95
ISBN 0-87483-196-2 (pbk : alk. paper) : $12.95
1. Presbyterian Church—Sermons.
2. Sermons, American. I. Title.
BX9178.J65C43 1992
252'.051—dc20   92-2289

First Edition, 1992

Executive: Ted Parkhurst
Project editor: Jan Cottingham
Design director: Ted Parkhurst
Cover design: Communication Graphics
Typography: Lettergraphics / Little Rock

A note to the reader: Most, but not all, scriptural quotations are taken from the King James Version. Any differing versions are noted only when reference is made to different translations for the sake of comparison.

This book is printed on archival-quality paper which meets the
guidelines for performance and durability of the Committee on
Production Guidelines for Book Longevity of the
Council on Library Resources.

AUGUST HOUSE, INC.   PUBLISHERS   LITTLE ROCK

For Bayard, Huddy, and George
without whose encouragement and assistance
this book would never have been published.

Contents

Foreword by James H. Daughdrill   *9*

Introduction by John M. Mulder   *11*

I. The Source of Christian Love   *13*

The Drama of the Divine Descent   *15*
The Everlasting Yea   *19*
God's Revelation and Man's Expectation   *24*
The Eternal and the Temporal   *28*
The Vanishing of the Partial   *32*

II. The Divine-Human Encounter   *37*

The Goodness of God   *39*
Saving Faith   *44*
What Does It Mean to Be Saved?   *50*
Saved From Our Self-despisings   *56*
Faith, Hope, Love   *61*
Christian Forgiveness   *66*
On Breaking Out of Jail   *73*
The Safekeeping of Jesus Christ   *78*
What Think Ye of Christ?   *83*
The Discipline of Time   *89*
The Time Factor in the Struggle of the Soul   *95*

III. Christian Love in the Family Circle   *101*

The Pattern of Family Life   *103*
Fixed Ground   *108*
The Wedding Cake   *113*
On Hanging Pictures   *117*
Where Goes Your Heart?   *122*
Where Faith Falls Short   *127*
The Words of Life   *132*

IV. *Christian Love in the Covenant Community*   *137*

The Church and Her Mission   *139*
Living in Love   *144*
The Continuing Samaritan Problem   *149*
The Private Preserve of Religion   *154*
Compromise   *160*

V. *Christian Love in the World at Large*   *165*

The Chain of Kindness   *167*
Reevaluation   *173*
Life Is Hard for the Fainthearted   *178*
Loss of Life   *182*
Lost Cool   *188*
Christian Character Judgment   *193*

VI. *Christian Love Out of This World*   *199*

Pilgrims of the Future   *201*
The Silence of God   *206*
The Eternal God   *211*
Interpreting the Times   *217*
The Secret and the Known   *221*
Your Portrait of God   *226*

Foreword

Throughout his ministry, Paul Tudor Jones has expressed a conception of theology that is desperately needed in today's society. For those grappling with their faith and with Christianity's application in their day-to-day experience, Dr. Jones provides a framework for thinking about God, about others, and about life.

This book of sermons is not only a sampling of Dr. Jones's preaching, it is a *consequence* of it. Members of his former Idlewild congregation, moved by Dr. Jones's message over the years, asked him to allow some of his sermons to be published.

Another purpose of this book of sermons is to show an alternative to the two primary shifts away from mainline Protestantism occurring in America: secularism and fundamentalism. Dr. Jones's ministry stands as a beacon of clarity pointing a wise and faithful way.

In contrast to secularism, Dr. Jones's sermons point beyond the single dimension of arid humanism, toward the spiritual wells of God's forgiveness and grace. For life to have real meaning, that meaning must have an eternal dimension.

In contrast to fundamentalism, Dr. Jones's sermons express a theology that embraces science and the use of reason and yet proclaims religion as the central purpose of life. His sermons are both pro-faith and pro-reason. They communicate that the discoveries of science are not a threat to faith but a revelation of God's design for the material part of the universe. They send a message that the lessons of history are not to be dismissed, that utopian social schemes cannot perfect either the individual or society, and that the best and strongest elements in our democratic society are grounded in religious faith and values. For those struggling to develop a theology they can accept rationally, Dr. Jones's sermons provide answers and hope.

Paul Tudor Jones is one of the century's most knowledgeable students of the Bible and of the works of the leading Christian theologians. He is not only one of the most scholarly ministers of our time but he is unexcelled in the pastoral care he has given to members of his congregation. He has attended to the needs of thousands in distress, bringing love, hope, courage, and faith to them. He has lived a life of dedication and self-sacrifice, has constantly dealt with the tragedies of others, and through it all kept and increased his confidence in God's purposes and his love for others.

Dr. Jones's understanding of the gospel has always included its application to the urgent moral and ethical issues of the day. His stands on civil rights and moral integrity in politics made him a prophet as well as a pastor. He never flinched from taking what he understood to be the correct moral and ethical stance even when he knew it would anger those with opposing views, which it frequently did. In the 1950s and '60s, for example, he was in the forefront of Southern ministers seeking to improve the condition of African-Americans and to foster better race relations.

This is a book for the thoughtful Christian and for those whose faith is troubled by elements of doctrine that do not square with their reason and experience. The sermons are the words of a minister who combines brilliant theology, deep compassion for human suffering and human frailty, and boundless optimism. Most important, they are the words of a man who lives by the principles he preaches, a man who has dedicated his life to Christ and to others.

—James H. Daughdrill
PRESIDENT, RHODES COLLEGE
MEMPHIS, TENNESSEE

Introduction

Recent research on mainstream Protestantism in America demonstrates the new world Protestant denominations confronted in the twentieth century. During the nineteenth century, these denominations seemed to dominate both American religious life and American culture. Historians now argue that this religious and cultural establishment of Protestantism has been gradually and decisively eroded during this century. In short, Presbyterians and other mainstream Protestants can no longer claim religious supremacy or cultural dominance.

Many observers believe that this shift of power and influence has had profound theological implications for these churches. In recognizing the pluralism of American society and the diversity of Christian belief, they have become less confident of the distinctive message and traditions that they bring to an understanding of Christian faith and discipleship.

Others argue that Protestantism itself is wracked by an internecine war, pitting conservatives against moderates or liberals. Tragically, these divisions have obscured the deeper challenge of secularity in the Western world.

The central challenge now confronting mainstream Protestant churches is the reformulation of their theological identity. These denominations cannot recapture their former supremacy over American religious life, nor are they likely to be the arbiters of cultural mores and values. They must also recognize that the foremost threat to their vitality does not lie *within* but *outside* the churches. In short, they must begin to recognize that the primary religious and spiritual issue today is not heresy but idolatry—the substitution of other values and beliefs for authentic Christian faith.

Dr. Paul Tudor Jones's sermons represent the work of a preacher who has not lost either his intellectual or theological bearings amidst the swirling crosscurrents of mid- to late twentieth-century America. As you read them, I think you will recognize three consistent features. First is his emphasis upon the Bible. For Dr. Jones, the text for a sermon was not a pretext for demonstrating some moral of human life, however hopeful that might be. Rather, the Bible serves as both a critic and an insightful guide to understanding Christian interpretations of the complexity and mystery of human life.

Second, Dr. Jones *reads,* and the breadth and depth of his reading in history, theology, literature, and contemporary affairs show a mind constantly inquiring into the wide range of human experience.

Third, Dr. Jones is a preacher to people. Here you will find a gospel that lives and breathes, that finds connections with people's lives, that inspires people to witness to the love they have found in Jesus Christ—even when that application may raise troubling questions about how we behave as individuals, as families, and as a nation.

Dr. Jones is a twentieth-century apologist—someone who defends the truth of Christianity. In his last sermon as pastor of the Idlewild Presbyterian Church in Memphis, he declared that throughout his ministry, his primary purpose was "raising the God question." In these sermons, you see him raising that question again and again. What does it mean to believe in God? What does the Lord require of us? What difference will it make?

What indeed? Dr. Jones's sermons serve as a model for raising the God question for our times and in the future and will summon the church to new and deeper understandings of its faith and the call to discipleship.

—*John M. Mulder*
PRESIDENT AND PROFESSOR OF HISTORICAL THEOLOGY
LOUISVILLE PRESBYTERIAN THEOLOGICAL SEMINARY

❦   ONE   ❦

The Source of Christian Love

The Drama of the Divine Descent

"Be ye therefore followers of God, as dear children; and walk in love, as Christ also hath loved us, and hath given himself for us an offering and a sacrifice to God" (Eph. 5:1-2).

There is a creation story as told by the Ik, an African tribe of hunters and gatherers who live in the mountains near Lake Rudolph. As the anthropologist Colin Turnbull recounts it in *The Mountain People,* their creation story used to go like this: God, or as the Ik called him, Didigwari, lowered the first Ik from the sky

> on a long vine, carefully and gently, and then when he saw that it [the small mountain of Lomej] was a good place he lowered others, more and more. They were big and healthy and strong. He gave them the digging stick and told them not to kill other men, but to hunt and to live by hunting and gathering. But the men hunted and got meat and refused to give it to the women, so Didigwari became angry and cut the vine so that man could not climb back up, could never again reach him, and he went far off into the sky.

That was the creation story as the Ik used to tell it.

But when Turnbull went to live with the Ik some years ago, he found they had stopped telling their traditional creation story to their young. Turnbull discovered the Ik had become a starving tribe, and in their preoccupation with the problem of survival, they had sloughed off all the religious and social customs that had characterized their lives for centuries.

For "progress" had come to their ancestral home in Africa. The Kidepo Valley, their ancient hunting ground, had been turned into a game preserve where it was now unlawful to kill animals. The new, emerging African nations began to enforce strict boundary controls and barred the Ik from their historic cycle of wandering from Kenya through Uganda and Sudan following the herds and flocks of game. The new order in Africa proclaimed the Ik, a hunting and gathering people, were to be transformed into a farming people and live on a rocky, mountainous terrain, which has now become drought plagued. The inevitable result has been starvation for the Ik.

As the Ik slowly starved and edged toward extinction, Colin Turnbull watched the deterioration of their culture and their character. All the conventions of society, family, and government were slowly stripped away. All compassion and mutual care for each other disappeared. The very old and the very young were the first to be driven out of the family to die. A cold, cruel individualism became the dominant Icien aspect in the daily struggle to survive.

One day, when Turnbull fed a starving, blind woman abandoned by her family and neighbors, she suddenly started crying. When asked why she was crying, the woman replied that all of a sudden the strangers reminded her, as they fed her, "that there had been a time when [her own] people had helped each other, when [her own] people had been kind and good." The memory of that long gone day brought tears to her eyes.

There is a creation story that Christians have told from generation to generation. It is the story of a God who put a man and a woman in a garden paradise and then drove them out because of their disobedience. But the Christian creation story does not end there, like the Icien story of a god who cuts the vine from the sky so people cannot climb up to him anymore. Rather, the Christian story of creation and alienation moves on to a climax of reconciliation and redemption. The Christian story tells of the divine descent drama of the God who, instead of hiding himself in the sky when people sin, comes down to earth himself and in the person of his own son is killed by violent men and is raised from the dead.

The key verses of Christian Scripture echo this message of the divine descent drama: "For God so loved the world, that he gave his only begotten Son.... For God sent not his Son into the world to condemn the world; but that the world through him might be saved" (John 3:16-17). That son did not count equality with God a thing to be grasped, but "humbled himself" and was born "in the likeness of men" and "became obedient unto death, even the death of the cross" (Phil. 2:7-8).

The creeds of the Christian church enshrine the same divine descent drama. They recite the faith that "the only begotten son of God ... who for us men and for our salvation, came down from heaven" (Nicene Creed) "... suffered under Pontius Pilate, was crucified, dead, and buried; He descended into hell; the third day He rose again from the dead; He ascended into heaven, and sitteth on the right hand of God the Father Almighty; from thence He shall come to judge the quick and the dead" (Apostles' Creed).

The central sacrament of the Church reenacts this divine descent drama. This is the action of the liturgy—the God-man, the Creator-Redeemer, the God who does not hide himself in the sky from sinful man, but who comes to earth to sit at the common table of mankind and says: "This bread is my body broken for you. This cup is my blood shed for the forgiveness of the sins of the many. This do in remembrance of me, for as often as you eat this bread and drink this cup, you reenact the descent of your God from highest heaven's bliss to the lowest depth of human woe and sin."

The Apostle Paul insisted that it was not enough to tell and retell the Christian creation-redemption story, not enough to summarize it in creeds and swear belief that the story is true, not enough to be present from time to time when the story is reenacted in reverent liturgy. Saint Paul insisted the only worthy response from man to the divine descent drama was actually to get into the act and participate in the drama.

Listen: "Be ye therefore followers of God, as dear children; and walk in love, as Christ also hath loved us, and hath given himself for us an offering and a sacrifice to God." The Revised Standard Version translates "be ye followers of God" as "be imitators of God."

What can that mean for us—sinful, weak men and women, here today and gone tomorrow—to be imitators of God? We are not unfamiliar with the notion of the imitation of Christ that Thomas à Kempis made famous in his classic book of devotions. To imitate Christ for Charles M. Sheldon, the clergyman and author of *In His Steps,* meant to walk in Jesus' steps, to think at every moment, "What would Jesus do?" and do just that as nearly as we can judge from his example and his ethical teachings.

But how does one imitate God? The only possible explanation is that we are to imitate God in the divine descent drama, that we walk through the life that is given us with that love of God that Christ brought into the world regnant in our hearts. That prevenient love of God for lost sinners who do not deserve it and who can never merit it—that must become our ruling passion if we are to be imitators of God.

In Africa today there is a tribe that is slowly dying. The Ik ceased to tell their creation story when their primordial order of life was upset by change and the fight for survival stripped their lives of every other value. Deterioration, starvation, and destruction followed when they ceased to live by whatever glimmer had been given of the nature of God and his relationship to them.

What happens if we cease to tell the Christian story of the drama of the divine descent because of the changes in our lifestyle and our affluence and our technological progress? What happens if our faith in the validity of that story fails? What happens when we hesitate to get into the act as imitators of God in the drama of the divine descent?

Colin Turnbull sees striking parallels between our Western culture and the more primitive society of the Ik. Some signs of rampant self-interest indicate that we, like the Ik, are rapidly on the way out. Individualism is dominant in our culture. Turnbull asks: "What has become of the Western family? The very old and the very young are separated, but we dispose of them in homes for the aged or in day schools or summer camps instead of on the slopes of Meraniang.... Responsibility for health, education and welfare has been gladly abandoned to the state."

Turnbull discerns in the Icien tragedy that qualities sometimes held to be basic to humanity—family, cooperative sociality, belief, love, hope—are not inherent human qualities at all and that they can be dispensed with, and will be junked, when and if men and women decide they threaten survival.

But this should be no new discovery for one acquainted with the Christian story of the divine descent drama. The gospel has always maintained that men and women are lost and doomed unless God rescues them. The keeping of the love commandment—to love one's neighbor as oneself—is always, as theologian Reinhold Niebuhr perceived, "an impossible possibility." Impossible from the point of human achieving by human capabilities alone. Possible only by divine grace. Man can love his neighbor as himself only via God. When man knows himself a sinner saved by grace, with the divine love reaching down to him and through him to his neighbor, then can be woven the glorious texture of family and neighborhood and community and world order that will hold together in mutual responsibility all the children of God.

The Everlasting Yea

"The divine 'yes' has at last sounded in him, for in him is the 'yes' that affirms all the promises of God" (2 Cor. 1:19-20).

Is life saying "yes" to you or is it saying "no"? Do you feel that the world is giving you the green light or continually flashing a red stoplight to impede your progress? What about your friends, business associates, and the members of your family? Do you count on them to open new doors of opportunity and good fortune for you, or are you always expecting them to do something that will thwart your desires and undercut your well-being and spoil your pleasure? Do you feel deep down inside that the cards of life are stacked against you, or do you feel in your bones that you are a favored child of destiny?

Now, I'm trying to quiz you into giving yourself a spiritual third degree, because, as a shepherd of souls, I have learned it makes a whale of a difference with people whether they believe life is saying yes to them or whether they believe it is saying no. So I'm asking you to search your own soul with this age-old question, "Is the universe friendly?" and honestly admit to yourself whether you have been living with the faith that life is saying no to your deepest hopes and longings or saying yes. For the way you believe about this sets the tone, the temper, the shade of color to your life.

In a certain ministers' association to which I once belonged, there was one minister who always objected to whatever was proposed. No matter how meritorious the proposal might be, this man would find fault with it. "Aw, don't pay any attention to him," said the Methodist minister one day when this fellow had opposed some good, cooperative project. "Don't mind him; he was born in the objective mood." So, indeed, it seemed. But after I got to know this fellow better, I learned his repeated "noes" and persistent denials were born of a negative sort of faith; he really believed all the world was against him, saying no to him. His way of meeting such a condition was shouting back his own defiant little no.

You probably are acquainted with some folks who are hypercritical of others. They criticize the other fellow's way of doing business, his method of bringing up his children, his peculiarities of dress or speech or walk. In nine cases out of ten, such an ugly, critical spirit is born of a negative faith, a faith that the universe is unfriendly.

Supersensitive folks always expecting someone to hurt their feelings or slight them, belligerent bodies going around with chips on their shoulders and always looking for a fight—these folks are fashioned outwardly into what they are by an inward faith that the universe is unfriendly, that life is denying them their rights and privileges, that the unseen powers of the cosmos are saying no to them. So it makes a great deal of difference what you believe life is saying to you.

A host of ardent advocates can be summoned, of course, to support either contention. There is no lack of sincere souls who swear that life says no to human hopes. There was old Koheleth, the writer of our biblical book Ecclesiastes, whose expressed faith was that all man's struggle and striving are destined to futility—a brief quivering of the flesh, a palpitation of the breast, and then, nothingness. "Vanity of vanities; all is vanity," said this gloomy preacher. And Thomas Hardy, coming out of a cathedral service, shook his head in sad disapproval, saying,

> *He who breathes "All's-well" to these,*
> *Breathes no "All's-well" to me.*

Yes, some heroic, sincere souls have lived by this faith that the final, persistent, irrevocable answer to all our hopes, our loves, our dreams is a harsh no.

On the other hand, innumerable blithe spirits have lived in the confident faith that life is saying an "everlasting yea" to the deepest desires and longings of each one's soul. These spirits have lived in the sure faith that the creating intelligence that conceived the universe, the primal power that is behind and before and pulsing through the cosmos, is keenly interested in each individual's well-being and working in friendly cooperation for each soul's supreme success.

Job was like that. When he was set upon by all earth's furies and knocked to his knees by adversity, yet he cried in unconquerable optimism, "I know that my Redeemer lives, and at last he will stand upon the earth; and after my skin has been thus destroyed, then without my flesh I shall see God, whom I shall see on my side" (Job 19:25-27). Job believed there was one who, conspiring through the events and circumstances of his life, through friends and enemies, was intent on championing his best interests. Thomas Carlyle finally worked out to this same positive faith. In his *Sartor Resartus* he affirms his belief that in the deepest soul of man and in the heart of the universe there is something that says an everlasting 'yea' to man's hopes and aspirations.

Listen to this rugged Scotsman: "The Universe is not dead and demonical, a charnel-house with spectres; but god-like, and my Father's!" And this: "What is nature? … Art thou not the 'Living Garment of God?'"

This surely was the faith of Saint Paul, for to the Corinthian Christians he said of Christ, "The divine 'yes' has at last sounded in him, for in him is the 'yes' that affirms all the promises of God."

Christ then has settled the age-old argument, Paul says. Never more need any one of us be in doubt and ask, "Is the universe friendly to me?" Now we know, for the divine yes has at last sounded in Christ, for in him is the yes that affirms all the promises of God. Because of Christ we can live in the faith that life is saying yes to us, that the universe is on our side, that God has given us the green light.

But why do we know, and how has it been proved in Christ, that life resounds with an everlasting yea for you and me? Here's why and how: Do you remember that thrilling news story of the woman who for five years scrubbed floors and saved and toiled and sacrificed until she had $5,000 that she used to accomplish the release of her son, who had been imprisoned on false charges? Her love and sacrifice and fidelity got him out and redeemed his life from disgrace and destruction.

Does that mother's son have any doubts now, if he ever had them, about the reality of a mother's love? Does he have any doubts about the reality of a mother's everlasting faith in her own son, even though he's a condemned outcast? Does that man have any doubts about the everlasting yea that rises in his mother's heart in response to his soul's deep desire for freedom and salvation from prison?

And how do we know that deep in the heart of the cosmos there is a booming yea to our deepest hopes and longings? Because while we were yet sinners, not falsely accused sinners, but convicted sinners, the fair son of God, Jesus Christ, who was and is the very image and essence of Eternal God, descended from his celestial glory into the suffering and tragedy and toil of our world and laid down his life freely for our sakes that we might be delivered from the prison house of sin and redeemed from our lost estate. How can any man or woman for whom Christ died ever doubt the reality of the Heavenly Father's love and care? In Christ the everlasting yea has at last sounded with unmistakable clarity, for in him are all the promises of God affirmed to us. Now we know that God's universe is saying yes to our deepest hopes and longings. We can live by that positive faith.

The trouble with so many of us is that we have not ourselves given an affirmative answer to Christ. We haven't said yes to the Divine Yes. So the universe, our world, seems always to be denying our hopes and dreams.

We are like the people in Plato's myth of the cave who lived subterranean lives, whose ideas of reality were derived entirely from the distorted shadows they saw moving grotesquely upon the cave walls. In the Stygian darkness where they continuously dwelt, these cave dwellers saw nothing directly. For now and then, whenever a man or a dog or a horse in the upper, outside world would pass before the mouth of their cave, high above their heads, they would see reflected on the opposite wall the creature's misshapen shadow and conclude that men and dogs and horses were just like those shadows. When brought up to the earth's surface and out in the bright light of the sun and shown real men and dogs and horses, these cave dwellers realized how far wrong they had been in their ideas of reality.

How many of us have lived in the thick, spiritual darkness of this world and accepted as real the distorted shadows of this world's false values? How often have we given our soul's assent, not to truth, but to a poor, misshapen shadow of truth? It has been too painful for us to come up into the realm of eternal reality and look at all things in the bright light of Christ's life. We have had false, misshapen ideas of what our real wants and needs and hopes are. That's why the universe seemed to say no to us. We have not been willing to say yes in our own souls to the Divine Yes, so it has seemed to us that life has been saying no to our ambitions and aspirations.

We need to realize, as Carlyle says in *Sator Resartus,* that for man there is something "Higher than Love of Happiness: he can do without Happiness, and instead thereof find Blessedness.... Love not Pleasure; love God. This is the Everlasting Yea, wherein all contradiction is solved; wherein whoso walks and works, it is well with him."

In Tolstoy's familiar story "Where Love Is, There God Is Also," Martin, the shoemaker, is miserable every day, thinking always of the great weight of sorrow he must bear. First he loses his dear wife. Then the little son whom he has idolized grows sick and swiftly passes away. Martin becomes inconsolable. He murmurs against God. His life is so empty he prays for death and reproaches God for taking the life of his only son instead of himself, an old man. Then one day, an ancient holy man comes to see Martin. The shoemaker begins to complain to his guest of his great sorrow, saying that all he wishes for is death.

> "You should not speak like that," said the old man. "God saw fit that your son should die and that you should live. Therefore it must be better so. If you despair it is because you have wished to live too much for your own pleasure."
>
> "For what then should I live?" asked Martin.
>
> "For God alone," replied the holy man. "It is He who gave you life, and therefore it is He for whom you should live. When you live for Him you will cease to grieve, and your trials will become easy to bear."
>
> "But how can I live for God?" asked the shoemaker.
>
> "Christ has shown us the way," said the old man. "Can you read?" he asked. "If so, buy a Testament and study it. You will learn there how to live for God."
>
> So Martin began to read, and the more he read, the more clearly did he discover and understand what God required of him and in what way he could live for God, so that his heart grew ever lighter and lighter.

The Divine Yes has at last sounded in Christ. But we must give the assent of our souls to the Everlasting Yea of God in Christ before the Divine Yes can sound for us, affirming all the promises of God to us in our own hearts.

God's Revelation and Man's Expectation

"Therefore the Lord himself shall give you a sign; Behold, a virgin shall conceive, and bear a son, and shall call his name Immanuel" (Isa. 7:14).

Whenever we stand on the threshold of a new adventure, we look eagerly for some sign of what the future may hold for us. A bride and groom would like a more concrete sign than that provided by the old superstition that their wedding day weather foretells their future. What more solid indications do they have for a blessed marriage than a bright, sunshiny wedding day?

As glad as we all are to get from our friends their best wishes for our health and happiness in the New Year, we had much rather have some sure sign of what the year 1991 holds for us.

All of us, right now, as the old year ends and the new begins, are eagerly looking for some sign of what we may expect from that confrontation of armies in Kuwait and Saudi Arabia. Will there be war or is there some sign of a peaceful resolution before the January 15 deadline?

We have read in our Scripture lessons from Isaiah's prophecy and from Saint Luke's Gospel about this very problem of human expectations and God's revelations.

The prophet Isaiah met King Ahaz at the aqueduct when Jerusalem was under threat of siege by enemy armies. The troubled king had gone to inspect the great pipeline of his city's water supply. One of the king's chief concerns for the immediate future was maintaining a steady flow of water into the city should the siege occur.

At the aqueduct Isaiah, the prophet of God, met the troubled king and announced to him, "Fear not, be quiet, the city will be safe."

Presumably the king listened with a quizzical look to the prophet's calm assurance about the future welfare of the city, for next the prophet said to the king, "Well, go ahead and ask for a sign from the Lord your God, that this security will be yours." But the king refused to ask for the sign on the pious ground that such would be tempting the Lord.

Then it was that the prophet spoke his famous, never-to-be-forgotten words, words picked up later in the Gospels and enshrined ever since in the glad Christmas story: "Therefore the Lord himself shall give you a sign; Behold, a virgin shall conceive, and bear a son, and shall call his name Immanuel," which means "God with us."

Is it impious or too superstitious for people concerned about their future or their country's destiny or the safety of their loved ones or the peace of the world to ask for a sign of what that future holds? The word of Scripture is that God, on his own initiative, has given people a sign. This is the meaning of revelation. This is the heart of the Christmas tidings of great joy: "For unto you is born this day in the city of David a Saviour, which is Christ the Lord. And this shall be a sign unto you; Ye shall find the babe wrapped in swaddling clothes, lying in a manger."

The great star in the sky was a sign. The singing of the heavenly choirs the shepherds heard was a sign. The inner consciousness of the wise men directing their search was a sign. The preaching of John the Baptist to herald the Messiah's coming was a sign. All these were signs of God to men about the future purposes of God in human history, that they might base their expectations solidly on God's revelation.

Now, the heart of the sign of God's revelation for men is the birth of a child. The promised sign of Isaiah to King Ahaz is not without its mysterious connotations. Certainly the prophet meant in this immediate context to assure the Jerusalem king and his threatened subjects that God's solution for their pressing problem of the moment was to be God's gift of a unique person, of the royal house, soon to be born. There is nothing here in Isaiah's assurance to Ahaz either to confirm or to deny the virgin birth stories of Jesus in the Gospels.

How many times the Scriptures show God solving the problems of his hard-pressed people in a baby's birth. God sends the needed person to be born at the right time, at the right place.

When God's people suffered slavery in Egypt and their future seemed hopeless, a child was born and providentially preserved from death in the very household of Pharaoh, the destroyer of the Hebrew children. Grown to manhood, Moses came forth as his people's deliverer and law giver and shepherd to guide them safely through their wilderness wanderings.

When later in their Promised Land God's people were torn by envious divisions and tribal warfare, God solved their problem by the birth of another providentially provided leader. Samuel, who was born of elderly parents past the natural time in life when people have children, came in response to prayer and was dedicated to the service of God. Grown to manhood, Samuel judged his people in righteousness and restored national unity.

Yes, at the heart of all human expectation and hope is the miracle of childbirth. "Therefore the Lord himself shall give you a sign; Behold, a virgin shall conceive, and bear a son, and shall call his name Immanuel." For this is God's way of coming to his people to meet their needs recurrently whenever the children of God are born.

But the ultimate and larger meaning of the prophet Isaiah's promise of God's sign in the birth of a coming child is more explicitly revealed two chapters later in his recorded prophecy in chapter 9, verse 6: "For unto us a child is born, unto us a son is given: and the government shall be upon his shoulder: and his name shall be called Wonderful, Counsellor, The mighty God, The everlasting Father, The Prince of Peace."

There is no evidence that Isaiah foresaw the coming of Christ exactly as the Gospels were to record three hundred years later. What the prophet did foresee in clearest detail were the cosmic dimensions of the coming deliverer who could fulfill human hopes and expectations.

That coming one in Isaiah's inspired vision must be, first of all, a charismatic personality whom people will call "Wonderful" because they discover that he is firing the imagination of artists, poets, musicians, and scholars to bring forth new treasures to enrich the lives of all God's children.

He must also be called "Counsellor" because his wisdom will lead people to fashion their relationships with each other in wider and warmer measures of justice, mercy, and righteousness.

That coming one must also be truly called "The mighty God" because people will find in him, not only a great humanitarian, but far more, satisfying their deepest religious yearnings for a companion God.

But even more, Isaiah's coming one must be worthy to be called "The everlasting Father," because with him people will have assurance that their future well-being is in his capable keeping.

Finally, he must be called "The Prince of Peace," for he must be able to give to the hearts of all people everywhere a sense of brotherhood. No dealing with our tomorrows that does not touch our bleeding and blasted relationships will be redemptive. "Let there be peace on earth, and let it begin with me." The only real and lasting peace must begin within the heart that has been reconciled to God and others by a divine redeemer.

No man has filled out in their uttermost meaning all these Isaianic names: Wonderful, Counsellor, mighty God, everlasting Father, Prince of Peace. No man, but one—and his name is Jesus.

He is God's revelation for our calm expectation for whatever the future holds. Let us go confidently into that future with our hearts in his keeping.

"Now unto him that is able to keep you from falling, and to present you faultless before the presence of his glory with exceeding joy, to the only wise God our Saviour, be glory and majesty, dominion and power, both now and ever. Amen" (Jude 1:24-25).

The Eternal and the Temporal

"Glory to God in the highest, and on earth peace, good will toward men" (Luke 2:14).

That philosophizing stage manager in Thornton Wilder's play *Our Town* says at the opening of the play's last act: "We all know that something is eternal. And it ain't houses and it ain't names, and it ain't earth, and it ain't even the stars ... everybody knows in their bones that something is eternal, and that something has to do with human beings.... There's something way down deep that's eternal about every human being."

And this something way down deep in every human being that is eternal is what the Christmas story is all about.

Perhaps as you've read the Christmas story you've been struck with its strange mixture of the temporal and the eternal. The details of the temporal are clear and rough and tough enough. A government order is issued concerning the payment of taxes on a specified date. Payment must be made, not just by mailing a check to the revenue official, but by making a trip to one's hometown and there enrolling for taxing. And the journey must be made on a given date, no matter if it inconveniently coincides with the anticipated delivery date of a child. And shepherds are working the night shift on the designated date. And at the crowded inn, where no reservations have been made, there is no more room. And the baby is born, from harsh necessity, in a stable.

And suddenly the eternal breaks through into the temporal. In the midst of the mother's birth pains, and on the fields where the cold, uninteresting night watch of the shepherds takes place, and in the unpleasant circumstances of the tax-paying pilgrimage, the heavenly chorus sounds forth triumphantly: "Glory to God in the highest, and on earth peace, good will toward men." And the eternal enters time. And God becomes man.

Certainly from the Christmas story it is clear enough that on that night at least the eternal is not something far off and removed from the temporal, but rather all mixed up with it.

But what is the nature of this something way down deep in human beings that is eternal? Christian theologians across the centuries have given an oversimple and much less than satisfying answer by simply calling this something the immortal soul of man. But what is the soul? What are the distinctive functions of the soul apart from the activities of the body, the mind, and the emotions?

Is the soul that which makes men and women capable of reverence, of feeling awe before the presence of beauty and greatness? For Mahatma Gandhi, Albert Schweitzer, Mother Teresa, and the ever-increasing number of environmentalists in our time, the human capacity for reverence for all of life is manifestation enough of this eternity set in human nature.

Some students of the works of Andrew Wyeth trace the secret of his greatness—his capacity to thrust through to the soul, to move the viewers of his paintings—to the overwhelming reverence he has for the simplicities of life. "You almost have to be on your knees before the thing you are painting," says Wyeth, "or the thing just doesn't come off." Is reverence the characteristic motion of that something that is eternal in human beings?

Or is the characteristic motion of the soul the outgoing of love toward others? Is this what transforms the temporal into the eternal? Is this the open sesame to throw wide the dark gates of our earthly prison so that the heavenly light may burst in?

The probation officer for young Lee Harvey Oswald when he was a chronic truant from school in New York said of the boy, "I get the feeling that his mother was so wrapped up in her own problems she never saw her son's problems.... I got the feeling that what the boy needed most was someone who cared. He was just a small, lonely, withdrawn kid who looked to me like he was heading for trouble."

Can it be that this thing that is eternal, way down deep in human beings, is that endowment in human nature that needs both to express and to receive love? Saint Paul must have thought so, or he would not have written as he did in 1 Cor. 13. And George Macdonald, the Scottish poet and novelist, has defined the very essence of temporality as being "always at the mercy of one self-centered passion or another." And if this is the essence of temporality, surely the nature of the eternal is just the opposite—to be delivered from self-centered passions by outgoing love.

In *The Brothers Karamazov*, Dostoevski pictures the rich and pampered woman coming with troubled soul to the holy man and asking how she can regain her faith in God and her belief in life beyond death. And the holy man tells her that if she would regain her faith in God and immortality, she must perform an act of unselfish love.

And if we have become so mixed up in the temporal that we have lost touch with the eternal and can't find it, the Christmas directive for each one of us is to look where the gospel story points for the eternal in the midst of the temporal.

The first focal point is, of course, the newborn babe. In a letter to his brother, Vincent van Gogh told of making studies to paint the portrait of the Roulin baby, the child of his friend the postman. And in the letter van Gogh observed, "A child in the cradle, if you watch it at leisure, has the infinite in its eyes."

That something which is eternal and deep in human beings is nearest the surface in children, even in their eyes; and busy bishops and business moguls and great ladies, if they are truly great, know this and warm their hearts at the altar fires of children's prayers. And one glory of the Christmas season is that it brings us all close again to the eternal in the heart of childhood. Phillips Brooks, the beloved Episcopal bishop, has in one of his Christmas poems this couplet:

> *The world has grown old with its burden of care*
> *But at Christmas it always is young.*

Then again, if we would find the eternal in the midst of the temporal, the Christmas story directs us to recapture the glory of the family circle. The gospel story reveals the holy family as each member is loyal to his or her relationship responsibilities.

A Dallas, Texas, minister told about asking people he encountered in the Christmas season, "What do you want most for Christmas?" He got some amazing answers. While everyone was making Christmas lists and buying jackets and toys and perfumes to give, here are some of the things people said they most wanted to receive: One woman said that more than anything else in the world she wanted a word from her husband that he still loved her and that he would give up the other woman. A boy told him that he wanted a chance to talk with his father, but his father was always too busy. A husband said that more than anything else he wanted to see a smile on his wife's face and to hear her laugh again.

Marshall Fishwick, in a December 21, 1963, article in the *Saturday Review,* observed that the real service of the existentialist philosophers in our American culture a few years ago was that they were pointing out that the real enemy in life is inauthenticity, pomposity, abstractions. The threat to our life is our deep involvement with the temporalities and our imperviousness to the eternal in the midst of time. "We are serious about trivialities (electric toothbrushes, sports cars, hair-dos), trivial about reality (life, encounter, death).... We accord ultimate meaning to the useful, but refuse to ask: useful for what?" Fishwick writes.

And the darkest depth of our existentialist tragedy is that we can become so remote and inauthentic in our most intimate relationships as to lose the eternal in the midst of time.

But, of course, the greatest glory of the Christmas story is that it links the past, the present, and the future—the near and the far—in this eternal soul stuff of reverential love. The babe born in Bethlehem is the long-expected King who has come to establish his rule of love in human hearts and who will come at the end of time to judge the world in righteousness. And the canon of his judgment is just the question, "Have you loved all your fellow men, my brethren, with the same love with which I have loved you?"

The Vanishing of the Partial

"The partial vanishes when wholeness comes" (1 Cor. 13:10).

Recently I ran out of second sheets for making carbon copies of my typewritten letters. The clerk at the stationery store where I usually go to purchase paper and refills for my ballpoint pen informed me that the store no longer stocked tissue-thin second sheets. "Most people nowadays," she said (a bit condescendingly to an out-of-date old fogy, I thought), "most people nowadays use copy machines like Xerox for their duplicating. We don't have any second sheets for making carbon copies."

I have a Mississippi friend who is an inveterate coffee drinker. For years he has traveled the whole state extensively. Recently he was bemoaning the fact that so many of the small towns along the highways are drying up, and shops and stores, particularly the restaurants and cafes where he used to stop for a cup of coffee, are all going out of business, and he was having a dickens of a time trying to find a place to get a decent cup of coffee.

No doubt you have been surprised on occasion by how some things that you had come to take for granted would always be there at your beck and call have ceased to be or mysteriously passed away.

Saint Paul, in evaluating with his friends of the Corinthian church some of their most highly prized spiritual gifts, sadly observed that with the passage of time, most of those spiritual gifts would vanish and pass away. He mentions three that would be outmoded, superseded, and supplanted: knowledge, prophecy, and speaking with tongues.

How quickly knowledge of one age fades away. Who knows this better than those of us who received our education before the age of computers engulfed us? Heraclitus, the Greek philosopher, taught his pupils this lesson by reminding them that they could never step into the same river twice, for the waters flowed on. So is it with the rapidly flowing stream of knowledge.

Prophecy, the capacity of one person to speak for God in that person's own age and generation—as crucial and indispensable a function as that can be—is nevertheless to cease, for the predictive elements in prophecy are ultimately all fulfilled, and the declarative elements in prophecy are ultimately unnecessary when history has finally run its course.

Speaking with tongues, either ecstatic speech or oratory, finally ceases. Even the eloquence of a Winston Churchill or a Franklin Roosevelt or a Ronald Reagan, our "great communicator," finally becomes dated and outmoded, losing its fire and power to persuade.

Man's disposition to see all things in flux and nothing as permanent or enduring is the most devastating temper of our times.

But Saint Paul says in this same paragraph of his Corinthian letter that there are three things that remain permanent in this world and the next: faith, hope, and love, and that the greatest of these is love. "Love will never come to an end," says Paul. "Prophecies will cease; tongues of ectasy will fall silent; knowledge will vanish. For our knowledge and our prophecy alike are partial, and the partial vanishes when wholeness comes" (1 Cor. 13:8-10). So Saint Paul urged his Christian friends in Corinth to hold on to love, time and eternity's greatest imperishable reality.

However, we need to be sure we understand the terms Saint Paul is using, lest we put our confidence of permanency in a very perishable commodity. Communication with words alone is a tricky business.

I heard an engineer remark that he and others of his profession had sat in a meeting and listened to specifications and directions for a contractual design. He came away from the meeting, made some calculations based on the words he had heard there—or thought he had heard—and then, the very next day, called a fellow engineer in another city who had been at the same meeting. He discovered in a few moments' conversation that the same words heard by himself and his friend had conveyed entirely different meanings to each of them.

When we listen to Paul's discussion of love, what does that word mean to us? The Greek word for love in Paul's day had come to refer almost wholly to sexual passion. That old Greek word for love, *eros,* lives in the word *erotic.* The Greeks had done to their word for love very much what TV and X-rated movies and Hugh Hefner and Larry Flint and the Madison Avenue soap salesmen have done to our word *love.* In our time the word love has become so sexed-up and sentimentalized, so perfumed and debauched, that it doesn't represent anything permanent. It fades faster than an early spring flower.

First-century Christians had almost to coin a new word for the love—that lasting commodity, the imperishable, perfect reality—Paul describes in 1 Cor. 13. "What was needed was a word that would express the Christian experience of the love of God himself, the love that is outpoured even on the loveless and the unlovable, the love that sent God's son to suffer and die with us and for us," Kenneth J. Foreman says in *The Layman's Bible Commentary.*

And the Greek word for this love, *agape,* whatever it may be in theory or story, is unintelligible without the deed of love. Frank Chamberlin Porter, in his remarkable book *The Mind of Christ in Paul,* says that in 1 Cor. 13 Paul is describing in a spiritual portrait the features of the divine love as revealed in Jesus Christ, though the name of Jesus is never used.

And in the 13th chapter of John's Gospel the deed of divine love in Jesus Christ is chronicled. Listen:

> Now before the feast of the passover, when Jesus knew that his hour was come that he should depart out of this world unto the Father, having loved his own which were in the world, he loved them unto the end.
>
> And supper being ended, the devil having now put into the heart of Judas Iscariot, Simon's son, to betray him;
>
> Jesus knowing that the Father had given all things into his hands, and that he was come from God, and went to God;
>
> He riseth from supper, and laid aside his garments; and took a towel, and girded himself.
>
> After that he poureth water into a bason, and began to wash the disciples' feet, and to wipe them with the towel wherewith he was girded.

And for us, the permanent and not passing quality, this complete and not partial reality, designated love, the love of God in Christ to be understood and experienced by people today, requires not only their hearing of it, but also seeing, feeling, and witnessing its fresh incarnation.

I took the elevator at the eleventh floor of a hospital. At the eighth floor the elevator stopped, and two young men in shirt sleeves got on. One was tall and talked with a sharp, clear, Midwestern, nasal tone to his shorter companion who responded in a mumbled Mississippi or Tennessee accent. I thought the mumbler was saying, "I'm going down." He was standing right beside me, and there seemed to be no significance in the statement "I'm going down" (if that was what he was saying), for we were all "going down" on that elevator. His companion made no comment. But a heavy, middle-aged woman across the elevator who could see the young man's face as he spoke later told us, after the accident occurred, that she realized he meant something different when he said, "I'm going down." For in just a few seconds, after he mumbled, the elevator stopped at the sixth floor, and as the door opened automatically, the young man lurched forward and fell prostrate across the threshold, cutting his mouth and loosening his teeth. It later developed that the two young men had just given blood. The shorter one began to feel faint and knew it. He gave verbal warning to his companion. He was really asking for help. But neither his friend nor any of the others on the crowded elevator grasped his meaning, only the woman who was looking straight into his face and saw his contorted expressions. She understood that his words "I'm going down" meant "I'm going to faint."

What hope the world is taking now that the leaders of the world's two most powerful nations are beginning to meet face to face, eyeball to eyeball, to exchange, not only words and challenges and bluffs and threats and ideas, but also emotions common to every human heart, emotions like hope and fear, and pride and ambition and anxiety and—is it too much to expect?—love.

Dr. Halford E. Luccock, in his book *Preaching Values in the Epistles of Paul,* says Dr. J. Robert Oppenheimer, the atomic scientist, urged "'world strugglers' to love one another as the only hope of the world. All will pass away except love." Luccock describes Oppenheimer closing an address with these words: "This cannot be an easy life. We shall have a rugged time of it to keep our minds open and to keep them deep, to keep our sense of beauty, and our ability to make it, and our occasional ability to see it, in places remote and strange and unfamiliar. But this is, as I see it, the condition of man; and in this condition we can help, because we can love one another."

What is needful for every one of us is that we make the conscious choice to live every moment of our lives under the dominant control of the perfect and the permanent rather than under the spell of that which is partial and imperfect. This means that we must make room for the mind of Christ to take over, for the love of God in Christ Jesus to motivate all we say and do.

For let us be well assured that whatever apparent triumphs and successes we may achieve under the spell of the partial, imperfect, and evil motives will soon perish, while the smallest and most insignificant act motivated by the love of God such as Jesus Christ revealed shall remain steadfast forever.

❦   TWO   ❦

The Divine-Human Encounter

The Goodness of God

"For the Lord is good; his mercy is everlasting; and his truth endureth to all generations" (Ps. 100:5).

Do you remember any of those fairy stories you listened to in your childhood about someone who had been transformed into a beast and could regain his human shape only through somebody else's love?

Certainly you recall the Grimm Brothers fairy tale about the frog prince. A wicked witch had turned a handsome young prince into a loathsome frog, and the spell could be broken and he returned to his human shape only by the love of a beautiful princess who would allow him to sit beside her and eat from her plate and sleep in her bed. And when this incredible love had at last been bestowed, the miracle of restoration to his lost human shape took place.

How fanciful is the fairy tale and yet how true to human experience! How many times has the bewitched spirit of some person under the evil spell of selfishness or greed or lust or violence or perverted emotions made that person act like a loathsome beast until at last a pure, sweet love, entirely unmerited, comes into that life and rescues it from beastliness. And behold!

the lost human shape is restored in the image of the handsome prince or princess that had always remained imprisoned in the human heart.

This, of course, is what the Christian gospel is all about—transformation through love. Yes, the gospel tells the story of the Eternal God who is holy and righteous and just, without any moral imperfection, who nevertheless has moved beyond the limits and demands of meting out justice to mankind, and by his love has rescued loathsome, sinful, unworthy creatures from their beastliness, broken the spell of sin, and restored them to their lost human shape.

"But God commendeth his love toward us, in that, while we were yet sinners, Christ died for us.... For all have sinned, and come short of the glory of God.... All we like sheep have gone astray.... For God so loved the world, that he gave his only begotten Son, that whosoever believeth in him should not perish, but have everlasting life."

Do you remember how Barbra Streisand used to sing, "He touched me. He touched me"? We have all listened to the television advertisement for the telephone company that says, "Reach out and touch someone." Well, that is the essence of the gospel. That is the meaning of the Incarnation. The Eternal God in Christ became man for us and for our salvation. He reached out and touched us in healing, redeeming, transforming love, touched our loathsome-ness, the beastliness of sin, and lo! the lost image of God in our hearts burst back into reality.

An old man had been an indigent in and out of a charity hospital for years. He had received treatment from the generations of interns there who practiced on him and his infirmities. He had become an unlovely, wasted, almost inhuman shell of a man.

Finally the day came when one of those interns was established in his own practice, and the same old man who had frequented the charity hospital entered the young physician's office and said, "I want you to be my doctor. I've come into an inheritance, and now I can pay, and I want you to be my doctor."

"But why have you chosen me?" asked the young physician. "So many of us treated you. Why me?"

"Yes," said the little man with the bent back, "all of you did and all of you were helpful and kind to me, but you were the only one who helped me with my coat."

The warmth that included treating him as a person, that reached out a hand and touched him as another human being—this was help and healing for the whole man. This established the relationship of persons that could not be broken.

This is a poor illustration, but nevertheless a faltering reach in the direction of the eternal reality over which the gospel exults. God in Christ touched us; his love bestowed broke the evil spell of sin that had enslaved us in beastliness, restoring our lost humanity and lifting us into a relationship of persons with God.

When the Bible speaks of the goodness of God, it usually refers to one of two things: providence or grace.

Providence is the goodness of God to all the human family: God's making the rain fall on the just and the unjust; his feeding the birds of the air; his clothing the lilies of the field; his ordering the natural world to bless all human life, whether people are conscious of God or not.

But grace is that goodness of God bestowed upon unworthy, sinful people that involves their consciousness of being made right with God, all the while knowing that they have not merited this goodness.

In Psalm 103, the Psalmist could see the goodness of God at work at many places in his life: providentially healing all his diseases, redeeming his life from destruction (snatching him from perils on land and sea), satisfying his mouth with good things (treasures of the earth in material prosperity, intellectual pursuits, and spiritual riches), so that his life was "renewed like the eagle's."

But see what the Psalmist puts at the summit of the mountain of God's mercies: the forgiveness of his sins. He mentions that first: "Who forgiveth all thine iniquities; who healeth all thy diseases; who redeemeth thy life from destruction." But he can't leave it. Over and over again in his hymn of thanksgiving he comes back to it. The Lord "hath not dealt with us after our sins; nor rewarded us according to our iniquities.... As far as the east is from the west, so far hath he removed our transgressions from us." His soul is obsessed with the unbelievable goodness of God in forgiving his multitude of sins, and he comes back to it over and over. This forgiveness is the goodness of God that is all grace.

Dag Hammarskjöld in his book *Markings* says of forgiveness: "Forgiveness is the answer to the child's dream of a miracle by which what is broken is made whole again, what is soiled is again made clean. The dream explains why we need to be forgiven, and why we must forgive. In the presence of God, nothing stands between Him and us—we *are* forgiven. But we *cannot* feel His presence if anything is allowed to stand between ourselves and others."

Saint Paul wrote to the Corinthian Christians, "I would not that ye should be ignorant, how that all our fathers were under the cloud, and all passed through the sea; and were all baptized unto Moses in the cloud and in the sea; and did all eat the same spiritual meat; and did all drink the same spiritual drink.... But with many of them God was not well pleased: for they were overthrown in the wilderness" (1 Cor. 10:1-5).

What was the difference? Why were not all who were the recipients of the goodness of God both in providence and grace brought through to the Promised Land? Here is why: They differed in the use they made of the cloud and the sea and the meat and the drink. As Paul Scherer, the Lutheran pastor and scholar, pointed out in his book *Event in Eternity,* some of them acted as if they were singled out for the purpose of enjoying the luxury of the divine favor, while others understood that they were being equipped for taking part in the divine mission.

Suppose, Scherer asks, "the crew of a ship sent to carry provisions to a sick and starving community should on their voyage forget their purpose? Suppose they drank the wine and ate the bread themselves as if the whole cargo had been stored on board for their sole comfort and satisfaction?"

When John Denver was in Memphis for a concert, he said in an interview that his principal reason for coming was not to sing, but to stir up public support for a campaign against world hunger.

What is your role and mine now—yes, and what is the role of our nation—in this crucial time of the transition of whole nations from communism to democracy? In a time when people in underdeveloped nations are starving and overburdened with debt? At this point in our life's voyage, what is our purpose? Are we feasting at the bounteous captain's table on the Good Ship American Way of Life, gorging ourselves on our plentiful provisions, acting as if the whole adventure were designed as our personal pleasure cruise, while indeed and in truth God's purpose in outfitting and provisioning and dispatching our ship is for bringing food—material and spiritual—to a starving world?

Pope John Paul II, when visiting a poverty-stricken slum in Rio de Janeiro, was so overcome by the human suffering he saw there he took off his heavy, golden fisherman's ring, the symbol of his office as Christ's regent on earth, and gave it to the parish priest to purchase relief for that wretched congregation. What an amazing sensitivity to the biblical understanding of the goodness of God in providence and grace.

On another trip Pope John Paul II visited Africa, and millions of people gathered to greet him everywhere he went. Christianity, you know, is growing now in Africa faster than anywhere else in the world. *Time* magazine, in its May 12, 1980, issue, says that in 1960 Africa was thirty percent Christian, while in 1980 the continent was nearly half Christian.

Why this growth in Africa, of all places, where white men's governments and business interests have exploited blacks for centuries? One would think that with the rejection of Western colonialism among the people of

Africa during the last three decades would go also a rejection of Western religions. But such is not the case. Rather, Christianity has kept on growing steadily. Why? The reason, say the Africans themselves, is that the Christian missionaries when they came fed the starving, healed the sick, taught the young and the old to read and how to improve their farming. In short, they brought love, expressed in sharing the best blessings, both material and spiritual, that God had showered on them.

Every Sunday when we come to church for worship we bring our offerings. We stand and sing, "Praise God from whom all blessings flow," and we pray a prayer dedicating our gifts and ourselves to the service of God's will in the world. How many times do we ask ourselves in that moment of prayerful dedication: Why is God, from whom all blessings flow, pouring out such an abundance on me? What purpose does the great, good, loving Heavenly Father have in mind by this miracle of grace he has wrought in my life, healing all my diseases, redeeming my life from destruction, forgiving all my iniquities, filling my mouth with good things, and crowning my days with his loving kindness and tender mercies? Why?

Is God nudging me to contemplate some grateful expression for his amazing grace in my life? Is he hoping against hope that I will wake up from my silly, selfish daydreams and see what my life is really all about? That God has provisioned and dispatched me, not on a pleasure cruise to consume in self-indulgence all he has put aboard, but in his infinite mercy he has loaded me down with life-giving supplies to sustain the bodies and souls of others so I may embark on a rescue mission of divine origin and universal dimensions.

Saving Faith

"This is the victory that overcometh the world, even our faith" (1 John 5:4).

Salvation means different things to different people at different times. To the one survivor of that Turkish plane that crashed yesterday morning, salvation meant a miraculous deliverance from death when his sixty-two fellow passengers instantly perished and he walked out of the crumpled and burning fuselage without scratch or scorch, saying, "I don't know why I'm still alive. It's a miracle."

Salvation to Gerald Kosh, that young American who was captured last week by the Chinese on Paracel Island, would certainly mean release from a Red Chinese military prison.

Salvation means different things to different people at different times. So also, saving faith is a many-sided reality with rich rewards for each of us at different levels of faith. Saint Paul in his writings tells what he discovered from his own experience about the glorious, multifaceted, saving thing faith is. Paul distinguishes among faith as conviction of the reality of the unseen world, and faith as trust in the promises of God, and faith as surrender to Jesus

Christ. For each level of faith, Paul says, there is a great and rewarding salvation.

First of all, faith is a conviction of the reality of the unseen world. "We walk by faith, not by sight," wrote the apostle to his fellow Christians at Corinth. Some people guide their course through their earthly existence only by what they can see and hear, by what they can reach out and touch and grasp. For them this is the only real world. Materialism is their philosophy, expediency their chart and compass.

But others insist there is another world, just as real, though unseen, of spiritual and moral values such as mercy, justice, truth, love, and honesty, and that these are the trustworthy channel-markers by which the voyage of life should be charted. "Sight is the physical vision of material things; faith is the insight which apprehends the realities of the spirit—goodness, truth, love," *The Interpreter's Bible* says.

Many years ago the Frenchman Alexis de Tocqueville came to this country hoping to find the source of America's greatness and genius. Upon his return to his native shores he wrote:

> I sought for the greatness and genius of America in her commodious harbors and her ample rivers; and it was not there. I sought for the greatness and genius of America in her fertile fields and boundless forests; and it was not there. I sought for the greatness and genius of America in her rich mines and vast world commerce; and it was not there. I sought for the greatness and genius of America in her democratic Congress and her matchless constitution; and it was not there. Not until I went into the churches of America and heard pulpits aflame with righteousness did I understand the secret of her genius and power. America is great because she is good, and if ever America ceases to be good, America will cease to be great.

Yes, this is one thing faith is, the assurance of the reality and worth of the unseen spiritual world and allegiance to it. And this is a saving faith for mankind. But what sort of salvation does it bring?

Faith like this saves a man from an empty materialism, from coming down to the end of life and having to see the material things go and realize too late he has put his trust and his heart in fake and perishable commodities.

Faith like this also saves a man from fear; if he is wedded to the eternal verities and courageously living for them, then he is unafraid of the partial powers of a lost world.

John F. Kennedy in his book *Profiles in Courage* told the story of how Sen. George Norris of Nebraska led the fight in 1917 to kill the armed ship bill, believing as he did that its passage would plunge our nation into war with Germany. As a result of his efforts, Norris was denounced all over the country as a traitor. Nebraska, his home state, was up in arms against him. He decided to go back to Omaha to defend his action. Friends advised him to give up the idea. Feeling is too high against you, they said. No one will come to hear you tell your story. If ever you should gather a crowd, they will be hostile. Don't go, they warned. But George Norris went anyway. He rented his own hall. When not one of his friends dared to introduce him, he went alone to stand before the three thousand silent people who had gathered. Nervously he walked out on the platform to face them. There was no applause, no hissing, just grim faces. Quietly, slowly he began, "I have come home to tell you the truth," and the audience burst into applause.

Life will not always give us the accolade of the public's approval for our espousal of truth, honesty, and justice, but it will give us the inner assurance of being in harmony with eternal righteousness, and that is more lastingly satisfying than the thundering cheers of a mighty multitude. It is a saving faith.

But faith, Christian saving faith, is more than this. Saint Paul speaks of faith as a trust in the promises of God. This is faith that goes a step further, you see. It embodies not only a conviction that the spiritual world is real, that truth, justice, mercy, purity, honesty are genuine commodities and real and solid as coal and iron, gold and diamonds, real estate and automobiles; it not only holds that these spiritual qualities are of the very nature of God and hence everlasting; but it goes one step further and believes that God is not just an oblong blur, a nebulous mass of moral statutes, but a person with a father's face of love whose gracious promises can be relied upon with implicit trust. Such faith builds its world, its home, its profession, on these blessed promises of God rather than the hope, promises, and collateral of a lost world.

For Saint Paul, the classic example of the man with this kind of faith was Abraham. God promised Abraham that he would give him a family and make of his direct descendants a nation as numerous as the stars in the heavens or the sands of the sea and through Abraham and his descendants bring a great spiritual blessing to the whole world.

This promise of God Abraham believed, he trusted; in fact, he launched his life upon it, even though the most important facts in Abraham's situation from the human point of view at the time God gave his promise were Abraham's own great age and his wife's sterility. Abraham and Sarah seemed to be the least likely couple in all the world to raise a family. Abraham considered these factors but did not weaken in faith. He did not shrink from facing truth even though it was forbidding and unpalatable, but neither did he allow such unwelcome truth to undermine his faith. He trusted in the promises of God. Such was the nature of Abraham's faith.

What are the promises of God to us? They are like the hairs of your head, without number. Every page of Scripture is crowded with them. You have but to open and read. But there are some more sweeping and comprehensive than others. Consider these: "I will never leave thee, nor forsake thee" "When thou passest through the waters, I will be with thee; and through the rivers, they shall not overflow thee." These are the promises of God's constant companionship with you in every experience.

Then there's this: "My grace is sufficient for thee," the promise of unlimited supplies of God's grace in every emergency. Paul, the persecuted and the prisoner, found that when he ventured his life in implicit trust in this promise, he was never disappointed. He wrote: "I have learned, in whatsoever state I am, therewith to be content. I know both how to be abased, and I know how to abound." And this: God "rescued me from so terrible a death, he rescues still, and I rely upon him for the hope that he will continue to rescue me."

Then there is God's promise that even death will be swallowed up in victory.

And what is the salvation procured by such faith? This trust in the promises of God is truly a saving faith, for it saves us from the heartbreak of loneliness, from frustration, despondency, and overanxiousness. It bestows poise on our spirits in the midst of storm.

But finally and supremely, saving faith in New Testament religion is surrender to Jesus Christ. "I am crucified with Christ," wrote Paul to the Galatians. "Nevertheless I live; yet not I, but Christ liveth in me: and the life which I now live in the flesh I live by the faith of the Son of God." The ultimate step of faith is surrender to Christ. We are not saved by acceptance of a dogma but by relationship to a person, and that relationship is established by our surrender to Jesus Christ.

We have, though, a distaste for that word *surrender,* and naturally so. It speaks of defeat or unconditional capitulation. And that is just what surrender to Jesus Christ is. Yet paradoxically, it is only through making this surrender that we have hope of achieving victory; through it lies our only chance of realizing our unique selfhood.

James Stewart of Scotland had a great sermon on the text "What God hath joined together, let not man put asunder." Of course, this text is meant primarily for the marriage ceremony, and that is where we always hear it used. But Stewart observed that there are some inseparable affinities, which God has joined together and which man puts asunder at his own peril and ruin. One of these eternal unions made in heaven by God himself is the human soul and its Savior, Jesus Christ. They were made for each other. Your soul and your Savior have been destined for each other, and you will never become what God purposed you to be until in love and surrender you are united through faith to him.

Have you ever built a boat or a little ship of your own? I shall always remember the summertime labors of some boyhood friends who had connived with me to make a boat. We got our plans, cut our lumber, assembled the parts, and caulked and painted our ship with care in the workshop far from the water. At last the boat was finished and trucked across the miles to the river. Then came the exciting moment for her launching. How often through all the days of our labors the thought had come to plague us, "Will she really float? Will she prove seaworthy and maneuverable?" I can see it as if it were day before yesterday—our little ship going down the improvised skids from the truck, hitting the water with a splash, and skipping along the surface with joyous, graceful bounds as if to say, "Why, this is what I was made for. I'm in my own element at last."

You were made for your Savior, Jesus Christ, and you will never know your real element until you become through surrender to him a new creature in Christ. You will never know the perfect freedom of the redeemed of God until by surrender of your will to him you become the bond servant of Jesus Christ.

And what sort of salvation is this? Why, such a faith saves man from the curse of sin, from spiritual death, from disunity and split personality, unto the life that is eternal.

Faith as surrender to Jesus Christ saves one from the tragedy of never becoming, never realizing what in the economy of the ages and the providence of God one was intended to become. What a catastrophe to come into this world, to have lavished upon oneself all the love of parents, the training of teachers, to have lived and loved, to have striven and fought, lived and died, and yet to have missed selfhood's supreme expression, failing the very purpose of the whole adventure.

And if this is what saving faith is like for the individual who surrenders to Jesus Christ, just see what marvelous salvation it effects in the whole social order!

Several years ago a friend sent me a clipping from *Newsweek* about the rescue work of the Mennonites among the families of Flint, Michigan, whose homes had been destroyed by tornadoes. The Mennonites arrived from several states, some as far away as Pennsylvania, without fanfare or publicity, and began to rebuild the homes of those most in need of help, the uninsured, and the badly injured. They took no money, no assistance, no thanks. Usually they just put the outer walls and roofs back, leaving the refinishing on the inside for the storm sufferers to do themselves. But when an owner was hospitalized or was a widow, the Mennonites rebuilt the entire home.

A union carpenter was asked whether his union objected to the Mennonite farmers doing carpenter's work. He scoffed and said, "They belong to a bigger union than we do. When there is trouble like this, I wish more of us felt like they do."

And why do the Mennonites feel and act as they do and turn loose such a stream of redeeming love in the world? There is just one plain, simple answer: They have a Lord and Master, Jesus Christ, whom by faith they serve in complete surrender, so that his love, compassion, and mercy find expression in the labors of their hands.

This is saving faith, what it is and what it can do for us and our world. Have you claimed its victory over the world as your victory? Are you trying to walk by sight or by faith? Are you trusting in the promises of God or still trying to rely wholly upon yourself? Have you surrendered to Jesus Christ?

What Does It Mean to Be Saved?

"Believe on the Lord Jesus Christ, and thou shalt be saved" (Acts 16:31).

To hear glib talk about the "saved" and the "unsaved" has always made my flesh crawl. Especially do I deplore it when it is another mere man I hear making the judgments about who is and who isn't "saved," especially when the criterion for judgment is church membership or a decision for Christ, verbally expressed once and for all in some public assembly. I just don't like it. It sounds so pious and smug and unrealistic.

Once, according to an article by Professor James Muilenburg in the May 1962 issue of the *Union Seminary Review,* someone asked Muilenburg, teacher of Old Testament at Union Seminary in New York, "What do you mean when you say you are saved?" Muilenburg replied: "I have never said this and have always found this kind of language hard to take. Throughout the years I have always studiously avoided such words as 'salvation' and 'saved.' The chief reason is that I was reared in a climate where people were always asking 'Are you saved?'" Professor Muilenburg went on to recall an incident during his junior year in college when he went to a revival meeting conducted by a famous evangelist. At the close of his address, the evangelist called upon all who were "saved" to speak to the "unsaved." Muilenburg could not find it in his heart to respond in any way, so he was approached by someone who asked, "Are you saved?" The college junior decided to give the man the answer he wanted, and said, "Yes." So then the interrogator pressed the question and asked, "How do you know?" Muilenburg said he didn't know and asked the man how he knew he was saved. Whereupon he quoted a passage from Scripture that seemed to be utterly irrelevant to young Muilenburg.

How many church people there are who share the revulsion of Professor Muilenburg and never talk about "the saved" and "the unsaved."

And yet, if the Christian church does not have salvation to promise men and women as the result of God's activity through the grace he has shown in Christ, what does the Church have to offer the world in general and every harassed person in particular? If it is not salvation that the Church offers, what commodity does it push? If we are not concerned about the saved and the unsaved, what is the Church's concern? Putting on church suppers? Paying off mortgages on new buildings? Having teams compete in athletic contests?

Certainly the New Testament is full of language and stories and ideas where the concepts of "the saved" and "the lost" appear over and over. Jesus said of his purpose in coming, "The Son of man is come to seek and to save that which was lost." He spoke of men being lost like a lost coin or a lost sheep or a lost, wandering, rebellious son. The gospel presents Jesus as moved with deep compassion when he beheld the multitudes of people who were scattered abroad like sheep without a shepherd. He invited all to receive the salvation God offered them through becoming his disciples, using those puzzling words: "Whosoever will save his life shall lose it; but whosoever shall lose his life for my sake and the gospel's, the same shall save it." And the early apostles in the Book of Acts and in their letters are repeatedly holding out to despairing men and women this one simple formula as the solution of their worst dilemmas: "Believe on the Lord Jesus Christ, and thou shalt be saved."

So our quarrel, it would seem, is not with the terms and the concepts of "the saved" and "salvation." These are biblical and crucial in the mission of the Church. Rather our revulsion is at the superficial, selfish, and smug use of these words and ideas.

A careful examination of the New Testament will reveal that Jesus Christ and the apostles never presented salvation as merely a passport to heaven or a new kind of life slipped into or over some character by virtue of the fact that he stood up some Sunday morning and made a public profession of faith in Jesus Christ as Lord and Savior, and then went out and did as he jolly well pleased with this own and other people's lives. To be saved in the New Testament sense is not merely making a decision once and for all, any more than one end of a piece of string is the whole ball of twine. The New Testament knows nothing of a salvation where only God is active and man is passive, where the saved is like one passenger out of many snatched in the nick of time from a doomed boat as it slips over the cataract to be dashed to destruction on the rocks below.

The New Testament very clearly states that to be saved means two very positive things. First, to be saved is to enter now into a living relationship with God through faith in Jesus Christ. This is a salvation that begins now, not when death severs our connection with this earth and we go into eternal orbit, not later and somewhere else, but here and now. It is bestowed only through faith in Jesus Christ. "No man cometh unto the Father, but by me," said Jesus in a strangely proud and exclusive claim. And the early apostles preached, "There is none other name under heaven given among men, whereby we must be saved."

"Does this mean then that all people who die without having heard the name of Jesus are eternally damned?" asks many a sensitive soul.

No, it does not. We can trust the God and Father of our Lord and Savior Jesus Christ to deal justly and mercifully with all his children in whatever situation their varying lots are cast. But it does mean that in this life the highest and best status that can be experienced by human beings is the saving relationship with God that comes through faith in Christ.

This, of course, involves making a decision for Christ now, professing faith in him, but it also involves acquiring knowledge of Jesus' teachings now and continually, recognizing his spirit of reverence for all life, experiencing his consciousness of the Father's presence and power, striving after the example of his obedience to the will of the Father.

Only such a full-orbed response by any one of us to the mercy God has shown us in Christ can result in tasting the genuine New Testament salvation that can best be described, as Muilenburg puts it in the *Union Seminary Review,* as "a sense of liberation, of being set free from the shackles of pride and ambition and anger and hostility and lust and emptiness and blindness … and from all the terrible demons that lay life waste and make it meaningless here and now."

But this New Testament salvation, though beginning in time and experienced in this world to a limited degree, has its ultimate and complete fulfillment beyond the life of this world. "I am the resurrection, and the life," says Jesus. "He that believeth in me, though he were dead, yet shall he live: And whosoever liveth and believeth in me shall never die."

The partial nature of our salvation in this world is one of Saint Paul's themes in his great eighth chapter of the Roman letter, but here Paul insists that it affords us a trustworthy sample of the glorious and incomparable magnificent salvation we shall experience beyond death.

But there is a second and too often neglected aspect of the New Testament teaching on salvation: Salvation by God in Christ involves the one saved in the saving plans and purposes of God for the whole world. The saved Christian can never be an isolationist salvationist. The New Testament does not tell me that God is interested in saving me from global holocaust or from my own little personal hell that my selfishness has created; the New Testament tells me that my salvation is included in and is a part of his salvation for the whole world. "For God so loved the world, that he gave his only begotten Son, that whosoever believeth in him should not perish, but have everlasting life.... And the life which I now live in the flesh I live by the faith of the Son of God, who loved me, and gave himself for me ... but not for me only, but for the whole world." And this gospel that is "the power of God unto salvation" for all men he has entrusted to us and made us your ministers in his stead.

Here is the exact niche where Jesus' perplexing, yet definitive, word on salvation fits: "Whosoever will save his life shall lose it; but whosoever shall lose his life for my sake and the gospel's, the same shall save it." What can one make of such a paradox? Can it be that this life we have in trust from God is like a rubber ball with an elastic cord attached—you have to throw it out and away from you in order to have it come back with an exhilarating rebound?

Here is where the God-ward and man-ward sides of our salvation are revealed. God has acted, moved mightily, reached low, to save us in Christ. But man must for his part make the venture of faith, trust, and reliance upon God in response. We must give, yea, even hazard, this life up to the hilt to be lived every day among others on the level Christ lived in order to be saved unto the uttermost.

In his *Intellectual Autobiography,* Reinhold Niebuhr, the theologian, tells about his first parish experience in Detroit:

Two old ladies were dying shortly after I assumed charge of the parish. They were both equally respectable members of the congregation. But I soon noted that their manner of facing death was strikingly dissimilar. One old lady was too preoccupied with self, too aggrieved that Providence should not have taken account of her virtue in failing to protect her against a grievous illness, to be able to face death with any serenity. She was in a constant hysteria of fear and resentment. ... The other old lady had brought up a healthy and wholesome family, though her husband was subject to periodic fits of insanity which forced her to be the breadwinner as well as homemaker. Just as her two splendid daughters had finished their training and were eager to give their mother a secure and quiet evening of life, she was found to be suffering from cancer. I stood weekly at her bedside while she told me what passages of Scripture, what Psalms and what prayers to read to her; most of them expressed gratitude for all the mercies of God which she had received in life. She was particularly grateful for her two daughters and their love, and she faced death with the utmost peace of soul.

Both women had made their profession of Christian faith and become members of the same congregation. But they did not have Christian salvation in equal quantity and quality. The first was not saved from the fear of death but the second was. Why? How? The second had found her life by losing it in the kind of redeeming love that Jesus brought into the world. And this love that redeemed the lives of others about her also redeemed, saved, and blessed her, psychologically, socially, existentially, and eternally.

Why should anyone think this Christian doctrine of salvation strange or otherworldly? It has its secular counterpart. Scott Carpenter says quite frankly that one of the reasons he volunteered to become an astronaut was that it "gave him a chance for immortality, for pioneering on a grand scale. This is something," says Carpenter, "that I would willingly give my life for, and I think a person is very fortunate to have something he can care that much about."

Arnold Toynbee, who made himself at home in every period of recorded history, tells us in *An Historian's Approach to Religion* that the Roman soldier had a zest for living unequaled in all lands and in all times until the Christian martyr stepped on the stage of history. Why did the Roman soldier possess this zest for living, this buoyancy and sense of meaning in his everyday existence, unequaled in all the world? Toynbee says it was because on the first day of every January each Roman soldier swore a solemn oath to defend the emperor and the empire with his life, and so he lived every moment for a cause for which he was prepared to lay down his life, and this gave unparalleled zest to living. Only the Christian martyr, whose allegiance to another lord and another kingdom outstripped the Roman soldier's courage and commitment, was lifted to a superior level of life.

To be saved from all life's deadly destroyers—sin and death and self and anxiety and fear and meaninglessness—is now and evermore shall be the deepest longing of every human heart. This is the salvation in its fullest and most satisfying form that can be yours and mine—now—as the gift of God through Jesus Christ—but only if we surrender ourselves to him.

Saved From Our Self-despisings

"And he bowed himself, and said, What is thy servant, that thou shouldest look upon such a dead dog as I am?" (2 Sam. 9:8).

Some people with a gift for writing publish their autobiographies. Last week I received notice of the publication of an autobiography by a friend of mine, a federal judge, who has recently retired. Some people who are artists paint self-portraits. But all of us, whatever our talents may be, have mentally painted our self-portraits and in our own minds have written our autobiographies.

You see, you have a mental image of yourself that you carry around with you all the time. It is truly a self-portrait, painted on the canvas of your self-consciousness. What is that self-portrait like? Do you paint yourself too big, like the bumptious guy who is all inflated with the wind of his self-importance? Or is your self-portrait too small, like the painfully timid soul who carries about a miniature picture of himself or herself as a dwarf or pygmy?

Rembrandt and van Gogh painted an incredible number of different self-portraits. At first blush, this seems a bit immodest. But on second thought, it is quite meritorious if a self-portrait is to be painted at all. Time changes things, all things, even ourselves. Just as on occasion it is a good thing to write down one's own, brief philosophy of life, so is it also a helpful thing from time to time to scrutinize one's mental self-portrait, observe how it has changed, or hasn't changed, and check it by truth and reality.

Have you had a photograph made recently? The proofs may surprise you with the realization that you have been picturing yourself as you were ten to fifteen years ago. And things are just not what they used to be.

Sometimes we observe that some people we know have matured while others have not. What about our own goals, values, objectives in life? Have these changed perceptibly for the better, matured any, or are they the same as they were when we were teenagers? How many disillusioned and frustrated elderly and middle-aged people there are whose disillusionment and frustration stem from the fact that the attractions and powers and capacities of youth are falling away, or have already gone, while the appetites, desires, and values of young manhood or young womanhood are still dominant and unchanged. T.S. Eliot in his play *The Cocktail Party* characterized such people as having only "the desire of desire."

It is not only time but also distaste that may dictate our doing a new self-portrait. One of the biggest troubles we have in life is the distaste we feel for our self-portraits, those mental images we carry around with us. And no wonder. An honest appraisal of our moral and spiritual stature reveals a very sorry spectacle.

Leslie Weatherhead, the British minister, in his book *Prescription for Anxiety* writes: "One of the inevitable things about life is that we have got to live with ourselves. What a misery it is to live with a person you despise, a person who has allowed fear to defeat him—even if it is yourself! And unaided we cannot help despising ourselves, the more we know ourselves."

The crippled Mephibosheth, bereaved of his father, Jonathan, and his grandfather Saul, despoiled of his kingly heritage and his house and lands, said to David, "Why do you take the trouble to look on such a dead dog as I am?"

The biblical record tells us the tragedy of poor Mephibosheth. He was a small boy, only five years old, when a messenger came rushing into the palace with the shocking news that the battle with the Philistines was lost and that his father, Jonathan, and his grandfather King Saul had been killed. In her terror, his nurse snatched up little Mephibosheth to run for safety and dropped the boy, crippling him. When King David summoned Mephibosheth into his presence, Mephibosheth called himself "a dead dog." That was the way he was picturing himself. Life's crippling and devastating blows reduce us often to such a state of self-despising.

We all have fallen so short of our moral code. There is such a wide gap between our goals and our achievements. We have violated and neglected friendships. Some of our best intentions in our closest and dearest relationships have resulted in chaos and confusion. We despise ourselves for what we are. It seems the only decent way to feel about the failures we know we are. We need a new self-portrait desperately, but how are we to get it?

Samuel Rutherford, the Scottish mystic, said, "Blessed are they who save us from our self-despisings." Surely here is a precious beatitude that is worthy of standing alongside the other Beatitudes of Jesus, not only because of our deep need for the miraculous rescue, but because of Jesus' amazing power to save us from our self-despisings. It is at this point that his saviorhood means so much to us day by day.

Do you remember that time Jesus met the leper by the roadside in Galilee? Leprosy does horrible things to people's bodies, you know. A hand or a foot will just rot away. Where the nose or an ear was, the leper might have only an ugly, red, scabby hole. But leprosy does horrible things to people psychologically as well as physically. It makes them feel guilty and cast off. In Jesus' day awful social and ceremonial laws controlled the lives of people sick with leprosy. The leper was cut off from his family and his city or village. He was forced to live outside the walls of the town. Everywhere he went he was compelled to cry, as a warning to others of his approach, "Unclean, unclean."

One day one of these pitiable people came to Jesus, crying, "Unclean, unclean." But in the roadway before Jesus, the man prostrated himself and in deep sincerity said, "If thou wilt, thou canst make me clean." Jesus stretched out his hand and touched him and said, "I will: be thou clean." And here is the wonderful part of the story: The man rose, not only cleansed in body, but healed of the deep psychological wound he had suffered. Others had hated and despised him so long he had come to loathe and despise himself, but the Son of God had loved him and touched his own hand to his festering flesh and healed him of his self-despising.

"When our hearts are filled with bitter shame (and we feel unclean and outcast), let us remember that Christ's hand is stretched out to us," says William Barclay in *The Gospel of Luke*. He would heal us of our self-despisings whatever their cause.

Do you remember that day in the gospel record when the responsible citizens brought to Jesus for judgment the poor woman taken in the act of adultery? Throwing her at Jesus' feet, they rudely reminded Jesus that the law of Moses was clear in such offenses—the transgressor should be stoned to death. And they said to Jesus, "Now, since you are a teacher in Israel, what do you say should be done with such a sinner?"

Jesus replied, "He that is without sin among you, let him first cast a stone at her." There followed a long, awkward silence. Then one by one, the indignant, violent men turned silently and slipped away until all were gone, and only Jesus and the woman were left. The miserable creature hesitantly lifted her shame-burdened gaze and looked into his eyes. "Woman," he said, "where are those thine accusers? hath no man condemned thee?" "No man, Lord," came the frightened reply. Then, said Jesus—and I feel his voice rang with triumphant courage and authority—"neither do I condemn thee: go, and sin no more."

So Jesus healed another defeated soul of her self-despising. His "neither do I condemn thee" is no brushing aside of the austere moral law. Never a man lived who had greater respect for the righteousness of the Father, the moral fiber of the universe, and the inspired commandments of God than did Jesus Christ, who so respected that law that he never transgressed it, cost him what it might in blood, sweat, and tears.

Jesus condemned the sin, but he knew it was no longer necessary to condemn the sinner, who already had thoroughly condemned herself in the court of her own consciousness. What she needed now was to be healed of her self-despising for her horrible failure. And as her Savior he began to act positively to whatever good he found in that poor, broken life of hers and to encourage self-respect to grow again based on the forgiveness of God and God's confidence in any man or woman who will try again. For what is God's forgiveness but his unlimited, unbelievable confidence in every person's ability to rise again through the grace and goodness of Jesus Christ?

There came a day in the dark and desperate life of that poor cripple Mephibosheth when on his consciousness there dawned the recognition that, as Joseph Parker put it, "sonship was the principal fact of his life." When preaching to his London congregation on Mephibosheth, Parker declared: "He was Jonathan's son. True, he was lame; true, he was in an obscure [and a precarious] position; true, he had counted himself as little better than a dead dog." But he was the son of Jonathan, whom David had loved, and David the king had vowed that if any of the sons of Jonathan could be found, he would show them the kindness of God for Jonathan's sake. And he sought out Mephibosheth and restored to him his father's and grandfather's estates and brought him to eat at the king's table all the rest of his days.

When will we learn that in the crucible of experience, in this vale of soul-making, in this comedy of errors that is our life, in the shame and mistakes and failures of our own autobiographies, the dominant factor that should undergird all our thoughts and emotions and self-analysis is the fact of our sonship or daughtership to the Eternal God, our kinship to Christ, our courageous elder brother, who has loved us and given himself for us.

Come what may, we are still God's children. We may indeed be broken down, but the fragments are majestic, the ruins are grand. Christ has come to seek and to save that which was lost. He saves us from our self-despisings, and blessed be his name!

Faith, Hope, Love

"So faith, hope, love abide, these three" (1 Cor. 13:13).

Always the Apostle Paul talks about faith, hope, and love. He concludes his magnificent prose poem on the supremacy of love in 1 Cor. 13 with the sweeping affirmation: "So faith, hope, love, abide, these three; but the greatest of these is love."

But that is not all. Over and over again in his famous correspondence we run across this triumphant trinity: faith, hope, love. In the opening paragraphs of his first letter to the Thessalonians, the earliest of his extant epistles, Paul writes: "We give thanks to God always for you all, making mention of you in our prayers; Remembering without ceasing your work of faith, and labour of love, and patience of hope in our Lord Jesus Christ." There it is again: faith, love, hope.

And in his Colossian letter, one of the very last the imprisoned apostle dispatched from his cell in Rome, he is still writing about faith, love, and hope. Listen to him: "We heard of your faith in Christ Jesus, and of the love which ye have to all the saints, For the hope which is laid up for you in heaven" (Col. 1:4-5).

What does Paul mean by faith, hope, and love? Are these just pious words he uses, grasped at random and thrust into reverent writing? Or is he talking about spiritual realities that sincerely mean something to him and ought also to mean something to us? Why is it always these three: faith, hope, love? Why not some others, like peace and joy and purity?

Does Saint Paul mean to say, "Here are the supreme Christian virtues: faith, hope, love; strive for them"? I think not. Roman Catholic doctrine has always held that they are not the supreme virtues. In fact, they are not virtues at all. They are spiritual realities that describe the total Christian life in relation to the three dimensions of human existence: the past, the present, and the future.

As Emil Brunner, the great Swiss theologian, says in his book *Faith, Hope, and Love:*

> Every man's existence is in the three dimensions of time. He lives in the past, in the future, and in the present. We live in the past—by memory. Without having our past with us, without remembering both our individual history and the history of man or mankind, we should not be *human;* we should be animals only. Man is the historic being, the being that has his past with him.
>
> But we live also in the future—by expectation, hoping, fearing, planning. Without anticipating our future we should not be human either. It is as well the foreseeing of what we might, could, and should be that distinguishes us from the animals. We live, of course, in the present, but for the most part we are not aware of the fact that this "being in the present" is most problematic.... Somehow it must be true that we do live in the present; otherwise we should not live at all.

These are the three dimensions of human life: past, present, and future. And we owe it to Brunner that he has understood the Apostle Paul's continual harping on these three chords, faith, hope, and love, and just these three and no others, because these reveal how the Christian lives in relation to Jesus Christ in each of these three dimensions of his life. The Christian lives in his past by faith, he lives in the present by love, and he lives in the future by hope.

First, look at what it means for the Christian to live in the past by faith. This is one dimension of your life and mine—the past. You have a past history and so do I and so does the whole human race. We cannot be too proud of that spotty record. We have an uneasy conscience about its innumerable failures and mistakes.

But there it is. As we survey it, guilt creeps in. What is guilt? Just our past seen in the light of a holy God. How can we handle that past, remove that guilt? We cannot remove it. The past is fixed by its very nature. Shall we just forget about the past and escape our guilt? Many have tried, though unsuccessfully, for we cannot forget and still remain human. The past remains as a dimension of our lives, and we find we must and do live in this dimension, either consciously or subconsciously.

But what we cannot do for ourselves and our past and our guilt, God can do. Christianity is called a historic religion, not because it is very old or very famous, but because it deals realistically with history, with this dimension of human life, our past. The Christian gospel affirms that God has acted in the stream of human history for our redemption and our salvation. The supreme, the culminating, acts of God's redemption are the historic facts of the Incarnation, the actual human birth of the Son of God, his life, and his death and resurrection. All this God did in human history, once and for all, to remove the stain and guilt of our sin.

If we can and will accept by faith what Christ has done for us in the Atonement, then our past is redeemed and our burden of guilt removed. The Christian is just the one who lives in this dimension of life—our past—by faith.

There is a second dimension of human existence—the present. The Christian lives in the present by love. The past is gone. We cannot change it. Our only hope for redeeming it is through faith in Christ. But the present is here, plastic as putty in our hands. We are making it what it will forever be by what we are doing with each flitting moment.

How does the Christian express relationship to Jesus Christ in every present moment? Saint Paul says the Christian's watchword for the present is love.

The Christian lives in the present by love and love alone. Not just any garden variety of affectionate feeling, however. Not love that is the Greek *eros,* our erotic attachments, our sexual desires in their most lurid or chaste expressions. It is not even love in the sense of the Greek *phileos,* or friendship, of give and take mutuality, a higher, but not yet perfect, love. Rather, the Christian lives in the present, says Saint Paul, in relation to Jesus Christ by incarnating the love of Christ, the Greek word *agape,* which is the love of God for sinful human beings. This is unmerited love, a love that goes out to give to the loveless and the unlovely, rather than a love that seeks to get. It is portrayed in Saint Francis's petition: "Lord, where there is hatred, let me sow love." It is made concrete by a contemporary Christian kneeling on this fifth day of May 1991, and saying, "O God, I pray today for Saddam Hussein and all the people of Iraq, especially for the suffering Kurds. Have mercy on

Saddam's soul and bless that afflicted nation." Jesus' words to his disciples interpret the character of this love, agape: "Love your enemies.... Pray for them which despitefully use you.... For if ye love them which love you, what reward have ye? do not even the publicans the same?" It is seen as Saint Paul glimpsed it in Jesus going to the cross, the Eternal God dying for the ungodly. The Christian lives in this present dimension of his life by love.

But there is a third dimension of human existence—the future. We can anticipate the future by worry and anxiety and fear or by hope and optimism. Saint Paul says that hope is the word that describes the Christian's relationship to this dimension of our life.

Most of us have done better by our first two dimensions than we have by our third. Perhaps this is the dimension of human existence that we should compare to an aging man's waistline. It is the future that most troubles modern people. Could Saint Paul speak to us now, he might well paraphrase his own famous words, "So faith, hope, love, abide, these three; but the greatest of these is love," by saying instead, "So faith, hope, love abide, but what you need most in the twentieth century is hope." For now worry and anxiety, fear and despair fill our hearts. People have lost their sense of purpose. Hope is almost gone.

How generate hope? By affirming with the philosophers of the eighteenth century Enlightenment that human progress is inevitable? That the procession of history is onward and upward forever? That hope should just naturally characterize this third dimension of human life? The fact is that two world wars have devastated the earth and blasted man's belief in automatic progress, and the scientific progress made in the discovery of atomic power has hung a mushroom-shaped cloud of doom over the human race. We've come to realize that all scientific development not only increases man's capacity for service to his fellows, but at the same moment and in the same degree increases man's capacity for cruel destruction of his fellows and the pollution of our earthly habitat.

No, the human race is not automatically related to the future with hope, and neither can we any longer accept the blasted doctrine of automatic progress. Is hope impossible then? Are we doomed to live in this third dimension—our future—with anxiety and fear and apprehension?

No, we can have hope, but only in Jesus Christ. For Christ is the lord of history. The future is in his keeping. And the Christian lives in this third dimension as he contemplates the future with a radiant hope only because of and through his relationship with Christ.

Very often when people despair of life and attempt suicide, they will give as their reasons something like this: "I have nothing more to expect from life. This, which meant so much to me, is gone. That dear one has died. This person has failed me. My health is gone. I have nothing to live for."

Viktor Frankl, the psychiatrist, says that the crucial thing for one in such a despairing state of mind toward his future is not so much to persuade him that he may yet expect something good from life as it is to help him see that life yet expects something of him. The rosy tinting of the future with hope is, therefore, not so much the expectation of good things yet to come for us, but rather the sense of responsibility that life expects, our Lord expects, specific things done for others that we ourselves can, by his grace, perform.

For one man who had attempted suicide, meaning to life and the will to live were restored when he realized that he was responsible for providing an education for a child he adored; for another man, when he was persuaded that life was expecting him to finish and publish his half-completed scientific studies.

"A person who becomes conscious of the responsibility he bears toward a human being who affectionately depends upon him, or to an unfinished work, will never be able to throw away his life," says Frankl in *From Concentration Camp to Existentialism.*

So hope of salvation for the Christian means, not only soul salvation in the coming consummation of all things in Christ, but the future fulfillment of sacred duties and responsibilities to others in Christ. Future responsibilities, not just future rewards, are a part of our joyously tenacious relationship to this third dimension of our life in Christ.

An observant young man was impressed by the poignant sight of an old woman whom he saw slowly trudging homeward from the Memphis Public Library on McLean Avenue and carrying a book titled *All Our Tomorrows.* Tragic? No. Hopelessly, incurably optimistic? No. There is the symbol of every Christian man and woman, moving on into the sunset, down the avenues of time, stepping into the shadows and confidently smiling, hopefully progressing, because our future is hidden with Christ in God. All our tomorrows are safely secure because that future is under the sway of him whom the Eternal has made King of Kings and Lord of Lords. And the Christian facing the future—any future—joins his voice in the mighty chorus of angels and archangels, martyrs and apostles who proclaim, "Hallelujah, hallelujah, for the Lord God omnipotent reigneth, King of Kings and Lord of Lords, forever and ever. Hallelujah, hallelujah. Amen."

Christian Forgiveness

"Lord, how oft shall my brother sin against me, and I forgive him?"
(Matt. 18:21).

For a full week the whole country has been in an uproar because President
Ford granted former President Nixon a full pardon last Sunday morning.
Some have been saying that it was a gracious and courageous thing to do.
Others have been saying that it was a stupid and unjust thing to do.

All sorts of questions have been asked: What about the other people in
the Watergate affair—Colson, Dean, Magruder, the Cubans—who are in
prison for their involvement? Should President Ford pardon them? What
about the court cases of those accused yet to stand trial: Erlichman, Hal-
deman, Mitchell? What about the president's proposal of amnesty for the
thousands of young Americans who during the Vietnam War deserted the
armed forces or eluded the draft because they had conscientious objections
about war in general or the Vietnam War in particular? Should they also be
granted full pardon and be restored to their families and their former status
of honorable citizenship in the Republic? What is the right thing to do about
forgiveness and pardon for all?

As Christian Education Sunday dawns upon us today, there never was a more apparent need among the American people for Christian teaching and Christian understanding to bring order into our confusion. If only our minds were enlightened by biblical teaching on justice and mercy! If only our hearts were converted to the spirit of Christian forgiveness! If only we had the divine wisdom to know when and how to pardon!

We could know the answers to all these questions now being raised on pardon and amnesty, on law-breakers and law-abiding citizens, if we were better instructed in Christian teaching on such matters.

The introduction to John Calvin's *Geneva Catechism* states categorically, "It has always been a matter which the church has held in singular commendation—to see that little children be instructed in Christian doctrine." But the fact remains that both adults and children are in singular ignorance and confusion about the Christian doctrine of forgiveness. Do you and I know what the Christian teaching really is on this knotty problem?

One day, as Jesus was teaching his twelve disciples, he said: "Take heed to yourselves: If thy brother trespass against thee, rebuke him; and if he repent, forgive him. And if he trespass against thee seven times in a day, and seven times in a day turn again to thee, saying, I repent; thou shalt forgive him" (Luke 17:3-4). And the apostles said to the Lord—well, what did they say? Did they say, "Yes, Lord"? Or did they say, "We will try it"? No. They said, Lord, "Increase our faith" (Luke 17:5).

How discerning, how wise, how honest, were those Galilean peasants! They were no pious hypocrites. They knew their own weakness. The forgiving spirit their Master demanded of them was too high for them. They knew it. It was no mere human possibility. So they begged him to increase their faith so they might be able to keep this commandment to forgive.

Jesus, in his teachings on forgiveness, was blazing a new trail. The Hebrew people had believed in the forgiveness of sins—that is, of Jehovah's forgiveness of the sins of a penitent people—but the Hebrew religion was not rich in its teaching of the obligation of man to forgive his fellows the sins they commit against him.

As the *Dictionary of the Bible,* edited by James Hastings, explains:

So closely, indeed, is the principle [of forgiveness in human relations] associated with the teaching and work of Christ, that forgiveness has been called "Christ's most striking innovation in morality," and the phrase, a "Christian" spirit, is commonly regarded as synonymous with a disposition of readiness to forgive an injury. The pagan ideal of manly life was to succeed in doing as much good to your friends and as much injury to your enemies as possible; and if it be not true that forgiveness was a virtue unknown in the ancient world, it was at all events not one that was demanded or proclaimed as a duty by any ethical system.

Jesus lays on his followers the duty to forgive their fellows the wrongs done them. It is no easily kept commandment. The first disciples told him they could not keep it unless he increased their faith.

Precisely what did Jesus teach concerning man's duty to forgive? First, he taught his followers that their willingness to forgive must be unlimited. As the Revised Standard Version has it: "If your brother sins, rebuke him, and if he repents, forgive him; and if he sins against you seven times in the day, and turns to you seven times, and says, 'I repent,' you must forgive him." George Buttrick writes in his masterpiece, *The Parables of Jesus:* "The Jewish law appears to have required forgiveness until three times. Presumably it allowed a man who had forgiven his enemy three times to regard him thereafter with implacable hostility." Jesus says to forgive seven times. Obviously he was not using the number in a literal sense. Among the Jews "seven" was the symbol of heavenly perfection. He desired to raise the duty to forgive out of the realm of numerical calculation. A similar passage from Saint Matthew's Gospel makes this abundantly clear. Peter came to Jesus and asked: "Lord, how oft shall my brother sin against me, and I forgive him? till seven times? Jesus saith unto him, I say not unto thee, Until seven times: but, Until seventy times seven" (Matt. 18:21-22).

On the other hand, it is equally clear from Jesus' words that something is required on the part of the offender before he can be the recipient of forgiveness: "If your brother sins, rebuke him, and if he repents, forgive him." This is the condition—repentance. The offender, before he can be forgiven, must have the consciousness of wrong done; he must make a free avowal of error, promise to turn away from it, and give evidence of a willingness to make amends. Jesus does not enjoin his followers to submit to any and all evil and injustice done them with a weak-kneed submission, saying always, "I forgive, I forgive." The spirit of always giving in, no matter what the issue, is no Christian spirit. A namby-pamby passing by of all wrongs done would dull and destroy all moral and ethical distinctions. Jesus does not command his followers to forgive unconditionally. He clearly teaches that there are conditions to be met before forgiveness can be granted.

Biblical teaching outlines four plain steps that must be taken in genuine repentance. First, admit the wrong done. Say, "Yes, I did it." Some call this by the theological term *confession.* The law of particularity is here most important. It is not enough for a man to say: "Forgive me, I'm a sinner. All men are sinners. I just did to you what everybody else does when he has a chance. Forgive me, a sinner."

That is no true confession. Biblical confession means to say: "I lied to you when I said such and such on Tuesday when we were talking about that friend of ours. It was a baldfaced lie. I should not have said it. I ask your pardon and forgiveness."

The second condition in Christian forgiveness is to give evidence of genuine sorrow for the wrong done.

The third is to promise not to repeat the wrong—to quit, to stop.

The fourth condition is to make restitution for the harm done to those injured by the sinful act. Zacchaeus was forgiven by our Lord when he promised to restore fourfold all the money he had fraudulently taken from the taxpayers in his district.

When we, peasants and potentates, people and presidents, fulfill the scriptural requirements for Christian forgiveness, we are in line for pardon, and only then. Jesus teaches that forgiveness—human and divine—is all of one piece, and there are no exceptions for the high and mighty or the weak and lowly.

Furthermore, Jesus very plainly places the burden of setting the wrong aright upon the shoulders of the Christian. It is not only cowardly but un-Christian to keep hiding a wrong, to keep covering up and excusing the evil we've done, to allow or force others to suffer for the wrongs we have done. The Christian has the responsibility of confessing explicitly the sin or wrong he has done.

But the Christian's responsibility does not stop there. In Jesus' teaching the Christian is not allowed to remain passive until his offender of his own accord comes to him penitent, begging for reconciliation. The Christian has to adopt all rational means he can summon to bring home to the one who has offended him the error and evil of his conduct. If one of the disciples of Christ is wronged and everyone knows without a shadow of doubt that none of the blame for the offense rests upon him, it is his duty nevertheless to go to that one who has trespassed against him and in a forgiving spirit point out the wrong done and be ready to forgive unreservedly when the offender admits his error. Here is what the Master said: "If your brother sins against you, rebuke him—that is, go to him, speak your piece—and if he repents, forgive him."

Our national constitution's provision for impeachment is an illustration of this principle in the affairs of government. The body politic inaugurates proceedings to give an orderly outline of wrongs done, if indeed they have been done, even by the one who holds the highest office in the land. Point it out. Rebuke the wrong in order that repentance, restitution, and reconciliation may take place.

Finally, Jesus' teaching on forgiveness clearly shows that the measure of our willingness to forgive men is the scale by which God forgives us. That clause in the Lord's Prayer, "Forgive us our debts, as we forgive our debtors," or, as it is sometimes rendered, "Forgive us our trespasses, as we forgive those who trespass against us," makes it evident that human forgiveness and divine forgiveness are strictly analogous. There is no difference between the forgiveness that the Christian wins from God and that which he in turn bestows upon his brother. God forgives us and in the same measure we must forgive others.

Jesus' parable of the unmerciful debtor shows that the absence of a forgiving spirit in our hearts prevents our being forgiven by God. An Oriental potentate, so the parable goes, left a large portion of his affairs under the supervision of a trusted steward. At the time of accounting, it was discovered that the steward had made away with $2 million. It was an impossible and extravagant defalcation, fitly representing the incalculable and undischargeable debt that sinners owe to God. The potentate was angry. He commanded the steward and his wife and children and all his possessions be sold in small payment of the huge debt. But the steward, falling on his face before his master, pleaded guilty and begged for clemency. "Master, have patience with me, and I will repay you all." With a boundless graciousness the master forgave his steward the whole debt and set him free. Going out immediately from the presence of his benefactor, this man who had been granted so costly a reprieve ran smack into a little fellow who for some time had owed him $20. Grasping the poor wretch by the throat, he demanded immediate payment. In the very same words with which the steward had begged for mercy, the poor man said, "Have patience with me and I will pay you." But the steward would show no mercy and threw his debtor into prison till he should pay all his debt. Then word was brought to the ruler of how the wicked steward had treated his fellow servant, and hailing him again into his presence, the potentate said, "You wicked servant. I forgave you all that debt because you asked me. Should you not also have mercy on your fellow servant, even as I had mercy on you?" So he delivered him to the tormentors, and Jesus said, "So likewise shall my heavenly Father do also unto you, if ye from your hearts forgive not every one his brother their trespasses." So Jesus clearly teaches both in this parable and in the prayer he gave us that the measure of our willingness to forgive others is the scale by which God forgives us.

These are the teachings of Jesus on forgiveness. What are we to make of them? Are they not commands hard to keep? How shall we obey them?

How shall we develop enough of a forgiving spirit toward all people in order that God may forgive us? It is here that I would return to the apostles' remark upon hearing Jesus' harsh command to forgive and forgive and forgive. We will remember that they said, "Increase our faith." This is a penetrating insight and one that we need to make our own, for there is an intimate relationship between faith and the development of Christ's forgiving spirit.

The basis of Jesus' teachings on forgiveness is a transcendent one. Such concepts for conduct could not possibly arise from human experience alone. They were not developed in the school of practical human morality. The duty to forgive, laid upon men by Jesus, evolves not out of the nature of man, but out of the nature of God. "Forgive," says Jesus. Why? Because it always works good in human relationships? Because you will always win your enemy that way? No. "Forgive," says Jesus, "because God forgives you and demands that you forgive your fellows." Jesus' precept on forgiveness—his greatest innovation in morality—has its foundation, its authority, not in human nature and human relationships, but in the divine nature and in the relationship between God and man.

Therefore, it is apparent that the forgiving spirit, enjoined and exemplified by Jesus, is no simple human attainment. It is a possibility only for the person of great faith. How wise were those disciples who, when Jesus told them to forgive those who trespassed repeatedly against them, said, "Increase our faith." It takes a lot of faith to forgive as Jesus demands it. Not only does it take faith in the existence of God, but also that God is just the kind of forgiving Heavenly Father that Jesus tells us he is, one who has forgiven us our multitude of sins. It is faith in such a Father that begets the forgiving spirit in the Christian. It comes in no other way. We cannot know this God unless we become acquainted with him through Christian nurture of biblical teaching within the Christian fellowship.

Our consciences must be instructed by the divine law, will, love, and mercy. Conscience is not automatically an infallible guide. Christian conscience must be instructed by Christian teaching, supremely set forth by the word and example of Jesus Christ.

The whole fabric of social life stands or falls on the point of equal justice and equal mercy to all. The Republic will be destroyed and respect for law and persons will go down the drain if all men are not kept equal before the law. The more responsible the position to which a man aspires, the more important it is for him to respect the trust placed in him by the people and by their God. If he fails, then he himself should require it of himself, in all good conscience, to make restitution to those whose welfare he has harmed or threatened. If others let him off, then the nobility or scurrilousness of his spirit will be clearly shown by whether he, himself, takes the easy way or the hard way to make restitution to the people who put their trust in him.

A forgiving spirit is the finest fruit of the Christian faith. It is not a spontaneous growth. Neither is it a chance occurrence. It must be nurtured by continuous Christian teaching and Christian fellowship. It is not a stronger will to have good will that we need, but rather we must pray with the disciples of old, "Increase our faith."

On Breaking Out of Jail

"He hath sent me ... to preach deliverance to the captives" (Luke 4:18).

Every now and then some dangerous criminal breaks out of jail, and a warning is broadcast to the public to be on the lookout for him. We are incessantly bombarded with reports of the overcrowding in all our jails and prisons. Most people are disturbed by the enormous number of felons who are walking our streets, out on bond, committing fresh crimes. For years one of our most pressing national preoccupations was the problem of how to spring from their imprisonment our fellow Americans who had been kidnapped and held hostage in Lebanon. One might say that we are a jail- and prisoner-obsessed people.

How to get those who ought to be in jail locked up and kept there, and how to get out those who ought to be free and kept from all harm, is for us all a very thorny problem. Being in jail is a terrible ordeal for both the guilty and the innocent.

Once I went to see a man in prison. I can still hear the locks clicking behind me as the guard led the way through one barrier after another. I can still see the expressions of shame and despair and bitterness on the faces of the prisoners. I can remember now how I then thought with a shudder, "What a fearsome thing it is to be a prisoner of the law."

But there are prisons, we all know, other than city jails and state and federal penitentiaries. I've seen prisoners who weren't behind bars, and you have too.

Fear imprisons people. I have visited with prisoners of fear. I have looked into their haunted eyes. I have heard them describe the miseries of their harsh imprisonment. I have seen whole communities locked up by their fears in a spiritual concentration camp. I shall never forget the feel of fear that hovered in the very air over a city caught in the grip of a polio epidemic back in those years before the Salk vaccine was perfected.

Sickness or crippling can imprison people. If you don't believe it, just wait till you or a member of your family has to spend weeks, months, or even years confined to a hospital bed or a sickroom.

The lusts and passions of the flesh can imprison the soul. What can be a more complete confinement than that of men or women shut up under the lock and key of a self-destroying habit, barred from the good life that goes on all about them?

A life situation can imprison us. How often circumstances in the middle years conspire to make people feel hopelessly jailed. It may be heavy family responsibilities; it may be a vocation or a job too hastily chosen years ago that does not now really satisfy the soul or intrigue the talents; it may be just the pressure of modern society, the piled-up requests and calls on one's time and conscience. Any one or a combination of these circumstances can crib, cabin, and confine us until we feel hopelessly jailed in a dismal prison.

Now, of course, the worst part of any form of imprisonment is what it does to the soul. When John the Baptist was imprisoned by Herod, he sent a messenger to ask Jesus if he really were the Messiah or should the world look for another Savior? Just think of it! That bold, fearless, reckless man who had been the first to discern our Lord's identity and the first loudly to proclaim it was now in the depths of doubt. "Art thou he that should come, or do we look for another?" See what continued imprisonment does even to the stoutest hearts? It gnaws away at one's vitals. It corrodes faith. It destroys deepest convictions.

"Once one of the Macdonalds, a Highland chieftan, was confined in a little cell in Carlisle Castle," writes William Barclay in *The Gospel of Luke*. "In his cell there was one little window. To this day you may see the marks in the sandstone of the feet and the hands of the Highlander as he lifted himself up and clung to the window ledge, as day by day he gazed with infinite longing out upon the border hills and valleys that he would never walk again.

Shut in his cell, choked by the narrow walls, John asked this question because his cruel captivity had put tremors in his heart."

Devilishly perverted people can do appalling things to the hearts and souls of longtime prisoners in the way of brainwashing. Human beings, created in the image of their great Maker, were intended to be free, and when they suffer imprisonment, they are most hurt where they are most like their Maker, in their immortal souls.

And it follows that the more sensitive, conscientious, and noble a person is, the more likely it is that any form of imprisonment will destroy him. In the play by Ketti Frings *Look Homeward, Angel,* based on Thomas Wolfe's novel, two brothers discuss their father's latest drunken spree. The younger asks, "If he hates it so much here, why does he stay?" His brother Ben, speaking as much about himself as about his father, replies, "It's like being caught in a photograph. Your face is there, and no matter how hard you try, how are you going to step out of a photograph?" Yes, the deeper one's sense of responsibility and capacity for affection and loyalty, the more cruelly imprisoning and soul-destroying many a jail can be.

Do you remember the popular song, "It's been a blue, blue day. I feel like running away. I feel like running away from it all"? That is about the way most of us have felt at times, isn't it? Those intolerable burdens, those impossible responsibilities, those irksome people. But breaking out of our prison ourselves is not the solution to our problem. Running away is not the real answer to our need. In fact, few if any of us can manage all by ourselves the particular jailbreak we need. We can't get the consent of our soul to step out of the photograph. What we really need is genuine release—full pardon. That, someone else will have to do for us.

Now Jesus Christ thought it one of his most important purposes in life to set the prisoners free. That day in the synagogue in Nazareth when he announced the objectives of his life's work, he put near the top this one: "To preach deliverance to the captives." And the early Church in its experience of the living Christ found him, as it is written in the First Epistle of Saint Peter, visiting the spirits in prison and setting them free.

As we read the Gospels we see clearly that this was Christ's life, this was the big business of the Son of God—to accomplish the release of all who had become imprisoned in life one way or another, to set the prisoners free.

Yes, and even yet this is the Great Redeemer's continuing work—to free even the violent terrorists, the hardened, dangerous criminals by forgiving their past sins, changing their hearts from hate to love, freeing them on the inside from the tyranny of evil, springing them from the jailhouse of destruction, and setting them free to serve God and man.

How does Christ deliver the captive and set the prisoner free? Not by granting physical release necessarily, though that so often follows, but primarily by bringing spiritual deliverance and granting the soul freedom, which is the very point where, as we have seen, all imprisonment pinches hardest. Yes, Christ has the remarkable power to transform forbidding prison walls into open doors of opportunity, a gibbet into a pulpit of truth, and handcuffs into swords competent to carve out new human rights. Many a person has felt as did Ben Gant about the impossible human situation in which he found himself—"how are you going to step out of a photograph?"—but discovered that the grace of Christ can put a new radiance on an old face and supply a new spirit for carrying accustomed responsibilities and so change the people and the grouping in that photograph as to effect a complete deliverance from within.

Where have we more remarkable evidence for this reality than in the experience of Saint Paul? The great champion of the Christian faith is thrown into prison. The intrepid missionary is snatched from his wide-ranging travels and chained to a Roman soldier. "Oh, what a loss," we say, "a tragedy beyond repair. Christianity is set back a hundred years." But how wrong we are. For Paul in prison writes, "The things which happened unto me have fallen out rather unto the furtherance of the gospel" (Phil. 1:12). How? In his letter he goes on to make it clear that he has two things in mind. First, his imprisonment has brought the unique opportunity to witness for Christ before his prison guards and win them for his Lord. Second, Paul has observed that his courage in bearing his imprisonment has not been without its effect on other hard-pressed Christians. But there is yet another way the gospel is furthered by Paul's imprisonment, of which he, in writing, was not aware, but which we, his spiritual heirs, see now so clearly: that prison correspondence of Paul's has become one of the Church's choicest treasures. Here Paul pours out his heart on what Christ means to him, and had not the imprisonment interrupted his missionary labors, he might never have had the time to do for us this incomparable service. So Paul's imprisonment by Christ's grace serves as the method for setting his spirit free to go campaigning past his own generation and down the centuries.

A beautiful young woman suffered a crippling illness. Circumstances sentenced her to life imprisonment in her own home. Yet Christ with his gospel came into that house and preached deliverance for her soul. Out from her bed went letters in a steady stream to missionaries all around the world. In correspondence and prayer she had fellowship with Christ's foreign legion. Amazing power went out from her life to distant lands. And what interest and exuberance of spirit flowed back into that little upstairs room from far away places because Jesus Christ had delivered a captive, not by healing her body and sending a robust young woman to the uttermost parts of the earth on missionary activities, but because he had proclaimed deliverance for her spirit.

I once knew a man who suffered a long imprisonment caused by alcoholism. He and his wife were separated because drink was destroying his life. He lost job after job. How often I'd seen him with defeat in his eyes and talked with this doomed prisoner about his dismal future. Then came a strange, unbelievable miracle in his life. The patient love and prayers and labors of a devoted son who never gave up on his father—a sort of prodigal son parable in reverse—finally paid off. The man maintained a level of sobriety for a number of months. He got a job and held it. He and his wife were reconciled. Finally, the day came when I saw him with all the lines of tension gone from his face. His eyes had lost their shifty, roving glance. Suntanned and poised, he stood before me. "My, you look well," I said. And he replied, "Well, I'm living right now." And he knew that I knew what he meant.

How had it happened? What had set the prisoner free? That man would say he became a free man after a long and bitter imprisonment because Jesus Christ had set him free, using as the human instrument of the divine love the man's own son.

Are you and I in a prison of our own construction? Have we let our lusts, our selfish ambitions, our precious luxuries, our indulgence in self-destroying habits imprison our souls? Do we feel caught in a life situation that is a jailhouse to us?

Well, Jesus Christ is interested in us and in our release. He came to preach release to captives. His continuing work in the world is visiting spirits in prison to set them free. All around and about us he is springing the lock and letting them go. Today he is knocking at the door of our imprisoned hearts to tell us he has come to let us out. Just turn yourself over to him. Put yourself in his hands. In trust and commitment, surrender yourself to him and see how free he can make you.

The Safekeeping of Jesus Christ

"To those whom God has called, who live in the love of God the Father
and in the safe keeping of Jesus Christ" (Jude 1).

The brief, two-page letter of Jude that comes so late in the Bible that it is
seldom noticed is addressed to people whom the author describes as "those
whom God has called, who live in the love of God the Father and in the safe
keeping of Jesus Christ."

Though unknown and unnamed, these Christians to whom Jude wrote
his little letter so long ago share with us Christians of every age these three
great experiences: (1) we are all called of God, (2) we are all privileged to
live in the love of God the Father, and (3) we all may abide forever in the
safekeeping of Jesus Christ.

All Christians are called; that is, all of us have been summoned from
what we are to what we should become. Calls of many kinds come to
everyone: friendly calls, anonymous calls, obscene calls, calls of sad tidings,
calls for financial assistance, calls for church or community service.

But the call of God is unique, decisive, prophetic. It is the call of the
Creator to his creature. It is the call to every person that is not so much audible

and from without as it is compulsive and from within, calling that person to rise up and live in the heights of the soul, to be about the work and witness for which the Creator has made his creature.

God has called you. He is calling you now. How are you responding?

The second great experience we have in common with those unnamed and unknown Christians to whom Jude wrote is that we are privileged to live in the love of God the Father.

The Christian is the one who has learned through Jesus Christ of the amazing reality of a Heavenly Father who loves every human being he has created as his own child, as if each child were his only child and the whole fervent torrent of omnipotent love were poured out on that favored child alone.

"For God so loved the world, that he gave his only begotten Son, that whosoever believeth in him should not perish, but have everlasting life.... God is love; he who dwells in love is dwelling in God, and God in him.... We love because he loved us first."

But so many Christians who are called of God do not live in the consciousness of the love of God. I recall a woman who was indeed in a sad plight. She was out of work. Her debts were piling up. She did not know what to do. As she talked of her many difficulties, she poured out the hostility, resentment, and bitterness she felt toward her children, who were ungrateful and uncooperative, toward her relatives, who refused to help her on her terms, and toward her former employers, who one after another had employed her for only a few days and then let her go.

What was wrong in this woman's life? As she saw it, everybody was against her, including God himself—getting in her way, obstructing her fortunes, withholding from her rights—and she was angry and resentful.

What was really wrong was her attitude. What she needed most was not a new and better job, not someone to pay her debts, not someone to make her children gratefully obedient and the family generous. What she needed most was the love of God in her heart—a changed attitude characterized by an unwavering conviction that she lived and moved and had her being in the love of God the Father. When she began to live in the consciousness of the love of God for her and let that love flow through her heart, her life was changed. First, came the change within, and then mysteriously, but oh, so practically, her outward circumstances were also changed. She found out the truth of what Frederick W. Faber wrote in his hymn "There's a Wideness in God's Mercy":

For the love of God is broader
Than the measures of man's mind,
And the heart of the Eternal
Is most wonderfully kind.

The third great experience we share with those unnamed and unknown Christians to whom Jude wrote is that we all abide in the safekeeping of Jesus Christ. The safekeeping of Jesus Christ—what is this? It is not immunity from disease. Christians get sick and need doctors and medicine just like pagans. It's not protection from catastrophe. Christians crash in airplanes; they have wrecks on highways. Well, what is the safekeeping of Jesus Christ? Is there some reality here, or are these just so many words, the safekeeping of Jesus Christ?

I had occasion to think about this question recently as I drove to the funeral of a boyhood friend who had been killed suddenly in a highway accident. I remember the first time I had ever seen him—a bright, agile little boy of four or five playing with the neighborhood children. Certainly he was the handsomest and best coordinated of all the children who played on the lawn that summer afternoon. Within the week he was stricken with polio.

Where then for this child was the safekeeping of Jesus Christ? Why, in the love and prayers and fierce fight of his parents for their child's life, in the dedication and skill of nurses, physicians, and surgeons who worked with him and for him across all the years of childhood.

Where was the safekeeping of Jesus Christ? Why, in the cheerful, courageous spirit of his mother and father, whose minds and hearts were kept from bitterness and remorse when this dark, crippling thing grasped their son's body and made a lunge for his soul. The safekeeping of Jesus Christ held their spirits from the damaging poison and through them structured their son into a debonair, blithe young man who faced life with courage, confidence, and love, even though his back was bent and his leg crippled.

But when grown to maturity with his own happy family about him this loyal churchman, responsible citizen, and faithful father met instant death on the highway last week, where was the safekeeping of Jesus Christ? Why, in his broken-hearted family's confidence that in the same moment he was taken from their arms, he was securely held in the arms of an eternal savior.

Yes, the safekeeping of Jesus Christ is real. First of all it is a reality of moral safekeeping. Temptations succumbed to can wreck life. It is the moral safekeeping that Jesus Christ gives that is paramount in Jude's mind as he writes. Some of the Christian community to whom he wrote had been called of God and lived for a while in the love of God and then strayed. Jude knew men needed more than good intentions and strong resolves to remain pure, so he ends his letter with that beautiful prayer and benediction: "Now to the One who can keep you from falling and set you in the presence of his glory, jubilant and above reproach, to the only wise God our Saviour, be glory and majesty, might and authority, through Jesus Christ our Lord, before all time, now, and for evermore. Amen."

Left to himself man is prone to stumble. Jesus Christ is able to safeguard him at this point and to keep him morally sure-footed.

What better example of both the reality and nature of the moral safekeeping of Jesus Christ could anyone ask than the life and death of Pope John XXIII? Here was a man not particularly gifted as a scholar or an intellectual or a political organizer, but whose distinction lay rather in the completeness of his subservience to the spirit of Jesus Christ, and the whole world bowed low to the otherworldly grandeur of this personality who was in the safekeeping of Jesus Christ.

But the safekeeping of Jesus Christ is not only moral reinforcement; it is mental redemption. People nowadays are troubled terrifically from within. The chaos that threatens is not the wild beast or the hostile man, but the tormented conscience, the uncontrollable thoughts, anxieties, worries of a man's mind. Peace, we crave, peace of mind.

And this is precisely what Jesus Christ brings us for our safekeeping. "Peace I leave with you," he said to those troubled disciples mourning his imminent departure. "My peace I give unto you: not as the world giveth, give I unto you. Let not your heart be troubled, neither let it be afraid." And when he had gone, all the way home to the Father, they found they had it—just as he had promised—his strong, untroubled peace.

When people would wonder at the remarkable strength and inexhaustible resources of Christian wisdom and work that came from a devout but very frail man, his wife would always explain, "Oh, it's because he works without tension. He doesn't ever need 'to blow his top' or 'get things out of his system' or 'off his chest.' He harbors no resentments, holds no hostilities. He works relaxed because his mind is so completely in the safekeeping of Jesus Christ."

But at a deeper lever still, the safekeeping of Jesus Christ is the safekeeping of our motives. Arthur Gordon, in one of his essays, "A Day at the Beach," tells of how when once life had grown flat and sour for him, he went to a trusted advisor who counseled him to reexamine his motives. And on reexamination he discovered that his work was no longer an end in itself. It had degenerated into simply a way to make money.

Gordon came to realize that "the sense of giving something, of helping people, of making a contribution, had been lost in the frantic clutch at security. Then I saw in a flash of certainty that if one's motives are wrong, nothing can be right."

And Jesus Christ makes such stern demands of his disciples: "But he that is greatest among you, shall be your servant" (Matt. 23:11), and "If any man will come after me, let him deny himself, and take up his cross, and follow me," and "Seek ye first the kingdom of God, and his righteousness; and all these things shall be added unto you." He makes these demands at the deep level of man's motives that he may be Lord of the heartland of the soul, to the end that his disciples may be enfolded in the safekeeping of Jesus Christ.

Are these ancient and universal experiences of all Christians your present possessions in the fullness of their glory? Do you know yourself to be called of God and responding obediently to that call? Are you living in the love of God our Father? Are you abiding in the safekeeping of Jesus Christ?

What Think Ye of Christ?

"While the Pharisees were gathered together, Jesus asked them, Saying, What think ye of Christ? whose son is he?" (Matt. 22:41-42).

The most important question that can ever enter the mind of man is this, "What think ye of Christ?" More fundamental than to ask, "Who am I?" More packed with passionate concern than to ponder, "Whom shall I marry?" More determinative of the course of one's destiny than to ask, "What shall I do with my life?" More comprehensive even than to ask "Whom or what shall I worship?" is this question, "What think ye of Christ?"

The Christian church through the centuries has insisted that every person must be confronted with this question, "What think ye of Christ?" And the Church has proclaimed that an adequate answer must be found, or one cannot enter into the fullness of life here or hereafter. Salvation or damnation, beauty or ugliness, social order or chaos, all turn on one's answer to this question, "What think ye of Christ?"

Why has Christianity staked so much on what people think about Christ? Why has the Christian religion insisted that the crucial question for all human history is now and ever shall be, "What think ye of Christ?"

Because, first of all, the answer we give to this question determines our theology—how we visualize God. Jesus said to his disciple Philip, "He that hath seen me hath seen the Father." The seeing that Jesus referred to here, of course, was not the glimpse of God in Jesus' physical form, but rather Jesus' revelation of God's moral and spiritual nature.

One of those early Christians writing to his Christian friends put it, to paraphrase Heb. 1:1-3, this way: God, in times past, spoke to our fathers in a fragmentary and imperfect way through the prophets, but in the fullness of time, there came the clear and full revelation of God in Jesus Christ. "For in him dwelleth all the fulness of the Godhead bodily" (Col. 2:9).

So complete and full was this revealing of God in Jesus Christ that Bishop James A. Pike writes in *A Time for Christian Candor,* "Whenever since [in human experience] we have observed examples of the revelation of God and of human goodness the most we can say is that this revelation is something like that which we have found in Jesus Christ." Pike continues, "Yet, while Jesus Christ is 'for us men and for our salvation' the Word made flesh, there is no reason for us to assume that—given the right historical context and given the right man responding aright—there could not be another such Incarnation."

But I must demur from the good bishop's suggestion that since there has been one Incarnation there could be another such Incarnation. Bishop Pike reasons thus: "Were there not the possibility of further incarnations, the Incarnation we know in Jesus Christ would be increasingly implausible as growing knowledge of the expanding universe continually reduces our sense of the uniqueness and relative importance of this particular planet."

For me this is a glaring non sequitur. Why must our awareness of an expanding universe diminish in any sense the uniqueness of any creation of the Almighty in his cosmos? Why should we assume that the possible existence of intelligent life on other planets should have to be a repetition of human life in the forms and problems we know here to exist? C.S. Lewis, in his science fiction stories about interplanetary travel by way of rocketship written years ago, pictured life on Mars as untouched by human sin, so needing an entirely different method of revealing the presence and power and love of the creator of the cosmos.

No, I cannot agree that the expanding universe and the dawn of the space era make it necessary for us to consider the possibility of other Incarnations. For us men and women and for our particular need, Jesus Christ was and is and ever remains the unique and all-sufficient revelation of God.

The blind eyes of the five Rotolo brothers in Sicily were opened to behold the wonders of sight. These boys, born with cataracts, had all their lives groped about in darkness until modern surgery gave them vision. But with sight there came also heart-breaking disillusionment. The country home where they lived with their unemployed father and work-worn mother seemed huge and wonderful when they groped in darkness from one corner to another. With sight there came the realization that their home was only one room with smoke-stained walls and rickety furnishings.

But the revelation of the moral and spiritual grandeur of God as revealed in Jesus Christ has never led people to disillusionment in twenty centuries, no matter what their progress, but from glory to glory after one's spiritual eyes are opened to behold the light of the glory of God in the face of Jesus Christ.

What think ye of Christ is a crucial question for every person, for the answer one gives to this determines one's theology—one's vision and knowledge of God.

There is a second reason for the crucial importance of the question, "What think ye of Christ?" It is determinative not only for our theology, but also for our soteriology. Our answer to this question determines the quarter to which we look for deliverance.

The nature of the human situation has always been such that man is looking for salvation or deliverance from something that is threatening him. Once it was dinosaurs and saber-toothed tigers; now it is the guided missile. Once it was the bubonic plague; now it is global war.

When Jesus in the temple courts turned to those Pharisees who had been trying for hours to trap him with catch questions and asked them, "What think ye of Christ?" he was asking primarily a soteriological question: "Where are you expecting your deliverer to come from?" The Jewish name for deliverer was *Messiah*. The Greek word was *Christ*. Long had Jewish hopes centered on a coming Messiah who would deliver God's people from their troubles. But people could not agree on the nature and the work of the deliverer. Some looked for a Messiah who would be a great general to lead Israel's armies in victory over her oppressors. Some expected God, himself, to appear with legions of angels to put evil to flight and to establish his righteous, heavenly kingdom on earth.

But when Jesus came, people's thoughts about the Christ did not coincide with what they saw in him. They were disappointed and disillusioned. "Instead of threatening Rome, he had warned Israel. Instead of rallying the leaders of Judaism, he had sternly denounced them. Instead of encouraging to action, he had talked of forgiveness and love," writes O. Sydney Barr in *From the Apostles' Faith to the Apostles' Creed.*

Jesus Christ saw the ultimate enemy of man as sin and addressed himself to effecting deliverance for man from that destroyer. With that concept of the Messiah's mission, he lived and died. For his trouble many despised and rejected him; some scorned him as inconsequential, but some adored and trusted in him.

What think ye of Christ, the Messiah? Where do you look for your salvation? To science? Henry Roth, author of the bestseller *Call It Sleep* said in the January 8, 1965, issue of *Life* magazine, "I think that automation and atomic science and technology will give us some new moral framework to replace religion."

Or do you look to the state as the most substantial quarter whence your salvation may come? Many have, in times ancient and modern, in cultures primitive and sophisticated. The cult of emperor worship in the long ago of Rome's heyday and the thriving of the omnicompetent state in twentieth century Russia and China are one and the same thing soteriologically—man's search for deliverance in his own social creations. So we see the rising tide of trust in the state to solve all our problems and to save us from all that threatens. For education, it is federal funds that will do it; for health and welfare, it is Medicare and eldercare; for city slums, it is urban renewal.

Or do you put your trust in your own initiative? An article in *Nation's Business,* "The Ultimate Weapon in War on Poverty," featured the stories of three men: one, a young black man from the Bronx slums; another, a former West Virginia coal miner; a third, a tenant farmer from Maryland. Each one fought his own battle against poverty with his own initiative, his own energy, and his own wisdom, and won out.

But it can never be the state or one's own initiative or science to which man can look for deliverance with complete confidence. For man and his political states and his sciences are all corrupted with the congenital human disease of sin. Something needs to be done to create within man a spirit in which he can believe in God and himself again and so strive, not trusting in self or his state as the ultimate source of all meaning, but as a favored and blessed child of God. He sees himself not as the castoff and deserted, but as the beloved and ransomed child of God.

George Buttrick, commenting on this text (Matt. 22:42) in *The Interpreter's Bible,* writes:

> When we probe to the depth of our desire, we find there a longing for genuine renewal. We crave a Messiah who will walk the road with us as companion, and yet carry a lantern that is far better than our human lamps. We crave a Messiah who will not shrink from the shame of our sins, but who yet in his purity can cleanse us of our sins. We crave a Messiah who can grant us power to rise above our dead selves to very life. We crave a deliverer who is willing to taste death, and who yet

conquers death to give assurance of eternity. In the depth of our desire
the Messiah is—Christ."

Finally, "What think ye of Christ?" is crucial for everyone, not only
because our answer determines the theological framework of our minds and
the soteriological trust of our hearts, but also because it sets up the ethical
framework of our daily lives.

Some of us who profess a staunch loyalty to a high credal statement
about the deity of Jesus Christ sometimes look down our doctrinal noses on
the low Christology of Unitarians and such, and sometimes we are shamed
by the ethical integrity of those who, though professing to believe less than
we about the deity of Christ, nevertheless prove themselves more loyal in
obedience to some commands of that Christ than we.

It was Thomas, the doubter, who, when his Lord proposed to go up to
Jerusalem where danger threatened, said to his comrade, "Let us also go, that
we may die with him."

The late Justice Felix Frankfurter, who early left Orthodox Judaism and
lived his life presumably as an agnostic, was nevertheless characterized by
legal scholar Alexander Bickel on Frankfurter's seventy-fifth birthday as
having an "utter inability to so much as modulate moral and intellectual
integrity." Frankfurter once said to his Christian friend Reinhold Niebuhr,
after hearing Niebuhr preach, "Reinie, may a believing unbeliever thank you
for your sermon?" To which Niebuhr replied, "May an unbelieving believer
thank you for appreciating it?"

Of course, the point is not that we should believe less that we may obey
more, but rather the contrary—that what we profess to believe should find
clear and courageous expression in what we do.

Unless Jesus Christ is our existential Lord—Lord and Master now in
this moment of our existence—influencing what we do and are, neither is he
our Savior from that which he calls sin in our hearts and our social order, nor
is he the revelation of the God whom we really worship in the sanctuary of
our souls. As Richard Watson Gilder's poem "The Song of a Heathen" says:

If Jesus Christ is a man—
And only a man—I say
That of all mankind I will cleave
to him,
And to him will I cleave alway.
If Jesus Christ is a god—
And the only God—I swear
I will follow him through heaven
and hell,
And earth, the sea, and the air."

"What think ye of Christ?"

The Discipline of Time

"Remember the sabbath day, to keep it holy" (Exod. 20:8).

One of the supreme services of religion is to train people in the discipline of time. As early as the seventh century, according to the *Principles of Church Union,* the calendar of the church year was fairly well set with Christmas and Easter, Advent and Lent designated. "In all this [making of the calendar] what was most at stake was the discipline of time, an ordered pattern of the year which helped keep the church mindful of what the faith of Christians cost and how it happened, and of the church's need to design a pattern of time which would reflect the wholeness of God's relationship to us," the *Principles of Church Union* states.

Historically, the Church's fundamental exercise in schooling people in the discipline of time has been the keeping of one day in the week for worship. For the Hebrew people it was Sabbath observance, saving the seventh day for rest and worship, enshrined in the Fourth Commandment, "Remember the sabbath day, to keep it holy." For the Christian it became the first day of the week, Sunday, saved for God and soul because this was the weekly anniversary of God's mighty act in raising his son from the dead.

I remember those stirring words of James Stewart of Scotland in his sermon "God's Glory in the Morning" from *The Strong Name:* "When the Romans built their great walls across the north of England, they placed at intervals of a mile apart, towers rising above the ordinary level of the wall; and there the sentinels were set to stand and watch. And when God built the battlements of our human life He placed at every seventh day a tower, a day thrust up above life's common levels, for the safeguarding of our souls."

One of the most disturbing aspects of present-day American life is the loss of Christian conviction about the crucial importance of the discipline of time. Modern men and women have lost all sense of urgency about nearly every discipline, especially the discipline of time. Central to this is the slipping away of the staunch observance of Sunday as a day set apart.

Church attendance is sharply declining in all denominations all over America. A church member said to me: "We Christians don't even attach the importance to attendance at worship that Rotarians do to their weekly meetings. If they miss they are under obligation to make up their attendance. We miss worship and think nothing of it."

Alexander Solzhenitsyn was interviewed by a *Time* magazine reporter at his home in Cavendish, Vermont. The famous Russian author, who spent many years in Soviet prisons and came at last to the United States in 1976 after being forcibly exiled from his native land on charges of treason, was far from uncritical of what he found in our American way of life. He discerned:

> a loss of the serious moral basis of society ... a sweeping away of duties and an expansion of rights. But we have two lungs. You can't breathe with just one lung and not with the other. We must avail ourselves of rights and duties in equal measure. And if this is not established by the law ... then we have to control ourselves. When Western society was established, it was based on the idea that each individual limited his own behavior. Everyone understood what he could do and what he could not do. The law itself did not restrain people. Since then, the only thing we have been developing is rights, rights, rights, at the expense of duty.

What's happening in America today is not any new, unusual departure. What is going on has been going on for a long time: the godless being ungodly, the faithful worshiping God and giving themselves to humanitarian service. What is distinctive about our time is that we have come to one of those continental divides in history when the descent is more rapid and precipitate, when the drift to godlessness is more general, when multitudes of people are being sucked into the maw of hell's destruction, when the world's accommodation to compromise spreads, not like ink on a blotter, but like a grassfire whipped by a fierce wind, when the rank and file of church members are following the god-despisers to perform all sorts of iniquities.

And the place for concerned Christians to peg this destructive drift, to break away from this collision course of contemporary culture, is at the point of keeping one day in the week for God and the soul, for as always, this is the fundamental point of beginning in the schooling of people in the discipline of time. People must be trained to accept the four fundamental principles of time: first, the origin of time; second, the divisions of time; third, the purpose of time; and fourth, the end of time.

First, then, see what saving Sunday for God does toward making people mindful of the origin of time. The account of the Fourth Commandment in the book of Exodus sets the origin of the observance of the Sabbath in the primeval event of creation. One way of saying that God made man is to say: It is God, the Creator, who gives man time—all the time he has—one day at a time.

People need to be reminded of this. If in the midst of time people never pause to remember their Creator in the days of their youth, they will soon cease to be aware of the divine origin of all their time, that all their days are reeled out to them by Another. To refuse to do this or to grow lax in maintaining this fundamental discipline of time is to fail to acknowledge God's sovereignty over all of man's time.

So we must be disciplined to pause one day in seven and say, "This is the day which the Lord hath made; we will rejoice and be glad in it."

A second function of the strict observance of Sunday worship in the discipline of time is that it helps people accept the varying stages of time. All time is not the same. The unfolding mystery of life is in clearly definable ages or stages: infancy, childhood, adolescence, young adulthood, middle age, and old age. Only a disciplined use of time marks the march of the Sundays, focuses upon the characteristics of each age, cultivates the fruits of each age, and guards against the follies peculiar to that time of life.

The great American heresy of attempting to live in a state of perpetual youth, the foolish refusal to accept the states of time, leaves one living in the pitiful illusion that time may be made to stand still and one may live out his days forever pegged at any given age—thirty, thirty-five, forty. This is so often the foolish fiction of one who has cut himself off from the weekly discipline of time.

In the third place, see what the keeping of one day holy unto God will do for clarifying our understanding of the purpose of all time, in all its stages.

As the Exodus account of the Fourth Commandment sets the origin of the observance of a day of rest and worship in the creation, so the

Deuteronomy account links it with the historic event of Israel's deliverance from her Egyptian bondage. The people of God are to remember to keep one day sacrosanct for rest and worship, not only for themselves and their God, but also for the sake of all people, especially those who are their servants, remembering that their God delivered them from the inhumane and unjust treatment of unscrupulous tyrants.

So the revelation of the divine purpose in the giving of time to man is that man may use all of his life, seven days a week of it, to glorify God and enjoy him forever.

Did you see the cartoon of the two barflies leaning over their beers with the caption, "I've found my niche in life—third stool from the end"? Such is the nature of man's use of time, that if he spends enough of his days anywhere—child of God though he is, fashioned in the image of God—that becomes his niche in life. Dean William Ralph Inge of London's St. Paul's Cathedral affirmed, "Our souls are dyed in the color of our leisure thoughts."

That Scottish saint Samuel Rutherford, out of the rock-ribbed discipline of his pious Presbyterian heritage, could cry: "What do we have our time and our life for, but to pour them out unto the Lord? What is a candle for but to be burnt?"

It is only out of a disciplined use of time devoted to God's glory in the service of others after the example of Christ that people can learn to use time for its supreme purpose—to glorify God and enjoy him forever.

In Thornton Wilder's play *The Angel That Troubled the Waters,* a scene is laid at the pool of Siloam, where at a certain hour of the day, the gospel story tells us, an angel ruffles the surface of the water and whoever at that moment is lowered into the pool is healed of his infirmity. In the throng of sufferers gathered expectantly around the pool one day, a physician is discovered. He suffers from a "heart in pain," a heavy feeling of sinfulness, and like the others, he is seeking a miraculous restoration of wholeness and health. But as he pushes forward he hears the angel of healing speak to him.

"Draw back, physician.... Healing is not for you.... Without your wound where would your power be?" the angel asks in Wilder's play. "It is your very remorse that makes your low voice tremble into the hearts of men. The very angels themselves cannot persuade the wretched and blundering children on earth as can one human being broken on the wheels of living. In Love's service only the wounded soldiers can serve. Draw back."

And so the physician learns the truth of what the Epistle to the Hebrews says of the Great Physician, "In Love's service only the wounded soldiers can serve."

The supreme purposes of time are understood and grasped only by those so disciplined in the use of time that they have learned to accept what God has done to us in the midst of time, even our crippling and our suffering, as part of equipping us for his service to others in the world.

But the ultimate service the Christian discipline of time renders God's man or his woman is girding one up for the ultimate adventure of this life—the end of earthly time.

As the faithful Christian keeps every Sunday for a day to praise his God, he is reminded of the mighty deed of his Heavenly Father in raising his son from the dead on the first day of the week and of that son's promise to his faithful disciples that they, through the amazing grace of God, would also be raised, for death could not hold the victory over them.

One day as I made my way up to a hospital room to see an elderly parishioner, I was wondering how I would find her. Her medical diagnosis was arteriosclerosis of the brain. She had been ill a long time, and I was afraid she would be so far gone as not to be able to converse.

On entering the room I saw how frail and thin she was, like a piece of wrinkled parchment on the bed. But her conversation was bright, crisp, and to the point. She talked of her concern for her husband, who was also ill in the same hospital. She asked me to go see him and to tell him that she sent her love and had enjoyed a good dinner. She talked of the visit of the youth group from the church to their home some weeks before to sing Christmas carols, recalling her conversation with some of the children, calling them by name, and linking them with other generations of their families she had known and respected in the congregation.

On leaving I asked if we might have prayer together. When I had finished my prayer, she began immediately to pray and said:

> *O God, grant that I may*
> *"So live, that when [my] summons comes to join*
> *The innumerable caravan, which moves*
> *To the mysterious realm, where each shall take*
> *His chamber in the silent halls of death,*
> *[I] go not, like the quarry-slave at night,*
> *Scourged to his dungeon, but, sustained and soothed*
> *By an unfaltering trust, approach [my] grave*
> *Like one who wraps the drapery of his couch*
> *About him, and lies down to pleasant dreams."*

Whence came these great words? What was the source of such calm courage in darkness and distress? The words, of course, came from William Cullen Bryant, but they were hers now only because an early discipline of the mind in memorization had made them hers. And the courage and the confidence behind the words and laying hold of them then was not a chance occurrence, but the result of the discipline of the years.

All things come from the Eternal God himself, but he has so ordered our lives in time that even he will not furnish his children such sinews of the spirit, such armor of the soul, without discipline of mind and body and spirit in the words of the faith and the chaste emotions of the faith and the noble deeds of the faith week by week, Sunday by Sunday.

The Time Factor in the Struggle of the Soul

"To day if ye will hear his voice, Harden not your heart" (Ps. 95:7-8).

I've picked a text from the ninety-fifth Psalm that goes with the Scripture lesson in Ecclesiastes about there being a time for all things.

The text sounds a note of urgency and warning: If today God speaks to you, offering you his goodness, his gracious salvation, don't refuse it. Don't be like Israel in the wilderness, whose distrust and disobedience in refusing God's offer of his Promised Land condemned the Israelites to forty years of wilderness wanderings and ultimately to death in the desert.

Much of the urgency to respond to God's offer of salvation has dropped out of modern theology, preaching, and church work. The old cliche "Preach the gospel as a dying man to dying people" is an interesting but archaic exhortation for young theological students of a far-off day. Few of us get worked up over that slogan now.

The time was when people were moved to accept the salvation of God in Christ through the preacher's proclaiming the brevity of life or the certainty of judgment. "Brother, you may be dead tomorrow. Are you ready to meet your Maker today?" or, "The world is soon coming to an end. Are you ready now for the final Judgment of God?"

But modern people have registered resounding revulsion toward too crude a proclamation of such a gospel urgency for decision, because everybody didn't die yesterday and the end of the world did not come last Thursday. And yet, the reaction of a sophisticated modern world to the claims of the Christian gospel has really been very unsophisticated. For there is a time factor that operates in the struggle and the salvation of souls, perhaps not as simply as sometimes suggested, but nevertheless as inexorably. How foolish people have been when they have acted as though there were no time factor, just because it did not always operate for everyone precisely as outlined by the fire and brimstone or end-of-the-world-a-comin' hot gospellers.

But everything, yes, everything, is caught up in the time form in this world in which we live. That old cynic Koheleth noticed the invariable operation of the cycle of time: There is "a time to be born, and a time to die; a time to plant, and a time to pluck up ... A time to weep, and a time to laugh." Who doesn't know as much and apply Koheleth's ancient wisdom to every realm of our worldly affairs?

There is a time for race horses to run, a span of just so many short years and then they are turned out to graze. There is a time of maximum performance for big-league ballplayers, and then the reflexes slow down. There is a time for peak capacity leadership that mature men and women can give to their business, their church, their community. For there is a time, a season for all things, a period when men and women can respond to opportunities for service and a time when they cannot. The time factor is a reality in our existence and we are caught in it.

Why won't we recognize that this inexorable time factor also operates in our opportunity to respond to God's call and his offer of salvation to us today? One afternoon as I was walking out of the Peabody Hotel, I heard the screaming siren of a cruising police car. Down Union Avenue in front of me the car sped, screeching to an abrupt stop in the next block where a crowd was gathering on the sidewalk. My step quickened with my mounting curiosity, and soon I was gazing down at the sickening sight that drew the crowd—the limp form of a man lying on the pavement. My eye followed the upward look of the bystanders until I saw, several stories up, the tilted painter's scaffold from which the workman had fallen.

Stabbing my conscience was the thought that my fellow citizen's time to respond to the grace of God in this life had come abruptly to an end, but my time was still to come. He was not less worthy to live than I, but he had died. Why? I do not know. I can observe this fact and know that for me, as well as for him, that time to respond to God's gracious call is not unlimited. All of life is caught up in the scheme of time. We have a time to respond to God's grace and goodness, but like all things in this world, that time comes to an end.

Why will we not be smart enough to see that the time factor looms large in the struggle, yes, even the salvation, of our souls and respond today. "To day if ye will hear his voice, Harden not your heart."

First, consider the time factor in relation to the psychological processes as they affect the struggle of the soul. One basic fact upon which all psychologists agree is that refusal to respond to any given stimulus renders a person less likely, even less able, to respond to the same stimulus the next time.

Charles Darwin, in his later years, confessed that in his youth he had a taste for music and poetry, but he shut his mind to these interests during the hurried, mature years when he gave himself completely to his study of science. Later, in old age, he discovered that the mind he had used so long as a sort of mill for working over and grinding out scientific data no longer would respond at all to music and poetry.

"To day if ye will hear his voice, Harden not your heart," for there is a time factor in the psychological world at work, and the time will come when your repeated refusals to hear and heed his call will render you insensitive, even deaf, to the entreating invitation of your God. The Eternal will not stop calling, but your time for comprehending and responding will be gone. You may not die tomorrow, the world may not end in atomic fission day after tomorrow, but such is the psychological law governing your life that your refusal to respond to God's grace today will render you a bit harder for him to reach tomorrow.

Then, too, there is a time factor operating in the social order as it affects the salvation of your soul. God uses other men and women and little children as his agents, his ambassadors of grace. Through them he is now struggling for your soul. Today, if you hear his voice speaking to you in the counsel, wisdom, or appeal of some servant of his, harden not your heart, for you and that person are caught in the time factor. Your messenger may never pass this way again. Refuse God's invitation through him and your soul may never be sent another ambassador to stir you to such a depth.

And it is not necessarily the eloquent or appealing or attractive person whom God uses to stir your soul to the depths. How often it is the devout but limited servant of God, like that lay Methodist preacher in Colchester Chapel whose halting efforts stirred the great preacher Charles Haddon Spurgeon to give his heart to Christ. After the service Spurgeon was heard to remark about the preacher's sermon: "The fellow had not much to say, and for that reason he kept repeating his text. But the text was all that was needed, at least by me. And his text was that word from Isaiah, 'Look unto me, and be ye saved, all the ends of the earth.'"

Yes, and it may be that in the changing pattern of personalities that God moves about us, his clearest call that stirs us the deepest comes, not in church, not even by way of high inspiration, but rather in an abysmal sense of shame. It was this way that salvation broke through to Saul Kane in John Masefield's poem "The Everlasting Mercy." Kane, coming out of a drunken stupor, hears first the poor widow Jaggard upbraiding him for his evil influence upon her boy, and then Miss Bourne, the mild little Quaker, speaking her cool but scathing words to him:

> *"Saul Kane," she said, "when next you drink,*
> *Do me the gentleness to think*
> *That every drop of drink accursed*
> *Makes Christ within you die of thirst."*

And it was under such tongue-lashing that old Kane's spirit came to birth, responding to the merciful call of the Father, and reverently Kane said:

> *"The water's going out to sea*
> *And there's a great moon calling me;*
> *But there's a great sun calls the moon,*
> *And all God's bells will carol soon*
> *For joy and glory and delight*
> *Of someone coming home to-night."*

And so, Saul Kane came home to God. But however or by whomever the call of God comes, the point is, don't let it pass without your heeding, for the time factor looms large. Never again may you be stirred to such depths.

And finally, there is the time factor operating in the historical situation as it affects your soul's salvation. That is what was in the Psalmist's mind as he spoke prophetically to Israel: "To day if ye will hear his voice, Harden not your heart." God had wrought mighty acts of salvation along the tortuous path of his people's history. God had showed his hand as the Lord of history in their deliverance from Pharaoh's slave labor battalions, in leading them safely through the parted waters of the Red Sea, in feeding them on manna and quail in the desert. Now they stood on Jordan's bank, the border of their Promised Land, and the voice of the Lord came commanding them to march in and take it.

But in that day the Israelites showed an amazing lack of trust in their God, who had proven his power of deliverance. They did not respond obediently. In distrust and murmuring they turned aside, and God gave them up to what James Baikie in his *The Story of the Bible* called "the aimless years" of wilderness wanderings when for forty years this was the weird enchantment that lay upon them: They must be ever striving but never achieve, ever be traveling but never arrive at their destination.

Such also is the oft-repeated experience in the spiritual pilgrimage of many a man and woman. God in his mercy shows his hand of deliverance in the very events of our experiences—that desperate illness, that financial catastrophe, that season of crucial temptation. We faced serious and dire calamity. We cried with all our hearts to God for merciful protection and escape. He responded more wonderfully than we dreamed possible. Then came, too, his voice calling us to cross over the border and dwell always in his kingdom and be ruled completely by the will of our Eternal Father. But we refused. Then inevitably came the aimless years when we cut ourselves loose from the purposes of God and existence lost its meaning.

My friends, the only way to get the best of the time allotted to us is to seize the purposes of the Eternal in the midst of time. Time begins to take on a new and more glorious dimension when the human spirit is synchronized into eternity by an act of human response to the grace of God as it meets us in our own experience. Haven't you spent days and days—years even—that seemed aimless, meaningless, wasted? Always striving but never achieving, always journeying but never arriving? Then comes the moment when in obedience to the divine voice we walk where Jesus walked, we take up the burdens he took upon himself, and the moments pulse with power; they gleam with eternal meaning. There is life, vitality, exhilaration in the flow of existence. We know we are caught up in the eternal purposes—and it is not just at the moment of decision for confession of faith, nor of accepting for the first time the forgiveness of our sins, but in obedience to God's call to a new opportunity for service, a new outpouring of sympathy, a new response to his will in the depth of our sorrow or loss.

Limitless, unbelievable, beyond man's imaginings are the mercy and grace of our God. But we are mortals. We are creatures. We are finite, limited beings. There is a beginning of our days and an end. We are caught in the time scheme. We know we must conform to it in laboring hours ("the night cometh, when no man can work") and in keeping social engagements (the party is set for an appointed hour, and if we arrive two hours late, the banquet is over). And we are fools if in the area of our most crucial relationships, in our spiritual salvation, we persist in acting as if we were infinite and had all the time of eternity yet waiting for us to respond to the mercy and grace of God.

"To day if ye will hear his voice, Harden not your heart.... Behold, I stand at the door, and knock: if any man hear my voice, and open the door, I will come in to him, and will sup with him, and he with me." Delay not. Now is the time.

THREE

Christian Love in the Family Circle

The Pattern of Family Life

"Be subject to one another out of reverence for Christ" (Eph. 5:21).

People keep saying that the family as we have known it is doomed. That's what the new morality cult has been saying in America for the last two or three decades, that the institution of marriage and the traditional pattern of family life are gone forever.

Of course, that's what the Communists were believing and preaching for the past seventy or eighty years. They were confident that all the sentimental, American hogwash about Mother's Day would fade into oblivion. For Marxist doctrine always held that with the destruction of the evil capitalistic system, some of the institutions that have been characteristic of capitalist, bourgeois culture would wither and die, and foremost among these, marked for inevitable destruction, was the family.

But now, on this Mother's Day with communism and all Marxist theories and teachings being discredited and thrown on the junk heap of history, can we take hope for the family's survival? Or would we be prematurely and naively optimistic, failing to discern all the glaring signs of the withering away of the American family's strength, produced, not by the blight of

Communist propaganda, but by a spiritual malignancy, entirely local and American, eating away at the American family's soul from within?

One of the principal concerns of the Christian church through the centuries has been to strengthen the family. In Thornton Wilder's play *The Skin of Our Teeth,* the family is depicted in successive ages and civilizations as always under attack, and Mrs. Anthropos—the woman, the wife, the mother—pleads, "Save the Family. It's held together for over five thousand years: Save it!" The Church, like Mrs. Anthropos, is driven by the same obsession.

But why is the Church so interested in keeping the family a healthy, going institution of society? Because the Church knows that strong, healthy, happy families furnish the best environment for growing souls. John Mackay, in *Heritage and Destiny,* puts it this way: "Life is a vale of soul-making, and souls are more important than civilizations. And souls are not made in solitude nor were they designed to live in solitariness." The home, the family, is the factory for soul manufacture, and the pattern of production there is of utmost importance.

In fact, the Church has always held that the family is a divine institution and that God himself has a pattern for ordering Christian family life. If this pattern is followed, the family will be a strong, cohesive social unit, able to stand against the hostile forces that attack it from within or without and able to perform its immortal function of soul-making.

What is that pattern? Paul in Ephesians puts it quite simply in easy, straightforward terms: "Submitting yourselves one to another in the fear of God." Or, as the Revised Standard Version translates his words: "Be subject to one another out of reverence for Christ." Wisely, Saint Paul does not go into minute or specific detail in outlining the pattern of Christian family life. Families vary from small units to large. Not all families have grandmothers. Some brothers don't have sisters. In some families father or mother is not there—or can't be counted on in the Christian pattern. Social conditions that impinge on family life change from generation to generation. Paul does not give detailed rules for ordering family life according to the Christian pattern. He just enunciates the great, overarching principle of mutual submission or subjection for all members of the family.

The term he uses is an old military expression pointing to the soldier's subjecting himself to the rule of company and commander for the sake of a common cause. The commentary on this text in *The Interpreter's Bible* states that "the spirit of mutual subjection is cardinal to the whole Christian conception of social relations. It is the antithesis of the spirit of self-assertion, of jealous insistence on one's rights, which generally characterizes the men of the world. In substance it rests upon the example and precept of Christ, who 'did not count equality with God a thing to be grasped, but emptied himself, taking the form of a servant'" This is, of course, the antithesis of the sentiment expressed in those words of the popular song, "I did it my way."

The Christian pattern of family life, then, is one of mutual submission on the part of every member of the family to one another in accordance with the love and spirit of Christ. It is a way of life summed up by an inscription in a wedding ring I have seen: "Each for the other and both for God."

But what does this principle of mutual submission involve in the varied family relationships of husband and wife, parents and children? Paul spells that out pretty plainly.

First, for the wife in relation to her husband, he says, "Wives, submit yourselves unto your own husbands, as unto the Lord. For the husband is the head of the wife, even as Christ is the head of the church" (Eph. 5:22-23). Sounds pretty patriarchal, doesn't it? Undoubtedly Paul had in mind the patriarchal family unit. But even though we have come a long way from his day to women's suffrage and feminine emancipation and the women's rights movement, let it be definitely understood that the Christian pattern of family life still demands mutual subjection, and in the wife's case this means, "Wives, submit yourselves unto your own husbands, as unto the Lord. For the husband is the head of the wife, even as Christ is the head of the church."

In *Christian Behaviour*, C.S. Lewis observes:

> The relations of the family to the outer world—what might be called its foreign policy—must depend, in the last resort, upon the man, because he always ought to be, and usually is, much more just to the outsiders. A woman is primarily fighting for her own children and husband against the rest of the world.... She is the special trustee of their interests. The function of the husband is to see that this natural preference of hers isn't given its head. He has the last word in order to protect other people from the intense family patriotism of the wife. If anyone doubts this, let me ask a simple question. If your dog has bitten the child next door, or your child has hurt the dog next door, which would you sooner have to deal with, the master of that house or the mistress? Or, if you are a married woman, let me ask you this question. Much as you admire your husband, would you not say that his chief failing is his tendency not to stick up for his rights and yours against the neighbours as vigorously as you would like? A bit of an Appeaser?

But what of the husband's relationship to his wife in the Christian pattern for family life? Again, the principle of mutual submission is invoked. Paul spells it out clearly: "Husbands, love your wives, even as Christ also loved the church, and gave himself for it" (Eph. 5:25). The heavier obligation of submission is laid on the husband. The one explicit command to complete sacrifice of self in all the precepts for Christian family relationships is directed to the husband or father in the family. He must love and give himself for it.

One of the most ancient symbols of Christ in his Atonement is that of the pelican in her piety. According to the legend, the pelican in time of famine would open with her own beak the great artery in her breast and pour out her life's blood for her young that through her death they might drink and live. This is a symbol of what Christ did for his Church, which in turn is the model of the supreme submission of the husband's love and self-giving for his wife. As the captain cannot leave his sinking ship, so, in the pattern of Christian family life, the husband must in love give himself for his wife.

Last, there is a third area of relationships in the pattern of Christian family life: parents and children. "Children, obey your parents in the Lord: for this is right" (Eph. 6:1). See, this business of mutual submission still runs all through the Christian family, and here the form the submission takes is that of a child's obedience to his parents, or literally his hearkening unto them in the Lord.

Parents are not just bosses to tyrannize over their children. Children are not born into a straitjacket pattern of family life and owe obedience to their elders just because parents are older and bigger, but in order "that it may be well with thee and thou mayest live long on the earth."

Rufus Jones, the Quaker philosopher, as a very young child was aware he had come into a world "where love was waiting for me, and into a family in which religion was as important an element for life as was the air we breathed or the bread we ate." In later boyhood and early manhood, Jones says, he encountered "every kind of temptation except bank-robbery," but he was kept safe and pure from participation in vulgarity by "that culture of the spirit in the family center." He submitted himself to the religious regimen of his family—obeying his parents in the Lord—and in later years he saw that this pattern of Christian life was exactly what had saved him and gave joy, beauty, and stability to his whole life. This submission and obedience to his father and mother in the things of the Lord did not destroy his affection for them but enhanced it. As Jones's biographer, David Hinshaw, writes in *Rufus Jones, Master Quaker,* his mother was so important to him that in the last years of her life, as her health failed, "when friends would ask him how she was, he would be unable to say a word."

If children living in a pattern of Christian family life find that submission to parents galls at times, let them remember that the submission is mutual. Parents in the pattern of a Christian home must submit themselves unto their children in the Lord. A man and his wife were showing me through their new, half-completed house. It was a magnificent structure. But what they seemed to be most enthusiastic about was the family room. "This is what we are most proud of," they said. "When our children get to their teens, we want them and their friends with us here rather than out on the town."

A grandfather was talking to me about his son and grandsons. The grandfather was concerned about his son, a mature man who had not been well, and he said, "My son has a big job cut out for him, educating those three boys." The father's health must be taken care of, his strength conserved, that he may submit himself to the divine commission to launch those three young lives.

The pattern of Christian family life is amazingly simple—all based on the principle of mutual subjection. "Be subject to one another out of reverence for Christ." And the family that unanimously adopts that pattern finds their home becoming a heaven.

The poet Carl Sandburg in *Always the Young Strangers* wrote of the beautiful bond of mutual subjection that was willingly taken in his family:

Mama's wedding ring was never lost—it was always on that finger as placed there with pledges years ago. It was a sign and seal of something that ran deep and held fast between the two of them. They had chosen each other as partners. How they happened to meet I heard only from my mother…. A smile spread over her face half-bashful and a bright light came to her blue eyes as she said, "I saw it was my chance." She was saying this at least twenty years after the wedding and there had been hard work always, tough luck at times, seven children of whom two had died on the same day—and she had not one regret that she had jumped at her "chance" when she saw it.

Here is our chance at life's most satisfying arrangement of these dearest relationships in family and home: "Be subject to one another out of reverence for Christ." Will we jump at our chance?

Fixed Ground

"My heart is fixed" (Ps. 57:7).
"Stand fast in the Lord" (Phil. 4:1).

Leslie F. Church in his biography of John Wesley, *Knight of the Burning Heart,* records the passing of John's father, Samuel, in these words: "The death of the old rector changed many things. With all his failings he had been fixed ground for his family."

Yes, old Samuel Wesley had many failings. He was always hopelessly in debt. He had served the tiny village parish at Epworth most of his life, and he was never called to a larger congregation. His parishioners were not too devoted to him. They resented his biblical preaching about their sins. He rebuked them for their violence and ill temper. Often in the middle of the night, the Wesley family would be awakened by a crowd of the rowdier element in Epworth beating on the side of the house with sticks, trying to drive their unpopular pastor out of town. Many were old Samuel's failings, but Leslie Church says of him: "The death of the old rector changed many things. With all his failings he had been fixed ground for his family."

Here's a tonic thought for tired, discouraged middle-aged folks suffering from the slump of the sixties, the failures of the fifties, or the fatigue of the forties—yes, and even for us of the three-score-years-and-ten-plus crowd: With all our failings, remember, we are fixed ground for someone. You can't quit or throw in the towel. You can't even stop for long enough to enjoy a brief respite of self-pity. There's someone depending on you, in the generation just ahead or the one just behind or one of your contemporaries who has suffered from life some crippling wound and is looking in your direction for steadying support.

What if you have failed here and there in this venture or that relationship? Who hasn't? Someone once said to me, "As I look back over my life I can see it has been just one failure after another." All of us have felt like that at times.

Even John Quincy Adams at forty-five wrote in his diary, "Two-thirds of a long life are past, and I have done nothing to distinguish it by usefulness to my country or to mankind." And later, nearing seventy, having distinguished himself as secretary of state, president of the United States, and an eloquent member of Congress, Adams recorded: "My whole life has been a succession of disappointments. I can scarcely recollect a single instance of success in anything that I ever undertook."

Though scores of failures stare us in the face, though the black clouds of disappointment and sorrowful losses are all about, remember there's not a single one of us who's not fixed ground for someone.

Often folks in the middle years come suddenly to the discovery that their personal ambitions have not been realized and that these ambitions are more than likely impossible to achieve. But even this is no occasion for despair. Though our dreams of personal glory and prestige may never come true, life has not lost its meaning. It may be that we are on the verge of life's greatest discovery—namely that we are here for someone else's sake, that we are fixed ground for another to stand upon, and through fulfilling that role, we'll get, not only life's greatest satisfaction, but our one chance at fame.

Jesus once said something that indicated he thought a personal discovery of this sort was the one and only entrance into the Kingdom of God. Remember? "If any man will come after me, let him deny himself [disown himself, think no longer of his own success], and take up his cross, and follow me."

Old Samuel Wesley never was much of a personal or professional success, but he and his wife, Susanna, nurtured and trained and sent forth into the world a remarkable family. One of his sons attended Charterhouse School and achieved such a life of distinguished service that to this day the little

British boys who go to that school proudly proclaim his name as they sing their school song:

> *Wesley, John Wesley, was one of our company,*
> *Prophet untiring and fearless of tongue;*
> *Down the long years he went,*
> *Spending, yet never spent,*
> *Serving his God with a heart ever young.*

And another of old Samuel and Susanna's boys, Charles Wesley, wrote dozens of hymns that are still sung, not only by Methodists, but by millions of Christians of all denominations all over the world.

And then, too, let's remember that it's not just financial support that's furnishing fixed ground for someone, important as that always is. It is moral, spiritual, psychological fixed ground that others are seeking in you. Your confidence that builds up their self-confidence, your faith in their future that hangs up a goal for them to shoot at, your expressed assurance that you are counting on them not to let you down—this is the fixed ground that is more important than financial support. A lack of financial support can be compensated for, while a failure of confidence is disastrous.

Samuel Wesley was pretty much of a failure in backing up his boys with cash when they went away to school, but no one ever outdid him in expressing high hopes, expectations, and confidence in their ability to take advantage of their education for the service of God and man.

Rufus Jones, the Quaker philosopher, once overheard his small son, Lowell, talking with a group of playmates. The boys were telling what each one wanted to be when he was grown. Finally, Lowell's turn came, and he said, "I want to grow up and be a man like my daddy." Jones said that few things in his life ever touched him more or gave him a stronger push to dedication. "What kind of a man was I going to be," he said, "if I was to be the pattern for my boy!"

A young businessman in talking of a more mature associate said: "He could have made much more money out of his business than he has, but money is not his first consideration. He has a passion never to do anything that would reflect on the reputation his father had and bequeathed to him in his name and his business."

Morally and spiritually you are fixed ground for someone. Never forget it.

And, of course, this business of furnishing fixed ground for other lives is not entirely the vocation of parents to fulfill for their children and of older brothers and sisters for the younger. Some of the strongest lines of influence have cut across all family connections. Here is where the Church, if it has any reality as a communion of saints, can perform its powerful ministry for fashioning personality.

How many young men and women in business and professional life are building their careers, their moral and ethical judgments, their standards of success, on the fixed ground of older men and women they admire and observe in church and community.

A promising young man, on a bold, brave venture away from home and the restraints and supports of society where he is known, gives his word that he is held firm on fixed ground and spiritual foundations by the faithful correspondence of a former teacher who contrives through every possible expression of her confidence and affection to lay stone upon stone for his sure foundation.

Don't despair, don't lose hope, hold on in the struggle. Remember, in spite of all your failings, you are fixed ground for someone.

But this would be empty counsel, sheer autosuggestion, unless there were some solid, unshakable ground upon which each one of us could take our stand. One of the surest things we know about ourselves in our more sane moments is how unstable we are. How quickly anger flares up hotly! How long resentment smolders! How suddenly unexpected opposition topples us over! So our stout resolves turn to water; our brave, firm stands become forsaken posts. Unless there is available to us, from some quarter outside ourselves, beyond our fickle emotions and wavering wills, some solid ground on which we can stand, we cannot furnish fixed support for others.

Historian Allan Nevins once said that great and admirable as moral courage is in itself, "it must be recognized that it never appears except as a part of that greater entity called character. Courage then is not an independent trait but springs from the nurture of moral breadth and poise."

How is this personality-making miracle accomplished? How is the chaos of conflicting desires in the soul of a person brought into order? How is the instability of our vagrant emotions solidified into fixed ground? How is the wall of character constructed?

Saint Paul says that it comes best and most naturally to a person who is "in Christ." God has created us each one in his image with the possibility of becoming godlike. God has provided us with a savior who alone can atone for, and deliver us from, our past sins and continuing sinful inclinations. If we will receive him for what God has appointed him, the Lord and Savior of our lives, then by his grace, as we live in him, character, Christian character, can be constructed within us, and dependable, fixed ground will appear.

This was what Jesus was talking about when he said that the people who heard his message of salvation, heeded it, and lived by his word every day could be compared to a man who built a house on a solid rock foundation. Then when the storms of life came and the winds blew and the rains beat down and the floods swirled about its foundation, it stood firm, built upon the rock of ages.

But the folks who hearing the gospel of Redemption refused it, obeying not the words and commandments of the Lord of Life, were like a man who built his house on sand without firm foundation. Then when the storms of life descended upon him, all was swept away.

The man or woman in Christ Jesus comes in time to possess what Phillips Brooks, the well-known Episcopal clergyman, called in his Lenten meditations, "the solidity of righteousness." Day by day the person dominated by the mind of Christ is, with each act of principle done, with each unselfish, merciful service rendered, laying stone upon stone the foundation of his personality set on the solid rock of Jesus Christ. It's not that he becomes indifferent to what people say or is unaffected by favorable or unfavorable events of the world about him. It's just that these have not the power to make or break him. Brooks said that it's just the difference that a storm makes to the fellow who's standing on the shore and one in a small boat at sea. The storm may vex the fellow on the beach in a hundred ways—blow sand in his eyes, whip off his hat, send a shiver down his spine, and make him button up his coat—but it sinks the poor fellow out at sea.

If Jesus Christ is the Lord of your life, if he really rules in the counsels of your personality, if his love and his word are accepted as the last court of appeals for the final decision in your personal, social, political, and business affairs, then you are on fixed ground. Though the scaffolding of time crashes about you, and the rugged masonry of ancient civilizations crumbles, and the steel girders of human custom and prejudice come crashing down around you, yet you shall not be moved. Your heart is fixed. Stand fast, therefore, in Christ.

The Wedding Cake

"Be subject to one another out of reverence for Christ" (Eph. 5:21).

Connie Francis sings a popular ballad about "The Wedding Cake," insisting that the wedding cake is not just sugar and spice but contains solid, serious ingredients like duty and patience and forgiveness.

But in spite of the philosophy of Connie Francis's popular song, which sums up in homey fashion the rationale for Christian family life on this Mother's Day in 1969, there is a sizable rebellion against the institution of marriage and all the family relationships connected with it. This is one of the things the eruptions on the college campuses are all about. A growing number of young people couldn't care less about cutting the wedding cake, for they don't intend to commit themselves to the solemn covenant the wedding cake symbolizes.

According to an article in the April 1969 issue of *Redbook* magazine, a psychiatrist and a journalist ran a brief notice in eight college newspapers a few months ago with these words: "Living together? Not married? Will you participate in a group discussion of alternate ways of family life with psychiatrists from the family institute sponsored by a national magazine?"

Those who gathered in response to the notice were living together without formal marriage, some because they wanted only a temporary relationship without the permanence of marriage, and some because they were rebels, rebelling against modern society and many of its institutions, not only marriage and the family, but university and college administrations, the Church, the government, and business establishments.

One couple drawn into these discussions said, according to the *Redbook* article, that "what they objected to was society's pressure on them to seal with a binding contract what they saw as an honest and free relationship like several million other young people in the United States, France, Germany and elsewhere. They have found an issue on which they do not care to be pushed around. At present, they wish not to marry as a part of a general feeling that the institutions of society should be de-sanctified."

Now it is utterly true that traditional Christian family relationships are based on what Saint Paul called mutual subjection "to one another out of reverence for Christ." A heavy load of responsibility for each other is bound up in the bundle of a Christian family. And a tremendous amount of liturgy and symbolism and moral and ethical teaching has been piled together to sanctify the institution of the Christian family. And as Connie Francis sings about it, that is what the wedding cake is all about. That's where it starts in the marriage contract of a man and a woman. Joy and privilege, duties and responsibilities, children and grandchildren, in-laws and out-laws, in sickness and in health, till death does part—it all comes with the wedding cake. That is a lot to load people with—children and grandchildren who did not ask to be the issues of that contract.

Yet mutual subjection out of reverence for Christ is the rule for all. For the wife, mutual subjection means she is subject to her husband as the head of the family as Christ is head of the Church. For the husband, mutual subjection means that he must cherish, protect, and sacrifice for his wife as Christ loved the Church and laid down his life for the sake of the Church. For children, mutual subjection in the family means obedience to their parents in the Lord, remembering the only commandment with a promise is "Honour thy father and thy mother: that thy days may be long upon the land which the Lord thy God giveth thee."

And parents in their turn subject themselves to the welfare and equipment of their children for life, always subjecting their desires for personal pleasure and ambition and wealth to the prior and more dominant claim of their children upon them. It all comes with the wedding cake, and it's a larger order than some of the youth today with their dreams of greater personal freedom want, so they don't cut the wedding cake. They aren't about to.

But not only the young are disillusioned with the institution of the family in Western Christian culture; lots of the older folks are, too. A friend of mine was telling me recently about a friend of his who, with his wife, had lived a respectable, exemplary Christian life. They had been diligent to bring up their children in the Church with the best of Christian teaching they could manage. To their horrified surprise a son went wild, repudiating all his training, even his family relationships. The very opposite of what they had intended and worked toward had occurred. It shook their faith, not only in the value of Christian training, but in the goodness and power of God. Little wonder.

But what we must all remember is that God has given our children, as well as ourselves, complete freedom. They can choose the lifestyle of alley cats and can repudiate any and everything we have valued. This is what it means to be human.

The ideal of the Christian family with its neatly balanced scheme of mutually subjected relationships is just one of the choices open to the free spirit of man. And for me, one of the recognizable glories of this Christian family system is its realistic grappling with the paradox of human freedom and servitude. Built into the pattern of the Christian family, mutual subjection is the recognition that utter freedom is only license whose undisciplined race through this life plunges to destruction.

The journalist Malcolm Muggeridge, in talking with college and university groups recently in Canada, said: "Young people ask me all the time about promiscuity. If I say my experience is that promiscuity destroys life, they won't listen to me.... They hope I'll say either, 'It's absolutely vile,' or, 'What does it matter?' I'm not going to say either. If you turn sex, which is procreative impulse, into pleasure to be sought as an end, you will destroy both the individual integrity of people and their collective life."

Unbridled license can become the most bitter slavery, while, as an ancient Christian prayer puts it, the service of Christ can be perfect freedom.

This is the mutual subjection of each family relationship out of reverence for Christ that glorifies each with an otherworldly splendor.

As wonderful as the husband-wife, the parent-child, the brother-sister relationships are when each lives for the other, a relationship is all the more magnificent, all the more creatively free and filled with blessing, when it is consecrated to the service of Jesus Christ.

Toward the end of his autobiography, Harry Emerson Fosdick has a chapter titled "Ideas That Have Used Me." This is the top-level option of all the Christian family relationships—not to exist for themselves alone, but to be matters of mutual subjection to one another out of reverence for Christ.

What ideas will inhabit you? A rapidly changing series of psychedelic lights of brilliant hue, or Paul: "This one thing I do,... I press toward the mark for the prize of the high calling of God in Christ Jesus"?

Dr. W.E. Sangster was a beloved British minister. As William Barclay writes in his book *In the Hands of God:*

> Soon after their marriage, Sangster said to his wife: "I can't be a good husband and a good minister. I'm going to be a good minister." He seldom took his wife and family out; he often forgot his wife's birthday unless he was reminded; he spent much of his time on preaching and lecturing tours at home and abroad.
>
> As his son writes in his father's biography: "It all depends, of course, what you mean by a 'good husband'. If you mean a man who dries up as his wife washes the pots, or a handyman about the house, or even a man who takes his wife out for an occasional treat, then my father was the worst of all husbands.
>
> "But if a 'good husband' is a man who loves his wife absolutely, expresses that love daily, asks her aid in all he does, and dedicates himself to a cause which he believes is greater than both of them, then my ather was as good a husband as a minister."

This is what our family relationships are all about at their best—just our chance of subjecting ourselves to each other out of reverence for Christ, that each may be stripped of the chains and slaveries of sin and ban selfish desires and all the walls be battered down that separate us from the service of Christ that is our perfect freedom.

On Hanging Pictures

"Thy word have I hid in mine heart, that I might not sin against thee" (Ps. 119:11).

You can tell a lot about a home by taking a look at the pictures hanging on the walls. The pictures people hang in their houses reveal in a measure the kind of living that goes on there. The ideals, the tastes, the interests, the loves of that home are placarded before you in the pictures on the walls.

You go into a home and see photographs of a beautiful young girl and a manly boy and you immediately conclude: "There is a son and a daughter in this family who are loved by proud parents. Mother and father are living for these children. In a measure this home is dedicated to that boy and girl."

Or you call in a home where you see on the walls bright prints of ducks and geese in flight or white-sailed yachts skimming a blue sea. It's a fair surmise that for someone of that house, hunting and water sports are absorbing interests.

Pictures on the walls of a house tell us lots about the folks who live there.

But have you ever stopped to think that each of us has an interior picture gallery—our imagination? The imagination is the picture gallery of the soul.

The pictures that hang on the hidden walls of imagination are even more important and influential on personality, and could we but see them, they would be far more revealing than the pictures that hang on the walls of our homes.

Ezekiel puts this quite plainly in one of his visions. In prophetic ecstasy Ezekiel is conducted to the wall of the temple in Jerusalem. He is shown a small hole in the wall and told to dig through. He emerges into a large hall. Looking about him, Ezekiel sees pictures on the walls of that secret chamber, "every form of creeping things, and abominable beasts, and all the idols of the house of Israel, portrayed upon the wall round about." In the hall stand seventy of the nation's leading men. Engulfed in clouds of ritualistic incense, the elders of the people stand gazing at the images, the degrading pictures on the walls. And the voice of the Lord comes to Ezekiel, saying, "Son of man, hast thou seen what the ancients of the house of Israel do in the dark, every man in the chambers of his imagery? for they say, The Lord seeth us not; the Lord hath forsaken the earth."

What is the meaning of this vision of the prophet? Just this: The imagination is the picture gallery of the soul. Could we dig in, as Ezekiel did, to the hidden hall of each person's imagination and see the pictures that hang there, we would know the secret of that life. On the walls of imagination are to be seen the images before which that soul bows down, whether they be vile, slimy, reptilian creatures or shining ones with angels' wings whose names are Truth and Love and Beauty. It's a sacred place, this chamber of imagery in every person's soul. There burn always the fires of faith, and there go up the incense clouds of religious devotion.

C.S. Lewis, in an incredible novel, *That Hideous Strength,* tells the story of a group of moral perverts possessing preposterous power in technical skills who almost succeed in gaining control of a nation. They force out of power in the government most of the people of good will, of humane instincts, of Christian morality. They invite to earth from outer space all the demonic forces of the universe. It is a tall story, of course, such as only C.S. Lewis could tell, but it is shot through with clever insights into human nature, one of which is this: To dehumanize their recruits to prepare them for positions of power in the new, evil order, the diabolical technocrats use a room filled with obscene, untrue pictures. The neophytes are taken to this gallery, shut in there for hours, and left to contemplate in this chamber of imagery the false, the vile, the unnatural. This is one of the initial steps in their training, an invasion of the imagination with abominable images. Then the new recruits are ready to be taken over, possessed by the evil spiritual forces, the demons, of outer space. In this novel Lewis presents us with a modern parable of the ancient truth that Ezekiel grasped in his vision of the chambers of imagery. The human imagination is the picture gallery of the soul, even the sanctuary of the soul, personality's most holy place. The images, the pictures enshrined there, could we see them, would lay bare to us that personality, show us what that soul lives for, believes in, and serves.

Educator Allan Bloom, in his book *The Closing of the American Mind,* decries the devastating effect that rock music has had on the students he has taught. He says that as a teacher he is not so much concerned with what rock music may or may not do to the students' morals, but rather what it does to the possibility of education in the higher reaches of the mind and soul. Bloom sees rock music poisoning the imaginations of young people at a crucial time, making impossible the "sublimation," that is, the "making sublime," of the emotions in a person's quest for truth and taste and nobler being.

Bloom also deplores the present-day antipathy students have for heroes; for without admirable characters, respected and adored and hung as portraits in the picture gallery of one's imagination, a strong and ennobling power is banished from the soul.

The power of imagination in structuring character has long been realized. George Buttrick, a modern Christian philosopher of rare perception, in his book *Prayer,* says of imagination:

> It fashions both the world and the man. As for the world, every journey or means of journeying is first imagined, any building is fancy frozen into stone, and any music is a dream caught in a net of sounds. As for the man, every crime is first imagined, every heroism…. That is to say, imagination is almost as momentous to character as a seed is to a flower. No man goes wrong *suddenly:* he falls slowly through a series of unworthy thoughts.

The psychologists have even tested the power of imagination and codified into law the comparative strength of imagination. This is one of the psychological laws: Wherever there is a conflict between the will and the imagination, the imagination will always win the battle.

The classic example is this: You can walk with no difficulty at all a ten-inch-wide plank laid along the floor of your living room, but walking the same board placed on the parapet of a skyscraper is an entirely different matter. Why? Your will to control your muscular action is no weaker fifty stories up, but your imagination plays havoc with your controls. There is before you the electrifying vision of yourself falling through space. Imagination makes you dizzy. Imagination in conflict with will is no match at all. Imagination always wins the day.

You will remember that story of the boy who pitched his best game of baseball on the Saturday after his blind father died. How did he do it? How could he play even at second best? What power of will, what emotional control were his? He did it, the boy said, because it was the first game his blind father had ever watched him pitch. Imagination fed by Christian faith turned the tide. "Compassed about with so great a cloud of witnesses," by faith the boy could visualize his father seeing him.

But how to control the awful power of imagination? If it's true that imagination possesses a propulsive power in personality, if the pictures in our soul's gallery determine action and character, it follows that great care should be used in the hanging of those pictures. But can we control our imaginations? Is it within our power to hang the pictures we choose in our chamber of imagery?

Not by force of will can we do it. We have seen that willpower always kneels to the power of imagination. But affection can control imagination. The hands of love can hang up the pictures in our souls' chambers of imagery. Stopford Brooke, when he was collecting material for his biography of the English minister Fredrick W. Robertson, went into a bookstore in Brighton, the town where Robertson served most of his years in the ministry. He saw hanging on the wall of the shop a picture of Robertson. "Did you know him?" he asked the bookseller, nodding toward the picture. "Yes," answered the man as he lifted his eyes to the photograph and a smile swept over his face. "Whenever I am tempted to do anything mean, I look at that face, and it recalls me to my better self." Just as lust can hang up an obscene image in the chamber of imagination, so also can love and admiration nail up a smiling saint.

The Apostle Paul had a lot to say about Christ being "the image of God." Of course, he had reference primarily to the deity of our Lord. For our human eyes to see, Christ is God incarnate, the very image of the Eternal. But I am convinced that the apostle also had in mind the placing of Jesus Christ at the center of our imagination, the putting there of that dear face in the place of honor in our soul's picture gallery. Listen to him, "Christ, who is the image of God, should shine unto them.... For God, who commanded the light to shine out of darkness, hath shined in our hearts, to give the light of the knowledge of the glory of God in the face of Jesus Christ.... That Christ may dwell in your hearts by faith; that ye, being rooted and grounded in love, May be able to comprehend with all saints what is the breadth, and length, and depth, and height; And to know the love of Christ, which passeth knowledge."

Paul knew the secret of controlling imagination through the power of a higher and superior affection: "(For the weapons of our warfare are not carnal, but mighty through God to the pulling down of strong holds;) Casting down imaginations, and every high thing that exalteth itself against the knowledge of God, and bringing into captivity every thought to the obedience of Christ."

In other words, the Christian who sets Christ in the center of his attention and fixes his thought on Christ sees the whole landscape of imagination judged and transfigured by him. The Christian, by habitual prayer, worship, and gospel reading, drives deep the picture of Christ, on whom to look is not merely to contemplate a picture, but to invite a friend. Christ becomes the center of reference for our whole scheme of imagination. The images in our thought-life incompatible with that dear face are quickly removed, and those congenial are kept. His image has expulsive power until all life becomes his world.

Where Goes Your Heart?

"But while he was still a long way off his father saw him, and his heart went out to him" (Luke 15:20).

If you go to see a cardiac patient in the intensive care unit of a modern hospital, you can watch the electronic diagraming of the patient's heart action, moment by moment, on a little, green glass chart by his bedside. A dancing point of light traces on the green graph each beat of his heart. This marvelous apparatus reveals the timing, the strength or weakness, the steady regularity or the wavering insecurity, of the patient's beating heart. And if the heart falters and stops, that, too, is instantly recorded.

Jesus, in the parable of the prodigal son, is saying that what religion is all about can be clearly diagramed for us in a few classic examples of heart condition. For the theme of this story—indeed, the golden text for all three of these remarkable parables in Luke 15, the lost coin, the lost sheep, and the lost son—is just this: "There is more joy over one sinner whose heart is changed than over ninety-nine righteous people who have no need for repentance" (Luke 15:7).

"One sinner whose heart is changed," as J.B. Phillips's translation has it. Changes of heart are what religion is all about, from heaven's point of view. It is not church buildings or church budgets, not Sunday school curricula or sacred music or scholarly sermons that the Christian religion is primarily concerned with, but rather the changes that can take place in the condition of the human heart.

The parable opens by charting the heart action of the prodigal son. What, in a word, is his heart condition? Why, his is the case of the wandering heart, a heart that is no longer at home in his father's house.

The boy has grown up. He longs for freedom. The house rules of his father are old-fashioned and oppressive to him. He's got to be free. His heart has already crossed the threshold of his parental home. His spirit already roams in distant ports. What can hold him? Nothing. So the father bows to the inevitable. He gives him his inheritance, and the boy with the wandering heart makes his journey into the far country of his dreams.

How did he go, this boy of the wandering heart? Did he join a camel caravan or ship out on a sailing schooner or hop a fast freight or thumb a ride on the interstate or take a trip on drugs?

However it may have started in noble dreams of freedom and creative self-expression and rejection of a shoddy establishment, the journey of his wandering heart soon degenerates into self-indulgence and foolish extravagance and, if the elder brother's suspicions are to be believed, into debauchery with prostitutes. Finally, his money all gone, his freedom follows not far behind. He has to go to work. And the best he can do is tend pigs. Soon he is hungry, lonely, and miserable.

Who is this prodigal? Do we recognize him at all, this boy whose heart condition is that of a wandering heart that roams from the father's house? Helmut Thielicke, in his book *The Waiting Father,* says the prodigal is every one of us. Everything we have comes from our Heavenly Father—our life, our time, our ability, our possessions. Our prodigality consists in our using what is his without him. That's what it means to wander from the father's house.

"[The prodigal's] body, which he adorns and uses, which so many are in love with—that came from [his father]. His possessions, money, clothes, shoes, food, and drink—they too came from his father, gained from the capital he gave to him. In themselves they are good things; otherwise the father would not have given them to him. But as he uses them they become his undoing, for he uses them for himself, he uses them *without* the father," Thielicke says. That's why his whole, sad, sick condition is traceable to his wandering heart.

The turning point in the story comes when the prodigal's heart is changed. The quaint language of the King James Version reads: "And when he came to himself, he said, How many hired servants of my father's have bread enough and to spare, and I perish with hunger! I will arise and go to my father, and will say unto him, Father, I have sinned against heaven, and before thee, And am no more worthy to be called thy son: make me as one of thy hired servants" (Luke 15:17-19).

The wandering heart becomes the homing heart. That's the change in heart condition. Instantly, the decision made, the prodigal is on his way home.

But how did the change of heart take place? What mysterious influences were at work? Was it just the hard practicality of hunger gnawing in his belly? Surely that, but was there anything else? Was it the subtle psychological image of the favored son that once had been contrasted with the haggard wastrel that now was? Did he change as the idealized image gained ascendancy over the sensual image?

Robert Louis Stevenson, writing in maturity about the struggles of his youth, simply said, "I came round like a well-turned ship." I heard a young man say not long ago in describing his experience of becoming a Christian, "It was a modern miracle."

The theologians have several words for this changed heart condition. One is conversion, a turning round and going back, the wandering heart turning homeward again. Another is repentance, which in the Greek carried the image of thinking and feeling together with another, namely, God, whose will and way and love had been cast off by the wandering heart and are at last reconciled and brought into agreement again.

How the repentance or conversion takes place remains a great mystery, and in all cases such changed heart conditions have their own individual records of change. But Jesus, as he talked with Nicodemus about this mystery of the changed heart, attributed it to the ever-brooding spirit of God, who as the relentless Hound of Heaven never—never—ceases to track down the wandering heart of his prodigal children.

The second heart condition charted for us in the parable of the prodigal son is the heart action of the waiting father. As the New English Bible puts it: "While he [the returning prodigal] was still a long way off his father saw him, and his heart went out to him. He ran to meet him, flung his arms round him, and kissed him" (Luke 15:20).

Consider the different possibilities of the heart action in the father waiting at home when at last the discredited and defeated and despicable wastrel shows up. The father's heart might well have registered disgust at the sight of the boy's rags and the long, matted hair and the smell of the pig slop about him. Or the father's heart might have boiled over in outrage at all the wealth the son had allowed to slip through his fingers. Or the father's heart might have been set on the just judgment that demanded righteous retribution, of where he might put this boy to work on the lowest rung on the ladder of his establishment until he could restore every wasted dollar. Or the father's heart might have risen in utter rejection as he said: "Away with you. When you clean yourself up and mend your ways and reform your character and regain your lost reputation, then come back and we'll see about letting you in this respectable house once more."

But no, the gospel record is that the father's heart went out to his son. He understood how deep was the change in the boy's heart. His was no longer a wandering heart, but an eagerly, hopefully homing heart. The only change that made any difference, a change in the condition of the boy's heart, had already taken place.

So the waiting father brushed aside his son's stumbling, humbling premeditated speech, "Father, make me as one of your hired servants," by giving orders fast and furiously to the servants: "Quick, off with these rags. Put my best robe on him. Bring a ring for his finger and shoes for his bare feet. And prepare a feast, for my son was lost and is found. He was dead and is alive again."

This is the heart action Jesus says every penitent prodigal can count on in our Heavenly Father. How do we know? Not just because Jesus told a story about it, but because Jesus lived a life and died a death that showed it. "For God so loved the world," runs John 3:16-17, "that he gave his only begotten Son that whosoever believeth in him should not perish, but have everlasting life. For God sent not his Son into the world to condemn the world; but that the world through him might be saved." Yes, the divine rationale for the Incarnation reveals the heart of God. And the old hymn proclaims it: "For the love of God is broader than the measure of man's mind; and the heart of the Eternal is most wonderfully kind." When any soul is lost, God is plunged in loss. When any human heart is wandering, the heart of the Eternal is going out to him, and God the Father's search for his lost world went as far as Calvary.

But there is a third heart condition charted in this parable—the heart action of the elder brother. It is a hardened heart, the heart that goes not out to others.

This elder son has stayed at home faithfully keeping everything running at the old home place while the prodigal sowed his wild oats. Coming home from work in the fields that memorable afternoon, the elder brother hears the sound of music and dancing and laughter. He asks a servant what's going on, and when he hears of his brother's return and the welcome his father has given the boy, he's angry and won't go in.

When his father comes out and pleads with him to put away his natural resentment at the waste of good money and time and at the scandal that's soiling the reputation of their respectable family, he won't listen. He's mad and he won't go in.

The heart condition of the elder brother is what bars him from the gala occasion, shutting out, not only the younger brother and the feasting friends, but even his father. His disposition casts a pall all round his world.

Here is Jesus' message for us in this parable: The life each one of us lives is heart action all the way.

If your heart has wandered, if you've rebelled against the rules in your Father's house and wasted the years and the substance and the ennobling relationships the Father has given you—and who of us hasn't failed somehow, somewhere at our great opportunity of life—then don't wait any longer. Don't sink any deeper. Let your heart be changed to a glad acceptance of his ways. Come home to him. Repent. Confess your wrongs. Renounce your rebellion. Don't wait another moment. Why? Because we can all be sure of the heart action of the eternal, the waiting Father. There is no question of his heart condition. He sees us a long way off. He knows the moment our hearts are changed. His great heart goes out to us. But he can't in his heart go out to us a moment before our hearts have allowed his love to turn us round. Just as he would not compel us to stay at the Father's house when we wanted to wander, neither can he hang out a Welcome Back sign for us before we are ready to come back. The unrepentant, the unchanged in heart remain forever in an alien land.

But the major thrust of the whole story for us church people is that elder brother part. Its message is directed at that in us which hardens our hearts against the prodigals who would come home to God but for us and our self-righteous, judgmental ways. Henry Drummond, the Scottish writer and lecturer, in his discourse on the elder brother's ill temper, raises the question, "What would have happened had the prodigal returned on an afternoon when there was no one home but the elder brother?"

The forbidding specter of modern, respectable, self-righteous, and judgmental Christianity stands across the doorway of the Church of Jesus Christ today, barring entrance to many a tired and homesick prodigal who is longing to come home. What each one of us in the Church today needs to do is to be sure our hearts are not casting that shadow, allow our hearts to be changed, and go out with him whose heart in Christ has already gone out to all the world.

Where Faith Falls Short

"'I have faith,' cried the boy's father; 'help me where faith falls short'"
(Mark 9:24).

As Mother's Day comes round again I'm reminded of the stunning surprise
my brothers and I experienced when we returned to our boyhood home to
close the house after our parents' death. We found here and there, tucked
away in chests and closets, quite a stock of unused gifts we had sent to our
parents through the years on various occasions—birthdays, Christmas,
Mother's Day, Father's Day. There were unworn scarves and ties, boxed
perfume and jewelry, unopened boxes of cigars.

Such a discovery gave me a strange feeling. I wondered if my feelings
would have been different had I found all the gifts and remembrances worn
out or used up.

Then came the reassuring thought that the real transaction in such gifts
on occasions of remembrance did not depend on their being used or con-
sumed. Such things simply symbolized the groping of the human spirit
through the material object for something beyond the tangible, sensate world
to assist in giving expression to the love and gratitude that the heart feels.

But is there anything real and lasting about that invisible world beyond and behind the material? Are there just momentary emotions and shadowy memories? Does anything there really exist, or is it just a fantasy, a self-deception of the human mind to believe that there does exist something solid and permanent and indestructible in close family relationships?

The gospel story today is all about this: the reality or unreality of the unseen world, the validity of belief or unbelief, the power or powerlessness of faith, the part that faith plays in the relationships of families.

Here is the essence of the story: A man concerned about the condition of his son brought the boy to Jesus. The child could not speak. In some versions of the gospel he is described as an epileptic. Others say he was possessed by a "dumb and deaf spirit." Presumably, the pent-up frustrations of the boy, denied the usual outlets of communication through intelligible speech, were expressed in violent fits, foaming at the mouth, muscular twitching, and jerking of the limbs.

You will remember that Helen Keller, as a blind, deaf, and mute child from Tuscumbia, Alabama, was given to violent fits of temper. The neighbors thought the girl was crazy. But when the teacher Anne Sullivan came and began to communicate with her through a code of touch symbols in the palm of her hand, the mind and spirit of a genius were discovered, and the real Helen Keller was set free.

The gospel record tells us that since Jesus was away when the man came with his disturbed child, the disciples tried to help but were unsuccessful. Finally, Jesus came back. He expressed impatience with his disciples for their incompetence. He blamed their impotence on their lack of faith, saying, "What an unbelieving and perverse generation! ... How long must I endure you?"

Then the distracted father turned to Jesus: "'If it is at all possible for you, take pity upon us and help us.' 'If it is possible!' said Jesus. 'Everything is possible to one who has faith.'"

"'I have faith,' cried the boy's father; 'help me where faith falls short.'" Jesus straightaway healed the boy. Later, the disciples asked, "'Why could not we cast it [the spirit] out?'" Jesus said, "'There is no means of casting out this sort but prayer.'"

In this gospel incident where we see the tragedy of the whole human situation in microcosm, everything turns on faith or the lack of it. The cry of the father, "I have faith; help me where faith falls short," is both the confession of the whole human condition and the necessary petition for every rescue.

Is it surprising to discover that the first place faith falls short is in the church of Jesus Christ, in that handful of Jesus' first disciples?

Quite understandably the world looks to the Church for help as the father of the mentally or emotionally disturbed boy looked to Jesus' disciples. What is the Church for if not to concern itself with every human distress? "What is the Church worth," asks Joseph Parker in his *People's Bible,* "if it cannot save the lunacy of the world? The Church, like its Master, has nothing to do in the world unless it be to heal and to bless and to save mankind. The Church was not instituted to amuse the world, but to save it; not to mock the world by speaking to it in a pointless and useless speech, but to redeem the world through Jesus Christ the Lord."

When people, with all their pressing, desperate needs, turn to the Church for help and do not find it, they are loud in their rebukes, and rightly so. But the rebuke of the Lord of the Church for her ineffectualness is louder and sterner. And notice that Jesus traces his disciples' impotence to their lack of faith. "What an unbelieving and perverse generation! ... How long must I endure you?"

The Church's resources in fine equipment and beautiful buildings and intelligently prepared educational materials and abundant financial backing have never been stronger, yet the Church is faltering in her ministry to a needy world because of a failure of faith. The disposition of the Church to put her trust both in her Lord and in the world, to believe in force a bit more than in love, to rely upon human efforts more than on divine grace, to seek first what we shall eat and what we shall drink and how we shall be clothed rather than to seek God's kingdom and his righteousness—these are the reasons that the Church is one place where faith falls short.

The second place where faith falls short in the recurrent human tragedy is the family. The poor father who brought his son to Jesus was expressing, not only his personal concern, but that of others in the tragedy that had befallen his family. "If it is at all possible for you," he implored Jesus, "take pity upon us and help us."

When one member of a family suffers, all suffer. Sometimes trouble, pain, disgrace come as a result of wild disregard for the laws of man or God. Sometimes we bring trouble upon ourselves. Sometimes our troubles are there because of a power beyond ourselves.

The novelist John Updike, that steady student of our American life, keeps tracing our troubles in America to a failure of faith in the families of our nation. Updike writes about the sense of accumulated loss that is ours and shows how our national past contained a wholeness and an essential goodness that have now evaporated. In one of his novels, Updike depicts the Puritan gods of America's past as having retreated to unawesome, half-deserted churches, while his principal characters are people in a stylish suburb caught up in a black mass of community sex.

Recently, consternation swept across our nation following the brutal attack on a woman jogger in New York's Central Park by a gang of young ruffians who beat her and raped her and left her naked and dying. People were puzzled to discover that the boys who had done this were not school dropouts or poverty-stricken but from respectable, middle-class families.

Undoubtedly, the dimensions of our national tragedy are to be reckoned in figures of diminishing faith in our families—families where faith falls short. But also just as surely are the prospects for our salvation to be reckoned in an increase of the same collateral and in nothing else.

Lou Holtz, the football coach at Notre Dame, in a letter written to America's next generation as part of an advertising campaign for Volkswagen, said:

> The basis of any society is the strength of the family.... The strength of a society is not found in the comforts of living but in its values, morals and concern for its fellow man. And I believe that these principles are predominantly developed in the family.... The qualities that we admire in people—honesty, cheerfulness, thoughtfulness, cooperation—must be learned in the home and developed by society. Our future, in my humble opinion, is contingent upon parents successfully developing these qualities so we can evolve into responsible, intelligent, compassionate adults.

In the gospel story, the cry of the father is, "I have faith; help me where faith falls short." This is the honest prayer of every believer. We are all fitful mixtures of faith and unbelief. Today we may say with all sincerity, "O Lord, in thee do I put my trust. Thou art my strong tower of defense." Tomorrow, in a despairing mood, we may whine, "Why go I mourning because of the oppression of my enemy? Where is my God, if God there really is?"

For faith falls short in the Church, and faith falls short in the family, and faith falls short for every individual unless faith is anchored in Jesus Christ. This is the supreme lesson in this gospel incident, indeed in the whole of Scripture. Jesus Christ and he alone can help us where our faith falls short.

What is faith? It is trust that there is a supreme power and purpose in the universe friendly to the truster, even though this reality is unseen and often contradicted by circumstances. And our faith would always fall short, doomed to fail us, were it not for Jesus Christ, who coming to us in human flesh reveals the quality of the divine love and depth and height and width of the divine power to deliver people from all the demons that assail them, assuring every person that from the divine point of view the relationship that exists between every soul and the Eternal God is that of a Heavenly Father and his well-loved child, and that nothing—neither life nor death, neither the fires of youth nor the ashes of age—can separate the souls that come to God through faith in Jesus Christ.

As *The Interpreter's Bible* says:

> Faith will not enable one to caress rattlesnakes safely, or to pluck money from the air, or to live without food. Yet in the wide realm of the Kingdom of God, and of God's continued action to bring in that Kingdom, whether for one human life or for the world, there is no barrier that can be set against the divine invasion: none but our own cardinal weakness—that often we believe more firmly in the power of the demons of evil than in the power of the God of Love.

Where faith stands tall, where faith is the margin of victory in the most desperate of circumstances, is always that tiny, one square foot of earth where a humble, honest man or woman has prayed to Jesus Christ, "Lord, I have a little faith. Help me where my faith falls short."

The Words of Life

"For you they are no empty words; they are your very life, and by them you shall live long in the land which you are to occupy" (Deut. 32:47).

I heard the announcer over a Memphis radio station tell of a man who was looking for a job. The announcer gave the man's age, his training and skills, his years of experience in his chosen vocation, and then ended with this statement: "The applicant seeking employment has moved his family to the Memphis area because he has a son with a health problem, a solution for which the family is seeking in the Memphis medical and hospital center."

A matter of health or sickness, a matter of life or death, for one member of one family gets the number one priority, so that job security for the father, convenience and comfort for the family, and the other children's educational opportunities are all sacrificed, or at least laid on the line, if only the necessary treatment and care can be secured for that one threatened life.

Moses had come to the end of his life. He knew it. Before he died he had some farewell words he wanted to say to his people. They had been a slave people whom he had liberated. They were a foolish and sinful people who had tried his patience over and over. They were a weak yet willful people whom he had borne in his arms in the wilderness and with whom he had grown exasperated. Time and again Moses had prayed to God for his people when the Lord Almighty had grown angry at their disobedience and threatened to destroy them. Moses had prayed, "Forgive them, O Lord. Forgive them, or blot my name out of your book of life."

Now in parting from his people, Moses, the great liberator and law-giver, knowing that he will no longer be there to guide, shield, and defend them, gives them his farewell message: "Take to heart all these warnings which I solemnly give you this day: command your children to be careful to observe all the words of this law. For you they are no empty words; they are your very life, and by them you shall live long in the land which you are to occupy after crossing the Jordan."

"It's a life and death matter," Moses is saying to the people for whom he had laid his life on the line. "It's a life and death matter that you reverence these words and obey them."

What are these words that Moses insists are no mere words but are the very essence of life for his people? Why, the whole contents of the book of Deuteronomy, the whole moral and religious law delivered by Moses to the people from God himself. The moral code is there, God's plan for people's behavior in relationship with each other: Do not kill; do not steal; do not lie; do not commit adultery; do not covet.

The religious code is there as well, God's plan for every person's relationship with God, based on faith and love and obedience: Worship one God with the whole of one's heart and mind and soul; honor the family relationships as sacred unto God; keep one day of every week for worship and rest and the nurture of one's soul in the midst of the covenant people of God.

Moses knew he was dying. God was raising up a new leader for his people in Joshua, Moses' successor. But the real leader, Moses knew, was God. God would guide and rule his people through his word. Therefore, they must reverence, learn, and obey God's word, for that word was no mere word—their very lives depended on it.

But don't times change the value, the relevance or irrelevance, of any given word? Surely ours is a day, a period of history, when there is widespread disdain for the old, the outmoded, the ineffective and ineffectual customs and systems and maxims of the past.

The young are particularly fed up with the preachments of moralistic Christian culture. The old rules and regulations that governed manners and morals, the canons of taste, the notions of the obscene and objectionable— haven't all these been washed away by the flood tides of rapid social change?

In his book *My Name Is Aram,* William Saroyan tells of his Uncle Khosrove's habit of shouting in all sorts of situations, "It is no harm; pay no attention to it." One day when Uncle Khosrove is in the barber's chair having his mustache trimmed, his son runs from their home, eight blocks away, to tell his father their house is on fire. True to form, old Khosrove sits up in the barber's chair and shouts, "It is no harm; pay no attention to it."

No matter how loudly we shout "It is no harm; pay no attention to it" in our impatience with old-fashioned moral integrity or in our exuberance over freedom from ancient religious scruples, the old words of moral integrity will not go away, and the ancient human values that the old words enshrine will not be transvalued. Still they remain; as Moses stated, "They are no empty words; they are your very life."

It was more than fifty years ago that Harry Emerson Fosdick, as he describes it in *The Secret of Victorious Living,* said to his Riverside Congregation in a time when free love and trial marriage were greatly in vogue:

> In its long history mankind has tried every conceivable experiment with the sex relationship—polyandry, polygamy, monogamy, promiscuity, wives and concubines, prostitution. Can you think of any basically new arrangement to be tried? And out of this long experimenting of the race there has arisen, so it seems to us, the great tradition: a man and a woman loving each other so much that they do not care to love anybody else in the same way at all, and so building a permanent home that puts around the children the strong security of an unbroken affection. That describes the loveliest family life in the world. That is the great tradition.... By no hook or crook can we ever make one step of real progress in this country if we give up the great tradition of the home.

In the making of every personality two mighty currents converge. One we call heredity and the other, environment. By heredity we mean what we get in physical, emotional, and intellectual equipment from our parents through biological transmission. Heredity is what the baby comes into the world with from the union of the male and female who produced him, legitimately or illegitimately, known or unknown, whether conceived in Christian wedlock or from a pad of communal cohabiting. Whatever is bequeathed through the biological process is heredity.

Environment, the other stream so powerful in the producing of every person, is the training, the schooling, the associations, and the atmosphere of home and street and playground and church and mass media.

But however strong and powerful in every personality are the twin currents of heredity and environment, the determining factor in the development of every person is his own personal response. What each person does with the treasure trove of heredity and environment determines human destiny. This is the point at which life or death is chosen. It's like Grandma Moses used to say, "Life is what you make it—always has been, always will be."

But how can words, any words, be so important, a matter of life and death? Words are symbols. Words enshrine values. The inspired words of God trap the imperishable values and qualities of individual and social life without which men and nations perish. When Charles de Gaulle died in his beloved France and the world was mourning the passing of a great leader, the November 23, 1970, issue of *Time* magazine summed up his life in these words: "Whatever the historical judgment on his leadership, De Gaulle demonstrated the importance of those great intangibles in the calculus of power—moral force, will, style, vision. To many men, these are only words; they were realities to De Gaulle, realities that the world often distrusts and yet yearns for more than ever today."

A mother was talking with her son about the son's son, her grandson. "Have you been taking him regularly to Sunday school and church?" Evasively, jokingly, the reply came, "I'll tell him that his grandmother is worried about his soul." "No," said the grandmother, "not his soul, but his life. I know and you know that the best place for a little boy, and, for that matter, for mature people, to learn how to live the best life is in Sunday school and church."

"For you they are no empty words; they are your very life, and by them you shall live long in the land which you are to occupy."

God's word of life remains unchanged, unchanging. Our response of obedience or rebellion to that word spells for us life or death. There is never any mystery about one person, or great masses of men and women, persuading himself that God's word is an empty word, an impotent or irrelevant word, a mere trifle, or a vain thing. That is his necessary rationalization in order to abandon himself to the worship of the god he has chosen to serve in the place of the God and Father of our Lord and Savior Jesus Christ. But God will not be mocked. Regardless of the fidelity or infidelity of people, the word of the Lord abideth forever. The races and generations of men and women come and go. They are like the grass that withers and dies. Our only hope of abiding is in embracing God's word of life, preeminently as revealed in his own son, Jesus Christ.

In *Markings,* the diary of Dag Hammarskjöld, the great secretary-general of the United Nations, these words of a prayer he had written and prayed were discovered after his death:

> *Give me a pure heart—that I may see Thee,*
> *A humble heart—that I may hear Thee,*
> *A heart of love—that I may serve Thee,*
> *A heart of faith—that I may abide in Thee.*

FOUR

Christian Love in the Covenant Community

The Church and Her Mission

"Now ye are the body of Christ, and members in particular" (1 Cor. 12:27).

Perhaps our first lesson on the nature and mission of the Church was taught us not with words but with hands. "Here's the church and here's the steeple. Open the door and see all the people." So we learned from this nursery routine that it is not the church building or the beautiful stained-glass windows or the organ or the pulpit that makes the Church, but rather the people gathered together for the worship and service of God.

And it may well be we shall never really understand the nature and mission of the Church until we understand it in terms of hands—our hands and others' hands—until we learn to use our hands in every way and for everything for which God made them.

First of all the Church is understood in the symbol of the extended and clasped hands of friendship and welcome. Once there was a minister who was about to give up trying to be a minister because he failed in every church he tried to serve. In despair one day he asked a fellow minister, "Why do I always fail? Why can't I be useful as a minister in the Church? Please tell me why?"

"It's your gestures," said his friend. "They are all wrong. Whenever you preach you gesture with your fists clenched. That's no way to preach the gospel of Jesus Christ. Can you imagine Jesus saying with clenched fists, 'Suffer the little children to come unto me, and forbid them not: for of such is the kingdom of God'? Can you imagine Jesus shaking a fist and saying, 'Come unto me, all ye that labour and are heavy laden, and I will give you rest'? Why, of course not. Whenever Jesus tried to teach or to minister to the people, it was always with hands wide open in love and welcome. When at last they killed him and nailed him to a cross, his hands were stretched out in welcome to the two thieves on either side of him."

The Church of Jesus Christ is a body of people who in the name and spirit of their master hold out their hands in welcoming friendship to all the people of the whole world. When we say the Apostles' Creed we parrot the words, "I believe in the holy catholic church," or perhaps some of us with all sorts of Protestant reservations won't join in this section at all because it sounds so much like professing faith in the Roman Catholic Church. But the creed pledges allegiance to the holy catholic church, that is, the one great universal Church of Jesus Christ, which is above and beyond all denominational differences, all geographical boundaries, all class distinctions, all language barriers, all time and space limitations.

The Church is catholic or universal in two ways: first, it is universal in that it meets the spiritual and eternal needs of all people everywhere, regardless of nationality, race, or culture; second, the Church is universal in that it is destined to cover the universe and gather within its protective fellowship all of Christ's redeemed. "The gates of hell shall not prevail against it," said Jesus. "Where Jesus Christ is," said Ignatius, bishop of Antioch and one of the early Christian fathers, "there is the Catholic Church." And the communion of saints is that warm, understanding fellowship those newly gathered in Christ find themselves enjoying because they have been saved from the damning, dividing barriers to human fellowship.

Would that there were more of us who understood this basic meaning of the Church as a universal fellowship of the saints, symbolized in the extended hand of welcome. There is no such thing as an isolated Christian in heaven above or on the earth beneath or in the waters under the earth. Just as there cannot be an individual hand or arm, for it is then cut off and dead, so there cannot be an individual Christian.

The second symbol of the holy catholic church, the communion of saints, is the open hand of sharing, a hand stretched out to give. (One might say it is more of a double motion, a combination: first, a thrust into the pocket or handbag and then a quick and willing offer.) Did you ever hear anyone whine, "They are always asking for money at church"? Well, did you ever reply, "Why yes, of course, how like the Church. Giving and sharing are congenital to the Church"?

In the letters of Paul we find him using that one Greek word *koinonia,* which means fellowship, to refer to a variety of Christian experiences. Now he uses it to describe his spiritual communion with the living Christ, now of spiritual communion with fellow Christians, now of sharing material substance with other Christians in need by chipping in cash for the contribution to the suffering saints in Jerusalem.

The congregation of a church that does not give, that does not share, ceases to be a church.

The third symbol of the holy catholic church, the communion of saints, is the uplifted hand of witness and testimony. The Church is composed of those people who have stood up to be counted for Christ. It is the social organism where men and women recognize Jesus Christ, the carpenter of Nazareth, as their Lord and Redeemer and act accordingly.

This involves two things, for the whole catholic church and the communion of saints have two characteristics dramatically portrayed by Simon Peter: confessor and apostle.

First, confessor. Peter, when asked by Jesus, "Who do you say that I am?" answered, "Thou art the Christ, the Son of the living God." As Emil Brunner, the Swiss theologian, says in his book *I Believe in the Living God:*

> Confession of faith is an unconditional declaration of loyalty, an oath of allegiance. Upon this confession the Christian community rests. After Peter came the other apostles; after the apostles, the three thousand on Whitsunday and then the expansion of the community throughout the whole world. All of them had to be ready at any time to be imprisoned, tormented, and killed for the sake of their oath of loyalty, their confession of this Lord, and many of them have paid this price from the first days of the Christian community on.

Second, apostle. Peter was not only the first confessor, he not only held up his hand in act and oath of allegiance, he was also an apostle. He raised his hand high in arresting testimony to others. As Brunner describes him, he was "the ambassador of God, whose witness to Jesus Christ awakens faith in other men."

And we must follow Peter in this manual of arms if we would know and experience the meaning and mission of the Church.

The fourth symbol of the holy catholic church, the communion of saints, is found in the ancient custom of laying on of hands in blessing. In *The Promise of the Spirit,* William Barclay recounts being taken by his father when Barclay was a very small child to visit a great saint of the church in the retirement of his old age. When the time came to go, the elder Barclay stopped at the door and said, "If I leave the boy with you for a moment, will you put your hands on his head and bless him?" Barclay recalls:

> So for a moment I was left with the old man, and he placed his hands on my head and blessed me, and I have not forgotten the feeling of that moment to this day, more than forty years after. It was not simply because he was an ordained minister of the church that the old man's blessing was so vividly effective. It was because he was who he was. There is only one truly apostolic succession, and that is not the succession of those who are within any denomination or who have been ordained in any particular way. It is the succession of those who themselves have the Spirit of Christ in any Church.

A mother noticed as she told her son repeatedly, "I love you. I love you," that it made him feel important. And then she sighed and said to herself, "In a better world, everybody must be made to feel important." In the communion of saints, where the love of God in Jesus Christ is the supreme reality, there is a remarkable power to bless all life the Church touches, as if the very hand of Christ were laid in blessing.

Finally, there are the folded hands of prayer. The holy catholic church, the communion of saints, is a praying fellowship, praying all for each and each for all. We do not trust only in ourselves. We know we are sinners. Kneeling before the Almighty, the Church confesses: "We have done those things we ought not to have done. We have left undone those things we ought to have done. There is no health in us. Lord, have mercy upon us." The Church is a society of confessed sinners who know that the love of Christ has forged them into a fellowship of the forgiven.

Confronted with the sins of self and society, the evils and perils of this awesome age, the communion of saints gives its heart neither to hate nor fear. The Church does not meet hostility with hostility or the unknown with suspicion. With admission of its failure, trust in God, and intercession for its enemies, using folded, praying hands as its spiritual compass, the Church moves forward into the unknown future believing that future is not only known to God but is also his coming kingdom.

As members of the communion of saints, we are not called upon to be cockeyed optimists and believe naively in crafty, unreliable human nature, but we Christians are called to believe implicitly in the invincible power of God's Holy Spirit, who can cleanse and empower the most unlikely candidates for sainthood, even such miserable failures as ourselves, and make each one a child of God and mold us together with all his children into a communion of saints.

The nature and mission of the Church is symbolized by hands, the various ways in which hands—human hands, yours and mine, even dirty or frail hands—may be put to work for God. And our hands, yours and mine, what of them? When we look at our hands today and tomorrow and tomorrow, can we say with Meister Eckhart, the German theologian and mystic, "I would be to the Eternal God what a man's right hand is to a man"?

Living in Love

"Never cease to love your fellow-Christians" (Heb. 13:1 [Revised English Bible]).
"Let brotherly love continue" (Heb. 13:1 [King James Version]).

Once two Presbyterians were not seeing eye to eye on a matter of considerable concern. In fact, they were working as hard as they could on opposite sides. They were canceling out each other's efforts. In exasperation one Presbyterian remarked about his brother, "I know he is a good man. I suppose he means well. Certainly he is a Christian, but I do believe that he is the most awkward Christian I've ever known."

Most of us, one way or another, are awkward Christians in the eyes of some of our fellow Christians. We cannot always agree. We get in each other's way. We stir up hostile feelings against each other. We work at cross-purposes.

The writer of the Epistle to the Hebrews sets down as his most important ethical demand for those first-century Christians to whom he was writing, "Never cease to love your fellow-Christians." Or, as the old King James

Version has it, "Let brotherly love continue." Sometimes it is pretty difficult to let brotherly love continue with some of the brethren we have.

Presumably, even in those idyllic days of the early church where the love of Christ still was very strong, brotherly love among fellow Christians was not always an easy achievement, else the writer of this epistle would not have thought it necessary to include the exhortation, "Never cease to love your fellow-Christians."

Certainly Jesus had repeatedly emphasized to this cardinal moral and ethical demand. He said all the requirements of religion could be summed up in the Old Testament command to love God with all one's mind and heart and soul and strength, and one's neighbor as oneself. He charged his disciples never to cease to love one another, because in the eyes of the world their love for one another was to be their badge of Christian discipleship: "By this shall all men know that ye are my disciples, if ye have love one to another."

And the Elder John wrote to the Ephesian Christians, "It's no new commandment but an old one, one we had from the beginning of our Christian experience: Love one another."

But always, in every age, it has been difficult for Christians to let brotherly love continue. Paul and Barnabas fell out over John Mark and for a while could not work together. Doctrinal differences from time to time have separated Christians. During the Arian controversy in the fourth century, when the church fathers were debating the human and divine nature of Christ, it was said, "All Christendom is split over a diphthong," referring to the controversy over two similar Greek words defining the human-divine nature of Christ. Christians in the separate denominations for a long time differed sharply in their views of how to worship: to kneel or not to kneel to pray, to be immersed or to be sprinkled at baptism.

But I suppose there has never been a time more difficult for Christians to let brotherly love continue than today in our American churches. Christians differ widely in their views on social, political, economic, and environmental questions. Conscience demands that sincere Christians contend for their convictions. In the controversy that develops, some Christians appear to be very awkward to other Christians, and brotherly love is often the first casualty.

The mother of the governor of Massachusetts listened to her minister one Sunday not so very many years ago and immediately was persuaded to go to Florida and demonstrate against what appeared to her to be unjust laws and inhumane customs. But some of the sincere Christian people in Florida were outraged at her conduct. They saw to it that she was put in jail for her trouble. The feeling of the Floridians was that Mary Parkman Peabody and her kind were just buttinskies who could better use their energies in cleaning up the wrongs and inhumanities in their own backyards.

When the World Council of Churches, headquartered in Geneva, Switzerland, appropriated $160,000 for financing the first missionary project ever undertaken in the United States—a project for educational and relief work among the black people of Mississippi—the Christian people in the whole mid-South viewed this "foreign mission" effort with consternation. We had been in the habit of thinking of the needy areas as being far away. It stirred us up.

Conscientious Christians in our time are finding themselves on opposite sides of the burning issues of abortion, homosexuality, and conservation of our planet's resources and people.

John Beifuss, reporting in the Memphis *Commercial Appeal,* noted:

> Many of the country's major Protestant denominations are grappling with social issues from sexuality to racism to the environment.
>
> Episcopalians, Presbyterians, Methodists and others are publicly struggling with their responsibilities during national conventions this year. Not surprisingly, sex has been the subject of the most heated debates.
>
> Many Christians believe the church is obligated to tackle social problems, even if it means becoming involved in political issues. Others think the church should stick to spreading the word that Jesus Christ is the savior of mankind.
>
> Why should churches take on the world and the flesh as well as the devil?

It's difficult enough for us to get along with our fellow Christians in the most placid of times—what with our varying temperaments and conflicting convictions and awkward ways of being able to see the mote in the other fellow's eye or the pigsty in our neighbor's yard better than in our own—but when a social revolution is in progress all over the world, and one of the hottest of the hot spots is developing right under us, and sincere Christians of widely divergent views begin to act on their convictions, we have double trouble on our hands. No wonder the storm warnings are out.

How can we now let brotherly love continue? How now never cease to love our fellow Christians? What will reconcile our differences? Who's to give in? The Christian answer, and the only Christian answer, is for us all to be reconciled to Christ. My brother and I, who see things differently, need to bring our convictions and our expressions of them to Jesus Christ and learn of him and of him be corrected. As we become more and more reconciled to

Christ, his teachings, and his spirit, the closer we will find ourselves together at all points.

Never before have Christians so much needed Jesus' parable of the vine and the branches.

> Ye are the branches: He that abideth in me, and I in him, the same bringeth forth much fruit: for without me ye can do nothing.
>
> If any man abide not in me, he is cast forth as a branch, and is withered; and men gather them, and cast them into the fire, and they are burned.
>
> If ye abide in me, and my words abide in you, ye shall ask what ye will, and it shall be done unto you....
>
> If ye keep my commandments, ye shall abide in my love....
>
> This is my commandment, That ye love one another, as I have loved you (John 15:5-7, 10, 12).

This parable of the vine declares the moral and ethical nature of Christian love, not its sentimentality. Christian love is something entirely different from just liking someone, even from liking someone very much, even devotedly. Christian love is willing the good for another as one wills good for oneself, as Jesus wills good for all people whether they deserve it or not. Remember, Paul says, "While we were yet sinners, Christ died for us." Christian love is affirming the fact of another's sonship to God. Christian love is working for another's welfare as one works for his own welfare. This is loving one's neighbor as oneself. Such love is more an act of the mind and the will than of the emotions, and it is not possible unless we abide in Christ, unless the teachings of Christ about God and God's love for all people abide in us.

Philip Vollmer, in his *Life of John Calvin,* records that Calvin, writing about his own personal religious experience, said, "God, by a sudden conversion, subdued my heart to teachableness." And John T. McNeill, in *The History and Character of Calvinism,* says of Calvin that when God made him teachable, the textbook used was the Bible.

So it is understandable why Calvin chose as his emblem a burning heart in an open hand—the hand of God. Once, in a passage about the Holy Spirit, Calvin wrote, "The Spirit inflames our hearts with the love of God."

And what is the result of such a God-subdued life? When the little council that ruled Geneva met after Calvin's death, it placed on record the impression the great reformer had left on those about him: "God marked him with a character of singular majesty." Those men who had worked most closely with Calvin sensed that a personal awareness of the directing and sustaining presence of the living God was for Calvin an almost uninterrupted state of mind.

Who of us is not troubled by what is most troubling the minds and hearts of Christian people today? Who does not deplore the excesses and sharp differences and the hostilities of these days? Do we really want brotherly love to continue among us, or do we thrive on contention? William Temple, Britain's great war-time archbishop of Canterbury, said in *Readings From St. John* that "love is not at our command. We cannot generate it from within ourselves. We can win it only by surrender to it."

"Jesus Christ is the same yesterday, today, and forever," and it is for us to abide in him and in his love and in his teachings rather than declaiming our prejudices and arguing our rights and fomenting our fears. When we abide in him, then by the miracle of his grace we shall be obedient to his love commandment, and our God-subdued lives will let brotherly love continue.

The Continuing Samaritan Problem

"They feared the Lord, and served their own gods" (2 Kings 17:33).

Well known and dearly loved by us all is the story of the good Samaritan. Jesus gave us this parable of beauty and tenderness, a parable that has brought new meaning to our conception of mercy and neighborliness. The parable of the good Samaritan will live forever in our hearts.

Not so well known is the story of the bad Samaritan, the sinful Samaritan. Yet it is a story that modern American church people need to hear and heed. Let me tell you that story, the story of the origin of the race and faith of the Samaritans.

The Scriptures' first mention of the Samaritans as a race of people is in the second book of Kings in the passage we just read. The time was the period immediately following the going away into Assyrian captivity of the ten tribes of Israel. The Assyrian emperor took away into captivity the princes, the noble families, and the leaders and rulers of the people to remove every possibility for revolt and rebellion among those left in the conquered province. The greater portion of the poorer population the Assyrians left in their Israelitish homes. Then, to take the place of the captives transported from Israel, the Assyrian emperor transplanted other captive people from the four corners of his empire to Israel and established colonies of these foreigners there. The mongrel race that developed from the intermingling and intermarrying of the Israelites with their foreign neighbors was called Samaritan after the name of Israel's capital city, Samaria. Such was the origin of the people called Samaritan.

The Scripture that furnishes us this account of the origin of the Samaritans also tells us the bizarre story of the beginnings of their religion. According to the narrative, ferocious lions began to appear in the old land of Israel, frightening and devouring the Samaritans. The notion arose among them that the damage and danger of the lions were due to the fact that the Samaritans were ignorant of the manner of the god of that land and were causing his displeasure. Apparently, the priests and prophets had been taken into captivity, too. So the Samaritans appealed to the emperor of Assyria to send them from among the captives a priest who could instruct them in the worship of the god of that land, and thus deliver them from the danger of the lions.

The priest came, so the story goes, and taught the Samaritans how they might properly worship God, but this was the tragic result: "They feared the Lord, and served their own gods." That is, they became syncretists in religion. They combined the religion of the lands from which they had come with the worship of Jehovah. They tried to worship the one, true God along with their idols. They attempted to mingle pagan practices with a righteous ritual. The Samaritans became mongrel in faith as well as in race. "They feared the Lord, and served their own gods."

All through their history this seems to have been characteristic of the Samaritans. When in later years Antiochus Epiphanes, the Syrian king, took Jerusalem and desecrated the temple there by putting up a statue of Jupiter in the holy of holies, the loyal Jews died by the thousands in their resistance to this abomination, but the Samaritans were quite ready to welcome Antiochus, to address him as god, and even asked his permission to call their place of worship on Mount Gerizim the Temple of Zeus Hellenius. The Samaritans syncretized; they combined; they made peace with idolatry and with evil.

An excellent example of the Samaritan spirit is to be found in the sinful woman whom Jesus engaged in conversation at Jacob's well. We read in John's Gospel in chapter 4 that when Jesus tried to talk with her about her personal morals, she attempted to turn the conversation into a discussion on theology. Jesus asked her why she was living in adultery, and she countered by asking which was the proper place to worship, Mount Gerizim in the land of the Samaritans or Mount Zion in the land of the Jews. The Samaritan woman whom Jesus met at Jacob's well was certainly the moral and spiritual child of those first Samaritans who "feared the Lord, and served their own gods."

Through the years this was their history. There was reason for a Jew's holding a Samaritan in contempt, reason for the common Jewish quip, "Thou art a Samaritan, and hast a devil." One of the chief reasons Jesus' parable of the good Samaritan created such a sensation was its almost impossible intimation that there might be a *good* Samaritan. For Samaritanism stood for intermarriage with idolatrous people, for adopting pagan ways, for laxity in morals, for becoming in every aspect of body and soul mongrel, low, and degraded.

Now I have been talking about the old Samaritan situation, and the Samaritan spirit, because here is to be found one of the most trenchant biblical analogies to modern American Christianity. Here is a parable of our times, not of the good Samaritan, but of the sinful Samaritans. For Samaritanism, this evil spirit of syncretism—a disposition to accommodate to the ways of a lost world—the most fearful of all "isms" that have come upon our troubled times, is with us yet. In the Church of the Lord Jesus Christ there are "those who fear the Lord, and serve their own gods."

There is in modern Christian faith and practice a continuous watering-down process going on, an insidious obliteration of the distinctions between right and wrong, a belief that openness is the supreme virtue, and that intolerance is the only unforgivable sin, a growing spirit that anything is all right. The modern Samaritan does any and every thing his pagan neighbors do. He fears the Lord and serves many strange gods. The observance of the Christian Sunday as a holy day, set apart, the abstaining from abuse of drugs and alcohol, the cultivation and display of certain noble traits of character— these acts were once the bright red badge that marked the Christian. But this badge of the Christian is becoming more and more conspicuous in its rarity. The spirit of Samaritanism is pervading modern Christianity. An eminent physician remarks that he can tell no difference between those of his patients who are Christians and those who are not by the manner in which they encounter and endure suffering, pain, tragedy, and death.

Back during the Second World War, Alfred Noyes, the celebrated English poet, traced the terrors and horrors of that awful epoch to a revival of the Samaritan spirit. In *The Edge of the Abyss,* Noyes said:

> The spirit of this evil thing which is assaulting civilization from without and within has no national or racial boundaries. It is not an isolated phenomenon. It is active everywhere, in art, in literature, in the drama and theatre. For 50 years the pseudo intellectual has been

preparing his way and making his path straight by scoffing at every distinction between right and wrong in private human relationships, in marriage and the home, as well as in wider spheres.... For a great part of the world, the authority of conscience, that God within the breast, has been lost.

Noyes pointed out then that the pseudointellectuals' practice of scoffing at anything higher than themselves undermined the foundations of civilizations, "picked the mortar from between the bricks," and prepared the hearts and spirits of men and women for that worldwide moral and spiritual collapse.

Do we not discern an incredible timeliness in Noyes' remarks for us today? Is he not describing vividly our spiritual condition now? Allan Bloom says in his book *The Closing of the American Mind* that we Americans now are justifying any way of life by calling it our lifestyle, providing a "moral warrant for people to live exactly as they please." If we call ourselves Christians and at the same time choose to live a life to the tune of "I Did It My Way," our golden text is, "We fear the Lord and serve our own gods of selfish indulgence and pride and plenty and careless ease."

So we are in the process of developing a new and more horrible form of hypocrisy than history has ever known, a hypocrisy that no longer says, "Thank God I am not as that publican," but "Thank God I am not as that Pharisee." In modern Christianity we have produced the astonishing hypocrisy of actually priding ourselves on having watered down our faith and our morality, on having blotted out the difference between right and wrong.

The horror of this modern Samaritanism—this religion of fearing God and serving our own gods, this easy acceptance of the moral laxity of our worldly neighbors as our own, this blotting out of the distinctions between good and evil, this attitude of just anything goes—is that it destroys the souls of men and women.

C.S. Lewis some years ago wrote an intriguing little book called *The Screwtape Letters*. It consists of a series of letters written by Screwtape, an important official in his Satanic Majesty's Lowerarchy, to Wormwood, Screwtape's nephew and a junior devil on earth. The letters are instructions in temptation, methods of corrupting and bringing to hell "the patient" to whom Wormwood has been assigned. At one place Screwtape writes:

You will say that these [temptations I have suggested] are very small sins; and doubtless, like all young tempters, you are anxious to be able to report spectacular wickedness. But do remember, the only thing that matters is the extent to which you separate the man from the Enemy [which is, of course, God]. It does not matter how small the sins are provided that their cumulative effect is to edge the man away from the Light and out into the Nothing. Murder is no better than cards if cards can do the trick. Indeed the safest road to Hell is the gradual one—the gentle slope, soft underfoot, without sudden turnings, without milestones, without signposts.

Yes, the result of Samaritanism is that people gradually give way more and more, here and there, little by little corrupting faith and practice until the soul is dead. And then stark, naked tragedy's hollow laugh croaks at the desolation through all the cavernous halls of hell.

Arthur John Gossip, in his book *In the Secret Place of the Most High,* notes that Carl Gustav Jung, the famous Swiss psychiatrist, has warned us "that all the evils of primitive man are still crouching, alive and ugly as ever, in the dark recesses of our modern hearts; and that it is only Christianity that is holding them in check; and that, if the true faith be neglected or forgotten, all the barriers it alone keeps in being against them will go down, and the old horrors sweep in a roaring flood across a dumbfounded world."

And Gossip quotes Nikolai Berdyaev, the Russian religious philosopher, affirming that "there is no longer any room in the world for a merely external form of Christianity based upon custom. The world is entering upon a period of catastrophe and crisis, when we are being forced to take sides, and in which a higher and more intense kind of spiritual life will be demanded of Christians."

My friends, we have been called to be the true servants of God, a peculiar people set apart for the purpose of righteousness and not a mongrel breed fearing the Lord and serving our own gods. Therefore, stand fast by your faith. Shun worldly lusts. "For what fellowship hath righteousness with unrighteousness? and what communion hath light with darkness?... Wherefore come out from among them, and be ye separate, saith the Lord, and touch not the unclean thing; and I will receive you, And will be a Father unto you, and ye shall be my sons and daughters, saith the Lord Almighty" (2 Cor. 6:14; 17-18).

The Private Preserve of Religion

"How shall I curse, whom God hath not cursed? or how shall I defy, whom the Lord hath not defied?" (Num. 23:8).

In Morris L. West's novel *The Shoes of the Fisherman,* Kiril, the pope, makes this entry in his diary: "Men who serve God professionally are apt to regard Him as a private preserve."

Now I would not disagree with this judgment on the clergy by West's imaginary pope, but rather I would apply more sweepingly his observation. For my experience with all people who profess religion, the professionals and the laity alike, is this: The gravest danger we all encounter in our religious life is our natural tendency to treat the God we worship as our own private preserve. Furthermore, the lesson history teaches us is that it is the tendency of every nation to think that it is the favorite nation of the Almighty.

This is what the ancient Bible story of Balaam and Balak is all about. How appropriate a Scripture it is for our meditation today as we begin a new administration in our national life, surrounded as we are by so much that threatens our future.

The children of Israel were marching out of Egypt—rather, God was bringing his people out of captivity and obscurity into freedom and serious world responsibility. They had passed through their wilderness wanderings. Now they were encamped just across Jordan and about to enter into their Promised Land. Their tents covered the hills and valleys for miles around.

Balak, the king of Moab, saw these ominous, nomad people suddenly appear on the border of his kingdom. They were moving in his direction. Fear gripped his heart. What couldn't those beggars of the desert do to his peaceful and happy kingdom?

So King Balak appealed to a man of God in those parts by the name of Balaam to curse the Hebrew people that they might be destroyed and his kingdom remain unmolested.

But Balaam replied that he must first consult God and discover what God's will was for this strange, threatening horde. And the revelation Balaam received from God was that God had blessed this unlikely and threatening band of vagabonds. So Balaam reported to Balak, "How shall I curse, whom God hath not cursed? or how shall I defy, whom God has not defied?"

But Balak, king of Moab, was a persistent man. He offered Balaam rich gifts if only the man of God would curse whom he wanted cursed. And for three whole chapters in the Book of Numbers we read of the shenanigans of Balaam and Balak as the king leads the prophet from one high mountain peak to another, offering sacrifices and seeking new revelations. But always there is the same result, the divine revelation that these are a people whom God wills, not to curse, but to bless. Finally, Balaam said, "If Balak would give me his house full of silver and gold, I cannot go beyond the word of the Lord my God, to do less or more" (Num. 22:18).

Then testily Balak turned from the prophet, saying, "I called thee to curse mine enemies, and, behold, thou hast altogether blessed them these three times. Therefore now flee thou to thy place: I thought to [reward thee richly and to] promote thee unto great honour; but, lo, the Lord hath kept thee back" (Num. 24:10-11).

And Balak returned to his people so soon to be swept under the swirling tides of conquest as Israel moved into her Promised Land.

Balak, king of Moab, represents man, humanity, religious men and women in every threatening experience turning to the source of their faith for deliverance. The king of Moab saw the host of Israel numerous and ominous. He concluded that in mere physical contest Moab must surely be destroyed. Therefore, he bestirred himself to bring into play forces from beyond the natural and the physical.

Here is a man of basic religious and spiritual motivation. Balak is no rank materialist. He is not an atheist. He believes that if only he can get at the ruling spirit of the universe and enlist that spirit on any given side of a controversy, that will be the winning side. He believes this so strongly that he is willing to put a whole lot of money into the project. We cannot find fault with Balak's basic religious faith and action.

Where we must find fault with Balak is that he brazenly attempts to manipulate God to suit his convenience. He would hire the lackeys of religion to perform the rites of religion to further his cause. Balak's faith has the weakness of a religion that is primarily intuitive, where the worship that takes place is reverence only for the god that is within.

The writer G.K. Chesterton warns of how dangerous this can be: "That Jones shall worship the God within him turns out ultimately to mean that Jones shall worship Jones."

Paul Tillich, the theologian, had a well-known sermon on the text from the 139th Psalm: "Wither shall I go from thy spirit? or whither shall I flee from thy presence?" Tillich points out that the "man who has never tried to flee God has never experienced the God Who is really God.... For there is no reason to flee a god who is the perfect picture of everything that is good in man,... a benevolent father, a father who guarantees our immortality and final happiness. Why try to escape from someone who serves us so well? No, these are not pictures of God, but rather of man, trying to make God in his own image and for his own comfort."

For God, as Rudolf Otto magnificently expresses it in his book *The Idea of the Holy,* is "the Wholly Other"—that one who is completely unlike man, but nevertheless is at work in human history performing his mighty acts, accomplishing his inscrutable purposes entirely apart from man's chicanery.

It is this objectivity of religion that biblical faith is all about. The Bible is the account of the mighty acts of God, performed on God's own initiative, wondrous and never to be dreamed of beforehand by man, but which once experienced as God's gracious mercy to unworthy men may be received, observed, and learned by men as the clear tracings of the Eternal's resplendent character.

Where Balak, a man of great faith in the supernatural, failed was in worshiping only the God within. He came to Balaam announcing: "This is the world that is precious to me. This is how I like things. Keep them the way they are. These are my people, and I want them saved. I'll pay handsomely to have this threatening horde of strangers cursed and destroyed."

Had Balak understood the theology of the biblical revelation, the objective side as well as the subjective side of man's religious faith, he would have come to Balaam and said something like this: "Balaam, I'm concerned. Here are these troublesome people of whom I am very much afraid. They are moving on Moab. Please tell me what you know about God's plans and purposes for them and for me and my people."

Then Balak would have been ready to receive the prophetic word: "God is blessing these people. They are a covenant nation. They are marked by the loneliness of election. Through them will all the peoples of the earth be blessed. The way of blessing for you and for your nation is not in cursing them and being belligerent, but through reconciliation and cooperation that you through them may receive God's blessing."

Biblical faith can never afford us the kind of religion that the Balaks of the world want and demand: a curse on the Tartars or the Huns when they threaten, or the Nazis or the Communists or the Libyans when each group in the exigencies of history overshadows our destiny ominously, or the unwanted young man who is about to marry our daughter, or the troublesome competitor who is about to take over our customers with his improved and superior product, or the new social arrangement that threatens our safe and comfortable way of life.

There is always something or someone threatening on the human horizon. Thus it has always been. Thus it will always be while the world stands. Ever our choice remains the same: either to use the offices of religion to curse whatever we see as threatening us, or to make use of the resources of religion to discover as best we can the way God is going in our time and offer ourselves as the servants of his purpose.

And it may just be that what threatens our nation—our American way of life with its horrendous federal budget deficit, our failing savings and loan system, our unsolved problem of atomic waste pollution, and all the rest—it may well be that what threatens us most right now is our freedom, our prized, unbridled American freedom.

In *A Touch of Wonder,* Arthur Gordon tells about listening to a Fourth of July speech:

> The speaker talked about the meaning of Independence Day. He spoke of the men who signed the Declaration, their courage, their dedication. He reminded us of our heritage of freedom, how precious it is, and how jealously we should guard it.
>
> We applauded when he was through. But suddenly, as the applause died away, a voice spoke from the crowd: "Why don't you tell them the whole truth?"
>
> Startled, we all looked around. The words had come from a young man in a tweed jacket with untidy hair and intense, angry eyes....
>
> "Why don't you tell them that freedom is the most dangerous gift anyone can receive?" he said. "Why don't you tell them that it's a

two-edged sword that will destroy us unless we learn how to use it, and soon? Why don't you make them see that we face a greater challenge than our ancestors ever did? They only had to *fight* for freedom. We have to *live* with it." He stared for a moment at our blank, uncomprehending faces. Then he shrugged his way through the crowd and was gone....

He was right: Freedom *is* dangerous; it *can* be a two-edged blade. Look at this country today. All around us there seems to be a drastic decline in morals: cheating where once there was honesty, promiscuity where once there was decency, crime where once there was respect for law. Everywhere there seems to be a growing laxness, an indifference, a softness that terrifies people who think about it.

And what lies behind all this? ... Perhaps we *do* have a blind and misguided concept of liberty. Perhaps we *are* using the freedom of choice gained for us by our forefathers to choose the wrong things....

... The freedom we now claim has come to mean freedom from all unpleasantness: from hardship, from discipline, from the stern voice of duty, from the pain of self-sacrifice....

As a nation, in short, we have clamored for total freedom. Now we have just about got it, and we are facing a bleak and chilling truth: We have flung off one external restraint after another, but in the process we have not learned how to restrain ourselves.

Before the awesome threats to our national and personal well-being in this crucial hour, our biblical, Christian faith proposes some safeguards on our human vagaries. First, we must make a sincere and systematic study of the mighty acts of God, the biblical record of what God has done in history, revealing his purposes and character. Then, we must look at our contemporary scene in the light of this revelation and judge for ourselves what schemes and actions of men God will bless and what he will curse. Then again, Christianity proposes this second check on the vagaries of too subjective a faith: the insistence that our prayer and participation in worship be not simply our directions to God on what to do for us in blessing whom we want blessed and cursing whom we want cursed, but rather that they be an unveiling of our spirits to God, unburdening our souls to him, and humbly seeking his directions and his corrections for us and our world.

Primitive, superstitious minds believe that worship is the business of bending the will of deity to perform the intents and desires of human hearts.

But in biblical theology worship has a higher purpose: that of gradually conforming the worshiper to the character of the one Eternal God.

Are we people of genuine biblical faith? When threatened by the troubles of the world, do we turn to God? Well, what is our stance before him in those crucial times? Do we move in to use the resources of religion to curse what we think is threatening us, or do we offer ourselves as his servants for blessing and redeeming his whole creation?

Compromise

"And Jacob awaked out of his sleep, and he said, Surely the Lord is in this place; and I knew it not" (Gen. 28:16).

At the door after service one Sunday morning, I was surprised at one worshiper's frank remark: "You were talking to me this morning, preacher. That's my problem—compromise. But you preachers just get after us for compromising our Christian convictions and conduct, but you don't ever tell us how we can keep from compromising. Why don't you do that sometime?"

Now, I liked that. It took my breath away, but I liked it. It's always wholesome when the pew talks back to the pulpit with constructive suggestions. And difficult though my friend's challenge is, that is just what I hope we can attempt: to discover what we all need to do to keep from compromising, to chart, if we can, some of the practical steps for people such as we are that will safeguard us from cheap and cowardly compromise.

The first thing we need to do is take stock of who we are, what sort of people we are, to determine why compromise is such a problem with all of us. An honest appraisal of the average Christian man and woman among us will reveal each of us to be a person of good intentions, but weak and fickle-hearted and hounded by strong temptations before which we fall in defeat, over and over. If we are honest with ourselves, we have to admit that there is a pretty even mixture of the evil and the good, the holy and the devilish desires rising within these hearts of ours.

Our human nature, yours and mine, is not much better or worse than that which Jesus gathered about himself in those first twelve disciples. In his book *Saints without Halos,* Alvin Magary speaks of Jesus on that night of his trial in the high priest's house as "the Embarrassed Messiah." Why embarrassed? Jesus was firm and courageous before his questioner. What was Jesus embarrassed about? Well, you see, the high priest asked about his disciples, among other things. The gospel record reads: "The high priest then asked Jesus of his disciples, and of his doctrine." And the record shows Jesus talked about his doctrine, but said not a word about his disciples. What reason Jesus had to be embarrassed about them!

There were James and John, those jealous-hearted brothers. The last Jesus had seen of them they had turned the final fellowship supper that love had prepared into a wrangle over who was to come first in honor. And there was Peter, the Rock, who boasted so loudly of his brave devotion. When Jesus had mentioned the possibility of his backsliding, Peter had said, "Not me, Lord. Though all the world should forsake you, yet will I not forsake you." And now Jesus could see out of the corner of his eye the same Peter (or was he the same?) cozily warming himself at the enemy's fire and shaking his head and sternly saying to a serving maid, "I tell you I don't even know the man." The three Jesus had asked to watch while he prayed in dark Gethsemane had fallen asleep. And then there was Judas, whom Jesus had loved and called and lived with for three years, gone for good now and whose betrayal was at the bottom of all this dark business. And the other disciples, where were they? Heaven only knows. At the first show of armed opposition they had scattered like frightened chickens.

Yes, when the high priest asked Jesus to tell him of his disciples, the Savior dropped his head in an embarrassed silence. And how often he must be embarrassed when the world is asking about the astonishing compromise we, his Christian disciples, make today. For we are just like they were—weak, vacillating folk, however well-intentioned we may be, so quick to forsake him and follow our own selfish ambitions or our inherited traditions and cultural patterns.

And what does all this add up to? Why, that we need help, of course. We compromise our Christian convictions and conduct because the balance in our lives is so easily tipped in the wrong direction. To remain strong and steadfast, resolute and constant before all temptations to compromise, we need an amazing amount of help. In our own strength alone we're doomed.

Even Saint Paul says this. If the disciples stood in need of outside help, surely we do, too. That help is of Christ who transformed the disciples' lives and can do the same with us, if we will let him.

Now, the next thing we need to see in our consideration of how to keep from compromising our Christian faith and action is this (and it may be a bit of a surprise for us): that ours is not so much a problem of strengthening the armor of our righteousness as of tightening the cord of our love.

There is the scriptural example of Peter denying his Lord. In the high priest's house that fearful night, the pressure of a hostile society was too much for Peter's ideals and his pledged loyalties, and the blustering disciple compromised so shamefully. "No, I don't know him," he said angrily with an oath to the maid. "I never knew him."

But later on the lakeshore, when Jesus had come victoriously through the Crucifixion and the Resurrection, see how the risen Lord deals with Peter's weak compromise. See them there in the dim, cold light of the early dawn, the morning mists rising like smoke about them, and Peter with his tormented conscience hanging his head before his approaching Lord. And Jesus? What does he say? Does he shame the culprit by saying, "How could you do it, Peter, after all we've been through together?" Does he begin to point out the weakness of Peter's faith? Does he upbraid him for his lack of courage to hold out alone for righteousness when the right was overwhelmingly outnumbered? No! Jesus comes to the penitent Peter with just one question, "Peter, do you love me?" That's all he says. "Simon, son of Jonas, lovest thou me more than these?" But oh, how fundamental, how incisive is that question: "Peter, where is your heart? What are the emotional bases of your life? Do you really love me more than all these other things in your life?"

Psychology tells us that when there is a conflict between the will and the emotions, the emotions will always win the battle. "To what are the ultimate love, loyalty, allegiance of your life pledged? Peter, do you love me?"

In this business of compromise as it plagues our lives—when we see how we've slipped, when a survey of our lives reveals the same sorry pattern of Peter warming himself before the enemy's fire in the high priest's house as the Prince of Light was under trial and unpopular and the powers of darkness were in the ascendancy—the thing we must come back to to discover why we compromised is to ask ourselves, "What do I really love?" Then if love and desires are weak where they should be strong, do something to strengthen them.

Simon Peter, searching his heart, found love, though wavering, still there. "Yea, Lord; thou knowest that I love thee." Peter's problem is ours. If we would not compromise, we must find some way to nourish that love and make it grow stronger in a hostile world.

And that brings us to this important junction, what we all know so well and apply so poorly: The ties of affection and devotion are strengthened by daily association; they are weakened and destroyed by long seasons of separation and neglect. Modern lovers have given the lie to the old adage, Absence makes the heart grow fonder, by adding that realistic phrase, For somebody else.

What have the saints of all the ages done to build the battlements of their lives against the destroying forces of this world that would pull them down in cowardly compromise? This they have done: Whatever experience of God they had in their lives, they held on to it. They ringed it round with sanctities. They returned to it day after day as to a shrine.

Jacob at Bethel, where he saw the shining ladder to heaven and the angels going up and down in solemn cadence, rose from his dream and set up a stone pillar to mark that place in his life as the very house of God. Later at Peniel, Jacob had another shaking encounter with God. Over and over through his life, Jacob made the actual or spiritual pilgrimage to these experiences. Something from God had been added to his life, and he wanted to hold on to it. He never let it go.

Four times in the New Testament there pops up the account of Paul's conversion on the road to Damascus. Why? Wouldn't one telling do the job? The account recurs because Paul is always telling and retelling it. This experience of the living Christ changed the direction of Paul's life, and if he was to be kept on that straight course, Paul felt the need of frequent recurrence to that hallowed event.

Sewn in the lining of the coat worn by Blaise Pascal at the time of the philosopher's death a piece of parchment was found. On the parchment, written in Pascal's own hand, were these words: "In the year of Grace, 1654, On Monday, 23d of November ... From about half past ten in the evening until about half past twelve, FIRE. God of Abraham, God of Isaac, God of Jacob, not of the philosophers and scholars. Certitude. Certitude. Feeling. Joy. Peace. God of Jesus Christ." Pascal called it his "Memorial." It was the record of a moving spiritual experience in the life of Blaise Pascal. For at least eight years, from the time of this experience of the reality of God and communion with him, Pascal had taken care to sew and unsew the parchment in the lining each time he changed his coat. Pascal always carried this memorial with him, so that in a moment of wavering faith, he could touch it, recall the exalted experience, and be renewed in love, loyalty, and strength.

During my pastorate at Grace Covenant Church in Richmond, Virginia, one of the ushers of the church brought to me a Bible that he had found in a pew rack in the balcony. He opened it and pointed to what he had just discovered written on the flyleaf. I saw there, written in pencil and signed by some person unknown to me, these words:

> Sitting in church this Sunday, October 24, 1939, I suddenly felt a great faith come over me. In a blinding flash of light I saw suddenly that the way of life I was following led to perdition. I wish to record this so when I return to this church ten years from today as I have sworn to do, a new man, a pillar of society and of the church, a friend of the underdog, and a true Christian in all respects, I will be reminded of the most eventful day of my life and the hour that changed the whole course of events for me.

What does all this business mean—Jacob at Bethel, Paul on the road to Damascus, Pascal's memorial, the unknown worshiper at Grace Covenant? Just this: Whenever they have an experience of God, people, instinctively knowing their own weakness and the distractions and temptations of life, seek to set up some sort of memorial to which they can return and replenish the fires of faith and devotion.

How important to preserve a nation as free, independent, and noble is the observance of Memorial Day, when a people's heroic defenders are remembered and honored. How indispensable to the individual Christian to remember his or her closest, most vivid encounters with the Eternal God.

What experience of God have you and I had in our lives? What have we done, or are we doing, to keep that experience real, insistent, in the warfare between heaven and hell that rages daily in our souls? Well, what are we doing, you and I, day by day, week by week, to keep in Christ's company, to live and move and have our being so really in his presence that the living Christ may have a chance to strengthen the bonds of our devotion that gird our lives to him? What are we doing? It is here that we lose or win the battle against cowardly compromise. In the words of the hymn:

> *I bind my heart this tide*
> *To the Galilean's side,*
> *To the wounds of Calvary,*
> *To the Christ who died for me.*

❦   FIVE   ❦

Christian Love in the World at Large

The Chain of Kindness

"And David said, Is there yet any that is left of the house of Saul, that I may shew him kindness for Jonathan's sake?" (2 Sam. 9:1).

King David was settled safely on his throne. All his enemies had been subdued. Jerusalem was built as a holy city. The boundaries of the kingdom were stretched farther than ever before in Israel's history. The warrior chieftain now lived in a fabulous palace. All that the heart of man could wish was David's to enjoy.

But David on his throne was unsatisfied. From the great soul of the shepherd king there came the question, "Is there not someone of Saul's house to whom I may show kindness for Jonathan's sake?" The remembered kindness of Jonathan, David's well-loved friend, stirred him with restlessness until one of Jonathan's kin could be searched out and helped.

Finally, there came a report: "There is yet one son of Jonathan's alive, but he is lame and his name is Mephibosheth." "Bring him to the palace," said David, "that he may eat continually at the king's table, and I will restore to him the land belonging to his father, Jonathan, and his grandfather Saul."

In the structure of the universe a chain of kindness stretches from man to man, from generation to generation, from country to country, from heaven to earth. The forging of links in that chain is one of our most urgent and rewarding duties. What about us, you and me? What do we know of the chain of kindness, and what are we doing about it from day to day? Are we forging new links for the chain or digging pits of despair?

This brief episode in David's life reveals to us some very important facts about this chain of kindness and our relationship to it.

First, there's this: Kindness has kindling power. Somewhat like the strange atomic power, kindness sets off a chain reaction. King David asks, "Is there yet any that is left of the house of Saul, that I may shew him kindness for Jonathan's sake?" Yes, for Jonathan's sake, for the remembered kindness of his friend Jonathan, whose love was sweeter to David than the love of women, for Jonathan's sake David would pass on kindness to another. In the next chapter in this Book of Samuel we read where David, hearing of the death of his friend Nahash, king of Ammon, and understanding something of the grief and uncertainty of Nahash's son, says, "I will shew kindness unto Hanun the son of Nahash, as his father shewed kindness unto me."

Henri Dunant, a young Swiss banker in Italy on business, witnessed the bloody battle of Solferino on June 24, 1859. The carnage sickened his soul. As the smoke cleared and the cannon fell silent, there before his eyes were the wounded and dying. When the armies moved away, leaving their casualties behind, untended, Dunant could not bring himself to depart. He organized companies of the humble villagers and townsfolk for rescue and nursing. He forgot all about his business schedule. He labored night and day for weeks. When finally he went home, the memories of Solferino lingered, and Dunant wrote a book about it, asking why some international organization of mercy could not be formed in time of peace to care for the wounded of both sides whenever war broke out. And so the Red Cross was born. The act of merciful kindness of Henri Dunant had kindling power. It set up a chain reaction of kindness that spread across the earth and has never stopped.

But why is it that when one does a kind deed it is like throwing a pebble in a pool of water and the waves spread out in ever-widening circles over the whole surface of the lake? Why did David feel some inner compulsion to do kindness to someone of Jonathan's family for Jonathan's sake?

Partly it's due to human gratitude and to the regnancy of example in fashioning human life. When we see a clean, unselfish kindness done, it glows like a sudden flare to light up the darkness of our selfish world and leaves in passing, not only a clear photograph for memory, but also a carefully cut pattern for our future action.

Someone's kind generosity provided a scholarship that opened the door to a college education for an eager, ambitious young woman. Years later when she and her husband had come upon prosperity and a thousand doors were open to them for luxurious living and self-indulgence, she found the way back to that old, familiar threshold of another's kind deed to her, and in recrossing it opened similar doors of educational opportunity to hundreds of young people. So the chain of kindness of the Gooch Foundation for college scholarships began.

But kindness spreads, not only because of human gratitude and example, but also because of divine inspiration. David said, "Is there not any of the house of Saul left that I may show him the kindness of God for Jonathan's sake?" In his friend Jonathan and all that he meant to him, David recognized the kindness of God. Once when David, as a hunted fugitive, was in mortal danger and his enemies were closing in on him, the Scripture says that Jonathan, David's friend, came to him in the woods and "strengthened his hand in God." Jonathan reminded David of God's care for him, of God's covenant with David, of David's invulnerability against all the schemes and spears of his enemies so long as David did God's will. So David had learned that the true source of all human kindness was Eternal God, that men are kind only because God is kind and inspires men and women to be kind.

Saint Paul put it this way: "Be ye kind one to another, tenderhearted, forgiving one another, even as God for Christ's sake hath forgiven you." And again, Paul explained his own kindness and concern for others, saying, "The love of Christ constraineth us." Christ's merciful kindness to us revealing the loving heart of God is the source of inspiration for any kindness we may show to any living soul.

But there is a third reason kindness has spreading power and the links of the chain of kindness reach farther and farther to bind mankind together, and it is this: We can never repay the kindness shown us. David could never repay the kindness of Jonathan, for Jonathan was gone. As Joseph Parker says in *The People's Bible*, "We can never repay, in the sense of being equal with, any man who ever did us kindness.... Men who suppose they have paid their benefactors are never to be trusted.... Justice may draw a line,—gratitude stretches out a horizon."

A young man wrote to an older friend who had helped him get his start in the business and technical world, "If I had three lifetimes to live and nothing to do in each one of them but to devote myself to paying back my obligations to you for your kindness, I could never repay the debt of gratitude I owe you." Extravagant expression? No, literal truth. So it is with each one of us. We can never repay, partly because the debt is too great, partly because our benefactor is no longer here or does not have need of what he bestowed upon us or what we are able to pay back.

But we can do this—what David did—find someone else who needs our kindness and perform it.

And that brings us to notice another fact about this chain of kindness—the world's unlimited and varied need for kindness. Mephibosheth was a very young boy, about four years old, when his father, Jonathan, and his grandfather Saul went off with their armies to fight for the defense of their homeland against the Philistine invaders. When the tragic news of Israel's defeat at Jezreel and the death of Saul and Jonathan on the field of battle was brought back to Jerusalem, the nurse caring for little Mephibosheth was so frightened she turned to flee for safety and dropped the terrified child, and he was crippled in both his feet.

How many there are who, like Mephibosheth, "bear the scars of an innocent sharing in human failure," *The Interpreter's Bible* notes. "How many little children there are in our world, totally innocent of participation in the world's evil, who will suffer to the end of their days from the ravages of war, from 'man's inhumanity to man.' How many more grow up with twisted, crooked personalities because of the failure of fathers and mothers, of older friends, of the home, of society, of the church." Now we are hearing of children born with AIDS because their parents had contracted AIDS, and of children born drug addicts because their mothers were abusing drugs during pregnancy.

How great is the need for someone to show kindness to these little sufferers in their vale of tears as David showed kindness to the little, crippled son of Jonathan. And, of course, not just the physically handicapped, the poor, and those on whom great catastrophe has fallen need kindness shown to them. Oh, the multitudes who need no material aid, no charity, who have an abundance of wealth in things, but are poverty stricken in friendship and in spiritual peace and comfort because they have suffered spiritual or social crippling, perhaps because of jealousy or slander or their own folly. How desperate is their need for kindness shown for Christ's sake.

And we, whoever we are, whatever we have or don't have, we are in a position to pass on some of this commodity that never goes out of style—the kindness of God for Christ's sake.

Then let us take note of this: Fashioning the chain of kindness is no sentimental making of a daisy chain. It's not simply doing a good turn daily because one good turn deserves another. It's not the philosophy of You scratch my back and I'll scratch yours.

We are talking about kindness unlimited, for that is what Christian kindness is, not polite reciprocation, nor even enlightened self-interest, but the kind of kindness Jesus enjoined on his disciples when he said, "But I say unto you which hear, Love your enemies, do good to them which hate you, Bless them that curse you, and pray for them which despitefully use you.... And if ye do good to them which do good to you, what thank have ye? for sinners also do even the same."

It's true that Mephibosheth was Jonathan's son and David owed Mephibosheth a debt of kindness for Jonathan's sake. And it's true that Mephibosheth was crippled, the innocent, pitiable casualty of social conflict and so deserving of someone showing him the kindness of God. But Mephibosheth was also the grandson of Saul, David's worst enemy, and heir to the throne of Israel in the old dynasty that David had supplanted. Ancient Oriental tradition taught that a new regal line could safely establish itself only if all members of the former dynasty were obliterated. For David, therefore, to take Mephibosheth into his own house and show him kindness instead of cutting his throat was to do an unconventional, improper, dangerous thing.

Can't you hear the wise men in the king's cabinet: "Why, Your Excellency, you cannot afford this foolish charity. If you care not for your own welfare and safety, how can you do this thing to your own children and your loyal subjects? As long as one heir of Saul's lives, he will remain a symbol about which insurrection may rally to destroy your dynasty, disinherit your children, and plunge your own loyal subjects into bloody civil war. This, Your Excellency, is an unwise charity, a cruel kindness."

No, the making of the chain of kindness is not sentimental slush, as David must have found out, but tough welding that calls for courageous hearts challenged by the world's deepest need on some of its most dangerous fronts.

I've known in my time devout Christian men and women who, constrained by the love and kindness of Christ, showed kindness to some of the neediest in our southland, and because of that kindness they suffered the loss of all things. Their only crime was that they showed the kindness of Christ to those whom others, their neighbors, did not want to receive his kindness.

And finally, this brief episode from the life of David reveals to us this about the chain of kindness: It awaits our forging, not only for the world's great need that kindness be shown, but also for ourselves, our own soul salvation. David, human, frail, erring man that he was, yet lived always with his soul windows open upon the Eternal, ready to receive tidings and inspiration from the other world. This was the secret of his genius. This is what made him a man after God's own heart. Because of this quality he could compose psalms. So even in the triumph and glory that was his as first citizen of Israel, the nation's ruler and adored hero, he felt in his soul that he must do the kindness of God to someone so his soul still might live, so what in him was most like God might remain alive and in touch with the Eternal. As God is eternal love and kindness, so he, David, God's child, must be kind, too.

Yes, the chain of kindness must be forged link by link, not only because our world needs to be filled with the goodness of God as the waters cover the sea, but more because we need to have our souls fashioned into the likeness of Christ, and that will not come without our showing kindness. It is more blessed to give than to receive. It is the giver's soul rather than the recipient's soul that is most filled with joy, beauty, and strength when kindness is done. Only as the love of Christ constrains us to do acts of kindness is our soul changed into his likeness.

Nothing is as important as souls. Souls are more important than comforts or kindness or kingdoms. Souls will outlast all powers and empires. And souls are not made perfect without showing kindness. It is not just that people in Africa and South America and disillusioned Communists all over the world need us to send missionaries to preach Christ to them; it is not just that the poor, the homeless, and the despairing people all around us in our city's slums and neglected rural neighborhoods need our kindness lest they starve or rise in rebellion; but we need to perform these kindnesses so our own souls may not grow cruel, hard, insensitive—so we may become more like Christ.

Reevaluation

"I have fought a good fight, I have finished my course, I have kept the faith: Henceforth there is laid up for me a crown of righteousness, which the Lord, the righteous judge, shall give me at that day: and not to me only, but unto all them also that love his appearing" (2 Tim. 4:7-8).

The whole world is startled and sickened by the horrible killings taking place in China. How difficult for us to understand this wholesale slaughter of the Chinese students, the nation's brightest, bravest, and best.

In his play *Dirty Hands,* Jean-Paul Sartre casts some light for us on this dreadful enigma. The leading character in the Sartre drama is an ardent young Communist in the country of Illyria who is given an assignment to liquidate a party member in a high position. The young man is sent as secretary to this commissar with orders to shoot him at the first opportunity. Party powers have decided to remove this particular commissar because he is following a policy of appeasement and peaceful coexistence with the capitalist forces of the country.

But the young Communist secretary with the assassination orders cannot—at first—bring himself to carry out his assignment. He is not by nature a killer. He cannot overcome his early bourgeois ideas about taking human life. Then, too, when he gets to know the commissar, his boss, he grows to like him. He cannot hate the man. But, more damaging still, he begins to approve of the commissar's policies. So he delays the assassination.

Nevertheless, at last, in loyalty to the party's commands and against his better judgment, his innate sensibilities, and his personal feelings, he shoots the commissar and pays the inevitable penalty of a prison term. Finally, in Sartre's play, the young secretary is released from prison only to discover that in the meantime the party has switched its policy, made a hero of the dead commissar, officially adopted his ideas of peaceful coexistence and now the top party officials are laying down as the condition for the young Communist's rehabilitation into the party that he flatly deny his role in the assassination.

The Sartre play ends with the idealistic young Communist frankly admitting his inability to reevaluate his life so sharply, to switch his personal commitments so completely. The final curtain comes down on the young Communist secretary opening the door for the goon squad waiting on the outside to come in and liquidate him.

All around the world today Communist nations are reevaluating their structures of government, their methods of doing business, and their relations with the outside world. China and Russia, the largest and most powerful nations committed to Marxist communism, have been going through the most rapid and radical changes because, as Zbigniew Brzezinski points out in his book *The Grand Failure,* their social system is going to rack and ruin.

The Chinese students who staged their peaceful demonstration in Beijing were demanding democratic changes in their system of government to match the changes already made in China's commercial coexistence with the capitalist nations. But China's top echelon of totalitarian control in its lust for power overruled the students' dreams of freedom and justice and mercy and launched the Beijing massacre.

But it is not only in Communist countries that the vagaries of politics and rapidly changing social conditions force on people painful reevaluation of the priorities to which they have given their lives. Changing conditions in church and family and in the heavy toll of the years through the aging process sometimes force catastrophic reevaluations on all of us.

Look at this business of growing old, for example. The French impressionist painter Claude Monet at eighty-six wrote to a friend, "Age and chagrin have worn me out. My life has been nothing but a failure, and all that's left for me to do is to destroy my paintings before I disappear."

Time was to reveal, however, that Monet's reevaluation of himself and his work at the middle of his ninth decade, though sincere and thoroughly honest at that point of infirmity and discouragement, was not the ultimate evaluation of his life and work that history would accord Monet, for his paintings are worth millions. But, more importantly, Monet raised such monumental questions through his life's work as to remain the most influential of all the French impressionists.

Then turn to marriage and the family. Every marriage counselor—professional or nonprofessional, doctor, lawyer, merchant, friend or relation—knows about that painful process of reevaluation that always takes place when some act of unfaithfulness or the long, slow process of thoughtlessness and neglect has wrecked a marriage. What reordering of values, what new priorities, what repentance, what forgiveness can be brought into that relationship to save it? These are the painful necessities of such a moment, regardless of how new or how old-fashioned have been the moral principles of a husband and a wife. A reevaluation must be made.

Changing conditions in the Church are also forcing painful reevaluations on us all. Now and then you hear someone say, "Where's so and so? I haven't seen him at church for some time," or, "Whatever happened to that family that used to sit in the pew next to us?" What's going on? Why, people are reevaluating their situations, their lives, in relationship to the changed world and their changed values regarding what is important now and what priorities should control their lives.

A friend of mine was in Chicago and chanced to remark to a taxi driver about the unprecedented, long, beautiful stretch of weather the country was having. The driver replied, "But we'll pay for it yet. I don't believe in God, but I've seen enough of life to know that there is an equalizer in control."

Subsequent conversation revealed that the young taxi driver had been raised a Roman Catholic but had become disenchanted with the changes he had seen in the established church and was now in complete rebellion, having renounced all faith. My friend responded on the spur of the moment, yet out of a lifetime of devout, disciplined, and dedicated Christian living, with a remark that stands in my estimate as one of the finest Christian contemporary witnesses I've heard. He said, "Don't let the troubles of the Church destroy your personal faith in God."

What a great thought for every one of us to clutch close in this time of reevaluation of all things! The Church, the body of Christ in the world, has always been and always will be an institution both human and divine. To it God has committed the incomparable riches of the Gospel of Jesus Christ, which carries the power of God unto salvation for all sinners who will believe. But the Church is always composed of human beings, weak, sinful, ignorant, and prone to enormous error. The Church has always had her troubles, but she has never been deprived of her power to point people to God in Christ. "Don't let the troubles of the Church destroy your personal faith in God."

Toward the end of his life, Saint Paul came to a season of ultimate reevaluation, and in his last letter to Timothy, he sets before us guidelines and goals that have proved to be unshakable before all forces, whether they be the ebb and flow of political fortunes, or the rise and fall of ecclesiastical structures, or even the steady drain of the years, or the success or failure of our personal ventures.

Listen to Paul's words: "I have fought a good fight, I have finished my course, I have kept the faith: Henceforth there is laid up for me a crown of righteousness, which the Lord, the righteous judge, shall give me at that day: and not to me only, but unto all them also that love his appearing."

Are these the top priorities, the essential guidelines that you and I are keeping in mind and heart and will for every reevaluation, whether in disappointment and defeat or in success and victory?

First, have we kept the faith? What faith? Keeping the faith for the Apostle Paul meant pressing on "toward the mark for the prize of the high calling of God in Christ Jesus." Have we lived for Christ? Have we so kept the faith that we have not let down those to whom we owe love and loyalty and service following the example of Jesus?

Second, have we fought a good fight? This life is a long warfare. It is often an obstacle course. The choice is ours—ever ours—to take our place on one or the other side of two titanic forces contending throughout all human history. Where do we choose to enlist our energies, to direct the weight of our influence? On the side of service to others and kindness and purity and honor, or on the side of selfishness and cruelty and callous disregard of human rights and human need and human hope? Where will we fight and for what? And will we really contend courageously, or do we intend merely to talk and make a show, a shadowboxing, at fighting a good fight?

Third, are we finishing our course, achieving our goals? Any realistic reevaluation by a Christian at any juncture must always include a fresh compass reading to determine whether we are on course or have strayed. From whom are we now taking our orders? Are we really receiving and carrying out Christ's orders?

The idealistic young Communist secretary in the Sartre play gave his all in loyalty, obedience, and devotion to the Communist party, taking all his orders in life and death, only to discover that he had entrusted his destiny to cynical, power-mad men. Only Jesus Christ, the Savior of all people, who gives himself completely for all, even the dirtiest and most lost sinner among us, only he is worthy to be trusted as the supreme Lord of the conscience of every person. Are we moving on to finish our course, which in reality is his course, the course of the Kingdom of God?

In *Catherine of Aragon,* Garrett Mattingly writes that the dying Cardinal Wolsey, on his journey to the Tower of London where King Henry VIII was sending him to be tried for high treason, was reported to have said, "If I had served God as diligently as I have done the King, He would not have given me over in my grey hairs."

These are our unchanging checkpoints for every season of reevaluation: Have I fought a good fight? Have I finished my course? Have I kept the faith?

And the unimpeachable assurance that comes from a reevaluation that sincerely includes these checkpoints is, "Henceforth there is laid up for me a crown of righteousness, which the Lord, the righteous judge, shall give me at that day: and not to me only, but unto all them also that love his appearing."

"Now unto him that is able to keep you from falling, and to present you faultless before the presence of his glory with exceeding joy, To the only wise God, our Saviour, be glory and majesty, dominion and power, both now and ever. Amen."

Life Is Hard for the Fainthearted

"I was afraid, and went and hid thy talent in the earth" (Matt. 25:25). "Wait on the Lord: be of good courage, and he shall strengthen thine heart" (Ps. 27:14).

If ever there was a parable of life, not only of the kingdom of God, but also of our ever-circling years, it is the parable of the talents. Here Jesus is saying to us: "This is the way life is, wherever you find it, in first-century Palestine or west Tennessee in 1988. Here is a parable of your life, and its overarching moral is, 'Life is hard for the fainthearted. Therefore, be of good courage. Wait on the Lord and he shall strengthen your heart.'"

A wealthy man of the ancient East prepared to take a journey. Calling in three trusted servants, he disposed of his property by assigning a given amount to each. Five talents of silver, or about $5,000, he gave to one. To another went two talents, or $2,000. To a third he gave one talent, or $1,000. He knew the ability of each man, and he divided his wealth accordingly.

This is not an improbable situation. In an economy without savings banks, government bonds, and commercial stocks, what better way to safeguard and invest one's resources than to place them in the hands of reliable people? I once knew a bank president who made such a remarkable success of running his bank that every January 1, stockholders in his bank received great big dividend checks, so much larger than the earnings from other banks in the city. The secret of his success? Why, he banked on people, not commercial collateral. He had an uncanny insight into human nature. He instinctively knew what people could be trusted with loans and with how much.

The master in the parable, having allocated his talents, went away and was gone a long time. Meanwhile, the servants were left to their own devices. So God, the Creator, endows us with whatever in his wisdom he knows is best for us and then leaves us in freedom to employ his talents and his time according to our inclinations.

Our human endowments differ. All men and women are not created equal in the sense of having equal capacities for business, literature, and government leadership. God gives to a Michelangelo five talents in art, to an Einstein five talents in science and mathematics, and to multitudes of his other children two talents or one, as it pleases him. All people are not equal in ability, but all are equal in that their Creator and Heavenly Father has endowed them with certain inalienable abilities. Each has been entrusted with his or her peculiar talent, which is needed and of incalculable value in the divine economy.

We return to the parable, which says that, at length, the master returned. He called in his three servants. (So the parable teaches not only endowment and freedom, but also judgment. We are called to give an account of our stewardship. We are free to use our talent as our heart directs, but our use will be judged by his standard, not ours. And that standard is revealed. The talent bestowed by God is not an outright gift, but a loan, an investment, and God will have an accounting.)

The five-talent man reported, "I have gained five other talents." "Well done, thou good and faithful servant," said the master. "Thou hast been faithful over a few things; I will make thee ruler over many. Enter thou into the joy of thy lord." The servant who had received two talents of his master's money came in with a similar report—he had gained two others. For him the master had the same commendation and reward: "Well done, thou good and faithful servant. Thou hast been faithful over a few things; I will make thee ruler over many things. Enter thou into the joy of thy lord."

Then came the fellow with one talent to report. Of course, you know Jesus told the story principally for this man. He stood in the center of the stage. The floodlights were on him. His report? "I know, Master, that you are a hard man, difficult to deal with, expecting the well-nigh impossible, so I was afraid and went and hid thy talent in the earth. Here it is. I give you back what is yours."

Whereupon the gracious master, who had just been so generous with his praise and rewards for his other two servants, turned on the poor, scared creature with vehement rebukes: "Why you wicked and fainthearted servant! So you knew me to be hard, expecting the impossible. All right, take his talent, which he would not use for me, and give it to the man who will make the most use of it. And throw this foolish, cowardly man into the cold darkness, where in remorse he can grind his teeth over his failure. For to him that hath shall be given, but from him that hath not, even that which he hath shall be taken away."

Harsh and cruel treatment, you say, for the kingdom of God? Perhaps so, but Jesus is just enunciating a universal law of life. These are not just the ethics of the kingdom, mind you; here is the stern law engraved in the granite of the centuries. Withhold a native endowment, refuse to employ a God-given faculty, and it will wither and die. If left unused, whatever God has given will be taken away, while the man who uses what life has endowed him with finds life adding to his endowments as the years roll by.

The failure of the one-talent man and his stern condemnation by the Lord of Life is a result, please notice, not of his greed or his tight-fisted stinginess, but entirely of his fear. "I was afraid and went and hid my talent." The man was not dishonest. He was not a drunkard, nor was he wasteful. What was wrong with him? He was afraid to hazard in use what his lord had entrusted to him.

"Life," Jesus is saying, "is hard for the fainthearted." As George Buttrick says in *The Interpreter's Bible:* "A man must venture for Christ at risk. He must not be content with 'things as they are.' He must break new soil. We miss the point of the story if we fail to see that Christ requires of his followers the hazard of the untried road."

The writer Charlotte Bronte said, "Better try all things and find all empty than to try nothing and leave your life a blank." And John Milton in his *Areopagitica* says, "I cannot praise a fugitive and cloistered virtue unexercised and unbreathed, that never sallies out and sees her adversary, but slinks out of the race, where that immortal garland is to be run for, not without dust and heat."

Life is hard for the fainthearted. God has so ordained it. He who gives lavishly to all men demands we risk with gallant abandon our all for his kingdom. To shrink back in cowardice is to find life difficult and hard with all its stern judgments against us. Therefore, my wish for you is for courage.

But courage is not had by wishing! If wishes were horses beggars would ride and cowards would all brave men be. No knave is proud of his shrinking, faint heart. But how can he change it? Where does courage come from? It is not necessarily an innate endowment, impossible of cultivation, else Jesus would not represent God as sitting in judgment on the man who fails because he lacks courage. Yes, courage can be cultivated, and that particular brand of courage exemplified in hazarding one's talents for God is born of faith.

Why was the fellow who buried his talent in the earth afraid? He tells us: "Lord, I knew thee that thou art an hard man, reaping where thou hast not sown, and gathering where thou hast not strawed." He was afraid because he had an utterly erroneous idea of his master's character. So, also, to many people God is a policeman who almost hopes to catch people in wrongdoing. They do not know God, the generous, trustful father expecting the best of his sons and daughters, waiting at the end of the day with a reward larger than the promised wages. The world, which he has created, is even that kind of a world—it finally rewards the venture of faith.

Robert Louis Stevenson in his essay "Old Mortality" says, "To believe in immortality is one thing, but it is first needful to believe in life." Immortality, everlasting life, heaven, waits for the one who believes courageously in life. You must enter the kingdom now, by taking the Lord's largess and employing it for him. Then, and only then, comes the reward: "Well done, thou good and faithful servant."

The cure for cowardly fear is faith—a good, long look into the face of the God and Father of our Lord and Savior Jesus Christ, a confident belief that he will keep his promises, live up to his commitments—and then stepping out into life on the basis of that trust. That kind of faith will destroy fear.

James Stewart, in his book *The Gates of New Life,* tells of Robert Stopford, who was one of Admiral Horatio Nelson's men: "Stopford was commander of one of the ships with which Nelson chased to the West Indies a fleet nearly double in number. And Stopford wrote, in describing the experiences and hardships of that desperate adventure: 'We are half-starved, and otherwise inconvenienced by being so long out of port, but our reward is—we are with Nelson!'"

At long last we shall all discover that the success or failure of our life's voyage will be reckoned, not by what we made out of the years, but by whether or not we have been with the great captain of our souls and what in love and faith we've risked for him. Faith and courage do grow together for every one of us when we make the venture of comradeship with Christ and volunteer for service in his name.

"Wait on the Lord: be of good courage, and he shall strengthen thine heart: wait, I say, on the Lord."

Loss of Life

"I am come that they might have life, and that they might have it more abundantly" (John 10:10).

Loss of life by death is always sad. Sometimes it is appalling. Last week, on April 3, that dire day when a whole cavalcade of tornadoes roared through the midsection of our nation, four hundred people were killed. They lost their lives by death. Since the first of this year, fourteen members of the Idlewild congregation have died—some young, some old. All lost their lives by death.

There's loss of life by sudden heart attack, by the slow attrition from the infirmities of age, by raging, uncontrollable cancer. Daily, our shocked attention is called to loss of life by death.

This Holy Week reminds us that even for the Son of God there was waiting for him on that dark Friday, as the price of his humanity and the cost of accomplishing his mission, the loss of his life by death on a cross.

But as bad as loss of life by death always is, there is something worse.

Have we begun to calculate that more appalling loss of life that is lost, not by death, but in the midst of life? This is the thing that disturbed the soul of Stephen Vincent Benet and wrung from him those never-to-be-forgotten words in *A Child Is Born:* "Life is not lost by dying! Life is lost minute by minute, day by dragging day, in all the thousand, small, uncaring ways."

As Jesus looked out on life, this is what sickened our Savior most, not loss of life by death—he knew how life could triumph over death—but rather Jesus was appalled by the loss of life in the midst of life. We know that Jesus very seldom spoke of sinners. That was the word the Pharisees and the Scribes used to describe the people whom they considered to be living lives of less moral excellence than their own. "Sinners," they said in scorn and disgust. Jesus used another term. He spoke of "the lost." What did he mean by "the lost"? He meant the people who were losing life in the midst of life, whose precious resources of life, time, energy, emotions, opportunities were all slipping away from them because they were investing in doomed enterprises.

Jesus said this precious possession of life can be lost in the midst of life in many ways. Sometimes life is lost as a coin gets lost, not through any fault of the coin, but through carelessness and mishandling by people. This is what happens so many times to small children. The precious possession of life is lost for them through the carelessness of others. Jesus said life can also be lost in the midst of life as a sheep gets lost through heedless wandering away from the good life at the shepherd's side. The lost sheep doesn't intend to get lost. He just follows his own selfish and animal instincts until suddenly he finds himself lost. Jesus said sometimes life is lost through calculated self-will, just as the son and heir of a wealthy and generous father can choose to renounce and to refuse the life at his father's side and take his willful way into the far country. Innumerable are the ways that life can be lost in the midst of life. But however it's lost, Jesus says it is always deplorable waste and pitiable tragedy, and it wrings the heart of God, who is restless and untiring in his search that the lost may be found. And, of course, this is what the Incarnation is all about, and this is what the cross as the climax of the Incarnation is all about, that we celebrate and experience by God's grace in the keeping of another Holy Week.

Are you and I beginning to understand the significance for ourselves and for our times of Jesus' clutching concern about this loss of life in the midst of life? Are we aware of how life may be lost, our own life or life dear to us, through overindulgence? Years ago, when we used this term *overindulgence,* it meant to most of us letting alcohol get the best of our lives. An old movie, *The Lost Weekend,* made this dramatically clear. It chronicled how a poor alcoholic lost, not only the consciousness of what took place in one weekend because he was inebriated, but his job, his family, his self-respect, and how someone's life was lost, all through his overindulgence. And, of course, the problem of alcohol for many people is still with us. But in our time there is the additional problem of drug abuse, which is causing so many of our choice young people to lose the best that life has to offer them in the midst of life.

But are we aware of how life can be lost through negative emotions, through harboring jealousy, pride, hatred, an unforgiving spirit, envy, and all those other negative emotions that are such destroyers of the inner person, that so poison our minds and spirits that it is not possible for a clear, clean, unselfish, helpful thought to swim in and motivate us? How many people who are the strictest teetotalers, who are so careful about guarding their lives from any sort of harmful drug abuse, are nevertheless subject to these deadly destroyers? Are we not aware of how these can disarm us before we fight the real battles of life?

Are we losing life in the midst of life, minute by minute, day by dragging day? If so, where are the leaks? How many times do we hear people say, "Oh, there is so little time to enjoy your family, your friends. We are so pushed by the frantic tempo of these days. Our lives are too crowded"? How many times do we hear someone say about a wonderful life that is cut short in youth or in maturity, "Why, life was just stretching out before that one and suddenly he is gone. What a pity he had just begun to live"?

And yet, are we among those people who squander what precious bit of time God gives us in fussing and squabbling and pouting and nursing hurt feelings and carrying a grudge, instead of loving and serving and enjoying every moment of these wonderful human relationships? Of course, it's in relationships that we win or lose this thing we call the opportunity of life. It's there that we find contentment or run into despair. This is where life is saved or lost.

I wonder if we have caught on to the compelling urgency of Jesus' warning to us and to our own nation this very moment that life be not lost in the midst of life. Just as we move toward the celebration of the two hundredth anniversary of our nation, are we going to lose the dream of the patriots who founded this nation on those enduring, high, idealistic principles? It can be lost, you know. I remember a striking book by that provocative Quaker Elton Trueblood that was published about twenty-five years ago in which he talked about the quality of life in the nation. He gave it the title *The Life We Prize.* Here is what he wrote:

> What we are now experiencing in the Western World is really a depression, but it is not the depression which has normally been expected, namely, an economic one. For several years various persons have warned that a depression might come, and we have said up to now that the prophets of doom were wrong about this, but actually the prediction has materialized, though in an unexpected way. What we

have is a *moral depression*. The stock market is still strong, and the price structure has not broken, but something more serious is happening and will become much worse unless we can take steps to check the movement....

... What is really tragic is not death for a reason, but the slow petering out of life in self-indulgence.

Well, that was more than twenty years ago, and the slow petering out of life in an avalanche of cheap and shoddy living has grown in intensity through the years, and now the stock market has broken, and the value of the dollar moves rapidly toward the ultimate of zero purchasing power as it dwindles week by week, and the spreading Watergate scandal involves more and more people in places of high trust and responsibility in our national life.

Collectively and individually in America today the world's corrosive stain is destroying the moral grandeur of a once great and spiritually sturdy people. Whether you call it the Watergate mess, or the era of electronic snooping to destroy the rights of personal privacy, or the epoch of income tax temptations—whatever you call it, it all boils down to this: We are losing, or we have already lost, the good life right here in the midst of life, little by little in a slow landslide of cheap and shoddy living. And it is not only in Washington but here. For Washington, alas, has no originality. Washington but reflects the image, the hopes, the fears, the convictions, and the conduct of Mr. and Mrs. America, Main Street, and RFD.

But the story of our condition is not all sad, because we still have the gospel of God's love for a desperately needy world. You see, the big business of religion is to save life from being lost in the midst of life. Oh, how strange it is that some people should get the idea, the very perverted idea, that religion is something designed to fence life in, to restrict, to deny, to keep people from certain delightful and enjoyable experiences. "Oh, no," says the man in the street or the person to whom you talk about the Church and the religious faith, "oh, no, I don't want to be fenced in. I don't want someone to tell me what to do and when to do it. I want to enjoy life while I have the time. Perhaps later, but not now."

There are people who really believe that the Christian religion dangles before people the prize of a promised heaven after this life on condition that one will renounce some of the joys and broader experiences of this life. How far this is from the mind and the message of Jesus Christ. Listen to him: I am come that they might have life, and that they might have it more abundantly." Jesus came to make it possible for every person to enter here and now into an abiding relationship with God through faith in Christ, a relationship that would immeasurably enrich and broaden and increase in every dimension that person's life. To the returning prodigal the father says, as he hugs him close to his heart, "This my son was dead, and is alive again; he was lost, and is found."

Any person who is away from this blessed relationship with God in Christ is lost, and life, the best of life, is lost. Any moment in time, any experience of human relationships, any event in history is lost if it is away from the redeeming, transforming power of Christ. In him was life and the life was the light of men.

But how not to lose life but to save it? What word has the Christian faith for us here? What does it tell us to do? It's the very simple but very difficult paradox: How to save life? Why, give it away. A compassionate woman went into a veterans hospital to cheer up the sick and the wounded. She came to a bed where a young veteran was sitting upright, and she noticed that the right sleeve of his pajamas was empty. She started back in horror, exclaiming, "Poor lad, how in the world did you lose your arm?" The veteran stiffened and said, "Madam, I did not lose it. I gave it for my country."

And Jesus, how did he lose his good, young life at thirty-three, cut short on a cross? He didn't lose it. He gave it. Listen to him: "No man taketh it from me, but I lay it down of myself" for "the life of the world."

It's all in the way we live it, you see, day by day. We need not be losing life to age or disease or negative emotions or pressures of the time, in all our small, uncaring ways. No, if with a will and a sense of dedication we give it, offer it up entirely with a holy passion and purpose to God through Christ, life is never lost—not even in death. For Christ's man or woman, death is only one other experience, an event in the life eternal. It's the turning of a corner, the going into another room in the Father's house where another phase of life, of the same life, is lived with God in a broader and more blessed way.

When Robert Louis Stevenson's *Treasure Island* was first published, one of the critics gave it a very unfavorable review. His opinion was that the work was too romantic, written undoubtedly by a man who didn't know anything about the harsh realities and tragedies of life. But, of course, it was just this seamy side, this suffering side of life, that Stevenson had always been up against. He had fought a battle against an incurable illness since he was a small child. He had to write all his thrilling adventure stories, not out doing some daring thing, but propped up in bed, usually with a raging fever. Yet the spirit of Robert Louis Stevenson was unbroken, unbowed, and unembittered because he had experienced this redeeming relationship with God through faith in Jesus Christ, which saved him from loss of life, precious life, in the midst of life.

When Stevenson died at forty-four and was buried in Samoa, the friendly natives there put these lines up above his grave, lines that he, Stevenson, had written for this purpose:

> *Under the wide and starry sky,*
> *Dig the grave and let me lie.*
> *Glad did I live and gladly die,*
> *And I laid me down with a will.*

> *This be the verse that you grave for me:*
> *Here he lies where he longed to be;*
> *Home is the sailor, home from the sea,*
> *And the hunter home from the hill.*

"Life is not lost by dying! Life is lost minute by minute, day by dragging day, in all the thousand, small, uncaring ways." But it need not be lost—ever—if we give it away, offer it up to him who says, "I am the way, the truth, and the life: no man cometh unto the Father, but by me." "I am come that they might have life, and that they might have it more abundantly." "Fear not … it is your Father's good pleasure to give you the kingdom."

Lost Cool

"And God said to Jonah, Doest thou well to be angry for the gourd? And he said, I do well to be angry, even unto death" (Jon. 4:9).

Jonah was angry. He was very angry. He had been cool and calm enough when he shipped out of Joppa that eventful day on his famous Mediterranean cruise. He remained cool through the storm at sea, sleeping calmly while everyone else on ship, including the captain and the crew, panicked. Jonah even remained coolly courageous when he told the sailors their only hope of surviving the storm was to pick him up and hurl him overboard into the boiling waters.

But Jonah finally lost his composure when God did not destroy the wicked Ninevites in fulfillment of Jonah's prophetic prediction and when God did destroy the gourd vine under which Jonah had sat for protection from the blistering sun. Then Jonah was angry, angry unto death.

Anger is a destructive fire that sweeps through a personality, burning up judgment and reason and wisdom, belching out hot words, and pouring out a smoke screen that make visibility of all reality well-nigh impossible. Anger is a fire that spreads through the interconnecting halls and corridors of human relationships in families, cities, and nations.

In the parable of the prodigal son, the record states of the elder brother that when he heard the merriment and the feasting his father had set in motion to celebrate the prodigal's return, he, the elder brother, "was angry, and would not go in." No, he would not go in and have fun with family and friends. He was mad and his own anger shut him out. Anger shuts out so effectively so many from the felicity and joy the family circle should always be including.

See the devastation that anger has caused in China today, when the reasonable, humane requests of the Chinese students were not given sensible consideration by China's totalitarian rulers, and in their wrath, they unleashed the power that comes out of a gun barrel.

The story of Jonah furnishes us a lesson in the causes and control of anger.

Jonah's lost cool began with an act of disobedience. He refused to carry out a command of God. We read, "Now the word of the Lord came unto Jonah the son of Amittai, saying, Arise, go to Nineveh, that great city, and cry against it; for their wickedness is come up before me. But Jonah rose up to flee unto Tarshish from the presence of the Lord" (Jon. 1:1-3).

When the command of God came to go to Nineveh, Jonah packed his bag and took off in the opposite direction. Nineveh, the capital of the Assyrian empire, lay overland to the east on the banks of the Tigris River. But Jonah went west, not east. He set out for the farthest known seaport west, Tarshish in Spain.

Why this reverse action by Jonah when the command of God came to him? Why does any person disobey the clear command of God? Why, because he thinks he knows better than God or anyone else what is good or best for him.

God says, "Thou shalt not steal," but man says, "I have to steal a little, or I can't compete with my competitors." God says, "Thou shalt not bear false witness against thy neighbour," but men and women say, "They lied about me first." God says, "Thou shalt not kill," but man says, "Somebody's got to stop communism." God says, "Remember the sabbath day, to keep it holy," but people say, "We can't this week. We have to get away to get some rest and recreation."

The word of God came to Jonah: "Go preach to the Ninevites. Cry out against the wickedness of those terrible sinners." But Jonah went off in the opposite direction, because he couldn't care less about those Ninevites. They were the people who had enslaved his fellow Jews. They had taken away their freedom, oppressed and persecuted them. It was only recently that some Jews had been permitted to come back to Jerusalem and rebuild their native land. In Jonah's theology it was unthinkable that a Jew should be concerned for the affluent, oppressive Ninevites. Indeed, for God to show interest in their welfare was, to Jonah, the equivalent of God's going back on his own nature. For the word of God to come to Jonah, the son of Amittai, "Go proclaim God's message to Nineveh," was like God commanding an orthodox Jew in Israel today to go preach freedom and mercy and reconciliation to the rock-throwing Palestinian youths.

For there was a strong exclusivist theology abroad in Jonah's day, and he had swallowed it hook, line, and sinker. He was an exclusivist in his attitude toward the Ninevites as European Christians were to become in their attitudes toward the Jews centuries later. Raul Hillberg points out in *The Destruction of European Jews* that the Nazi destructive process in Germany before World War II did not come out of the void. It was the culmination of a cyclical trend that began with the unsuccessful efforts of Christians to convert Jews after Constantine had made Christianity the official state religion of the Roman Empire. The missionaries had said in effect, "You have no right to live among us as Jews." The secular rulers who followed them said, "You have no right to live among us." The German Nazis at last decreed, "You have no right to live," and herded them off to the crematoriums.

The exclusivist sentiments of Jonah that left no room in his heart and mind for compassionate concern for the Ninevites drove him to disobey the word of the Lord that came to him, saying, "Arise, go to Nineveh, that great city."

But the second thing that the story of Jonah reveals about the cause of anger and the loss of control is that action is not so important as attitude. It wasn't Jonah's contrary action to the command of God that undercut his cool, so much as his contradictory attitude. The first duty of God's servant is, not obedience to a given command, but reconciliation to God's point of view, becoming of one mind with God.

When Jonah was given his second chance to obey, after being thrown overboard in the storm and being rescued by the great fish, Jonah repented of his disobedience to God's command, but he was still of the same point of view with reference to the worthless Ninevites. His was an obedience based on a false theology. Therefore, Jonah's preaching to the Ninevites was vindictive crying out against their wickedness.

How popular it is today to cry out against the wickedness of the great cities. There is no lack of prophets. Everyone wants to get into the act. The prophets of the poor and the homeless cry out against the arrogance, the luxury, the cruelty of the rich. The prophets of the establishment cry out against the crimes of violence, looting, and arson of the impatient poor. The prophets of the electorate and the press and the media cry out against the corruption and unethical behavior of the politicians.

Jonah proclaimed the coming judgment of God upon the wicked Ninevites with a hot hostility toward them. He was unprepared for both their repentance and God's merciful withholding of the predicted destruction. He couldn't stand to have his word proved false, even by a miraculous deliverance. It was this that blew his cool. Then Jonah poured out his peevish soul in denunciation: "I knew you to be a God of soft, loving kindness. That is why I ran away to Tarshish when you first called me to go to Nineveh. Now look, you have made me a laughingstock. You told me to preach, 'In forty days Nineveh will be destroyed.' But you didn't do it. When the king and all these sinful people repented, you changed your mind. I'm sick. I'm mad. I want to die."

In *The Layman's Bible Commentary,* Jonah's experience is described as an instance "in which a prophet succeeded in proportion as his prediction failed. It was not the Lord's purpose, of course, to destroy even Nineveh; his purpose was to save it. Prophecy was directed to the salvation of the people, and so the prophetic word was always somewhat conditional—if the people repented, destruction would be stayed; if not, it would come to pass."

It is not enough for the servant of God merely to obey the commands of God; he must also adopt God's attitude toward a lost, sinful world, an attitude of love and forgiveness and willingness to accept and save the penitent. It's when one gives obedience without adopting the attitude of God that one runs the risk of losing his cool.

When Dave Brubeck, the great jazz pianist and composer, was in Memphis for a concert 20 years ago and he was questioned about his oratorio, he said, according to *The Commercial Appeal:* "It's based on Christ's words—words almost totally ignored, even by churches. It has a new concept. Christ said to love your enemies, do good to those that hate you. If you can't do this, you're not a Christian. If your minister can't help you, switch churches. If you hate any person or any country, you don't understand love."

When we try to be obedient to God's commands but remain unreconciled to his attitude of forgiving love toward his world and his redemptive purposes for all his human children, we are heading for a terrible disillusionment in the judgments of God in history and perhaps for petulant spells of deep anger.

But the most penetrating lesson from the Book of Jonah on the causes and control of anger is Jonah's poignant failure to learn from his most fundamental personal experiences of pleasure and pain what his attitudes and actions must be toward all his fellow human beings.

The maddest Jonah becomes—when he is so angry that he wants to die and even justifies his anger in response to God's question, "Doest thou well to be angry?" with his reply, "I do well to be angry, even unto death"—is when the pretty little gourd vine that God made to grow up over Jonah's lean-to and shade his head from the hot sun dies because God sends a worm to cut the stem and a dry wind to wither it away. Then Jonah is really angry.

And the Book of Jonah ends with the awful, yet merciful, rhetorical question God puts to Jonah: "If you care so much about your gourd, for which you neither labored nor made to grow, which came up in a night and perished in a day, how much more should not I, the Lord and Father of all mankind, care to spare that great city, Nineveh, where there are 120,000 little children who know not yet their left hand from their right hand?"

How pitiful when men and women cannot apply the simple, fundamental experiences of pain and pleasure to their concept of theology, sociology, anthropology, and religion! Shylock, in *The Merchant of Venice,* uses the same argument in his famous words: "Hath not a Jew eyes? hath not a Jew hands, organs, dimensions, senses, affections, passions? fed with the same food, hurt with the same weapons, subject to the same diseases.... If you prick us, do we not bleed? if you tickle us, do we not laugh? if you poison us, do we not die?"

And when men and women do not take this fundamental application from personal experience of pain and pleasure into the realm of their attitudes and actions toward others, rage, anger, even hatred, result.

In the Academy Award-winning movie *In the Heat of the Night,* the harassed police chief, Gillespie, whenever threatened or pushed into a corner or humiliated by the mayor, the town council, or its toughs, takes it out by getting angry, not with those who outrank him or outnumber him, but by getting angry with his subordinates or prisoners and venting his hostility on them.

Oh, what a timely tract is the Book of Jonah! If ever we find those things that have given us comfort and protection and security threatened or destroyed, instead of being like Jonah and growing angry, should not this serve to make us more aware of the merciful intentions of Almighty God, our Heavenly Father, toward all his children who are suffering from hunger, homelessness, discrimination, unemployment, lack of dignity and respect, and spur us to offer ourselves as the instruments of God's intent for their salvation?

Christian Character Judgment

"Barnabas wanted to take John Mark with them; but Paul judged that the man who had deserted them in Pamphylia and had not gone on to share in their work was not the man to take with them now" (Acts 15:37-38).

Saint Paul was rough on young John Mark. He sized him up as a quitter and scratched his name from the missionary team, even though this broke permanently the beautiful partnership of Paul and Barnabas. Some have seen this harsh character judgment of John Mark by Saint Paul as a fatal flaw in Paul's personality. They say Paul should have remembered Christ's admonition, "Judge not, that ye be not judged."

This raises the question for all of us of the ethical nature of our character judgments. Sometimes we hear it said as a compliment of someone we know, "You'll never hear him say an unkind or critical thing about anyone." Is this ability to refrain from critical judgement a hallmark of a Christian? Is the person most to be admired among us the one who lives by the adage, See no evil, hear no evil, speak no evil?

Yet practicality demands that choices be made between competing personnel. Programs languish when inefficient people are not removed from places of responsibility. Wasn't this what Paul was doing with reference to John Mark? On the first missionary journey the young man quit after the first stage of operations and went home. Why? The record does not say. There have been many guesses as to his reasons or excuses: that he was young, inexperienced, and grew tired early; that he had conscientious scruples against taking the gospel to the gentiles; that he got sick, was perhaps bitten by a mosquito in the lowlands of Cyprus and developed malarial chills and fever when the missionary party reached the higher altitudes of the Asia Minor mainland. Why he quit, we don't know. That he did quit, we are sure. And we do know that from this point on, in the missionary expansion of the Church, Paul became the dominant leader, not only in shaping the plan for the geographical spread, but also in shaping the organizational structure and the theological framework of the early Church, and that Paul made the character judgment that branded Mark a quitter and removed him from the Christian mission.

Whatever Jesus may have meant by his admonition, "Judge not, that ye be not judged," the gospel record presents the Master in the act of making repeated judgments on character. He called the Pharisees "hypocrites," "blind guides," insincere paraders and posturers of a virtue they did not really possess.

Jesus told a parable in which he represented God as judging a rich man, calling him a "fool" for living his life to collect wealth and not being rich in spiritual values. And the moral Jesus drew from the parable was that men should make the same character judgments on themselves and others lest they gain the whole world and lose their own souls.

Character judgments must be made all the time by every person—for we are moral creatures. We have our standards—low or high, good or bad—for all things, for buying a suit, for shopping for groceries, for casting our ballots, for advising and admonishing our children.

The question is not, should I, as a Christian, make character judgments? For the answer is apparent that I, as a moral creature, can never refrain from making character judgments. The crucial question is, on what basis should I, as a Christian, make character judgments? What must be my frame of reference, my yardstick, by which I make character judgments?

Gilbert Stuart, the early American portrait painter, on seeing for the first time the face and features of the crafty European statesman Talleyrand, is reputed to have remarked, "If that man is not a scoundrel, God Almighty does not write a legible hand." Stuart, judging by his understanding of what God expects in man and reading the features of Talleyrand's face as only a portrait painter can read the emotions and principles of character in that one's soul, made his character judgment of the man.

In a radio broadcast to the British people during the darkest days of the Battle of Britain, William Temple, the archbishop of Canterbury, reviewed the evils perpetrated by their Nazi enemies: the firebombing of their English cities, the enforced slave labor of the German concentration camps, the mass murders of Jewish men, women, and children. Then Temple cut to the heart of that monumental wickedness by saying, "The most horrible thing about our Nazi enemies is, not just that they do these atrocious things, but that they believe it is right that they should do these things."

Friday's *Commercial Appeal* story on the Memphis State confrontation between black students and the university administration quoted one student as expressing this sentiment: "Stop thinking about what is right or wrong or what is appropriate—but just do it, whatever it is, to achieve our demands."

This is the point at which all hell breaks loose on a campus, in a nation, in a family, in a human personality—when the basis of character judgment is not firmly fixed in what God has revealed he wants of men.

The sacred writings of Holy Scripture make crystal clear that the hallmark for Christian character judgment has two features. First, the frame of reference is Jesus Christ. His character, his personality qualities remain the standard by which we are to judge ourselves and others.

If some may think Saint Paul was hard on John Mark and others in passing judgment, let it be noted that he was even sterner with himself. Often he referred to himself as the chief of sinners. He wrote the Philippians that he did not count himself to have attained what he ought to be, but "I press toward the mark for the prize of the high calling of God in Christ Jesus." And to the Romans Paul wrote that God's intention for all men is that they each one become like Christ. Listen: "For God knew his own before ever they were, and also ordained that they should be shaped to the likeness of his Son, that he might be the eldest among a large family of brothers" (Romans 8:29).

C.S. Lewis in his *Screwtape Letters,* that famous imaginary correspondence between a senior and a junior devil on the subject of temptation and the opposing war aims of these spiritual forces of darkness and light, has Screwtape pen these significant lines:

[The Enemy] really *does* want to fill the universe with a lot of loathsome little replicas of Himself—creatures whose life, on its miniature scale, will be qualitatively like His own, not because He has absorbed them but because their wills freely conform to His. We [demons] want cattle who can finally become food; He wants servants who can finally become sons. We want to suck in, He wants to give out. We are empty and would be filled; He is full and flows over. Our war aim is a world in which Our Father Below has drawn all other beings into himself: the Enemy wants a world full of beings united to him but still distinct.

The first hallmark of Christian character judgment is that the standard is Christ: "The world, life, and death, the present and the future, all of them belong to you—yet you belong to Christ, and Christ to God" (I Cor. 3:23).

The second hallmark of Christian character judgment is that it is always made with a view, not to condemnation and destruction, but to redemption and salvation. The tone of the voice, the look in the eye when a character judgment is made make all the difference in the world in the result of a given judgment. Then the revelation is made of our motives in passing judgment— whether we are judging to cut someone down to a smaller size, or to prove how excellent or right we think we are, or to justify our actions in the sight of others when our consciences can't justify us, or, as Jesus always made character judgments, with a view to reformation of character and salvation of souls.

When the woman taken in adultery was brought to Jesus for judgment, he did not condemn her, not because there was nothing to condemn, for there was plenty to condemn, but because there was no more need for condemning since the woman herself had already given the most damning condemnation of such behavior in the highest court of human appeals—her own conscience. Jesus' word to her was, "Go, and sin no more."

Need we be reminded that character judgments are not just negative, critical judgments—especially Christian character judgments? Jesus was always looking for something praiseworthy in human nature, even though it be a wee, faint glimmer of good, and reacting positively to that. About a Roman centurion Jesus said, "I haven't found such faith in all the Holy Land among all God's chosen people as this so-called pagan has."

Once Robert Louis Stevenson was asked by a friend about his literary labors and successes, "Is fame all that it is cracked up to be?" "Yes," replied Stevenson, "it is when I see my mother's eyes."

There is character judgment that is positive as well as negative, encouraging as well as discouraging, and we are all called to exercise and express it. For failure at this point has far-reaching influence, not only on the developing character of our family and friends, but even on world history.

Arnold Toynbee, after a lifelong study of the history of the world, wrote: "My own view of history is that human beings do have genuine freedom to make their own choices. Our destiny is not pre-determined for us; we determine it for ourselves. If we crash, it will be because we have chosen death and evil when we were free to choose life and good. The three wars and the rising tide of mutual hatred make me wonder whether we are not going to wreck ourselves, as our predecessors wrecked themselves a number of times—as I see the pattern of the past."

The more confused and disturbed the times, the greater the demand for men and women of integrity. In an age of permissiveness, how precious those characters who consciences cannot be seduced by any siren song. God's standard for the characters of the men and women he needs today remains the same—Jesus Christ. We must be concise and consistent, courageous and compassionate, in our character judgments of ourselves and others, for from the human point of view, in the performance of this solemn, Christian duty lies the hope of mankind.

SIX

Christian Love Out of This World

Pilgrims of the Future

"Now Christ is the visible expression of the invisible God.... He is both the first Principle and the Upholding Principle of the whole scheme of creation" (Col. 1:14,17).

The earliest childhood recollection of Pierre Teilhard de Chardin, the French paleontologist and philosopher, was a terrifying memory. It was the event of his first haircut. Vernon Sproxton, in *Teilhard de Chardin,* quotes Teilhard's description of that experience: "My very first memory is of my mother clipping off a few of my curls. I picked one up and held it to the fire. It was burned up in a flash. Terrible grief overcame me. I learned that I was perishable."

The first haircut and curl-burning experience stirred the young Teilhard to begin a lifelong search for the durable. He became intrigued with a piece of iron from an old plough he picked up about the family farm in the south of France. It became his talisman, for in his childish understanding of reality, he thought nothing could be more durable than this wonderful substance. But, when he learned that even iron rusted and crumbled, he cried.

Soon afterward he transferred his interest to the rocks and stones he found in abundance in the mountain ranges of his native Auvergne. Surely here in the solid granite he had found something indestructible. So he became in manhood a paleontologist who traced in the rocks and fossils of the earth the developing plan and purpose of the Creator through the centuries and the millennia of evolving life.

Then surprisingly, during his successful archeological work in China when he was in his early forties, Teilhard suffered a season of depression and despair. He lost confidence in himself and in the significance of his labors. Finally, the depression passed, and as he emerged from the gloom of his doubts and despondency, it was the future, tomorrow, that came to dominate his thoughts. "What counted now was not reconstructing the past, reanimating the fossils; but the future," Sproxton writes in *Teilhard de Chardin*. "He came to speak of himself as a pilgrim of the future on the way back from a journey made entirely in the past. That future, he came more and more to believe, would disclose some direction and destination which would give shape to the whole of life and bring together into a harmonious whole the palpably diverse and discrete elements of mankind."

So he found, at long last, the durable and the secure for which his anxious and frightened heart had been searching, not in the iron and the rocks and the least perishable elements of God's creation in the material world, but in the discernable purposes of the Creator and his future.

Sproxton says that the writings of Teilhard reveal his conviction that "life must be judged, not from the point of view of the slime from which man has emerged, but from the greatness to which he may aspire. It is the oak tree which gives the acorn significance."

The passage of Scripture that became the organizing center for the life of Teilhard as a pilgrim of the future was the first chapter of Colossians. Here Saint Paul reaches the pinnacle of his thought on the nature and work of Christ. "Christ is the visible expression of the invisible God," writes Paul. But he goes further than this. Paul and other apostles had said this and more beforehand. Now Paul asserts that all things in the created universe were made through Christ and for Christ. It is Christ in whom is to be discerned the originating principle and the sustaining principle of the universe. He is the goal toward which all things move. Christ is the prototype of all men and women. What Christ was and is, God has destined that all people should become. Christ's redeeming death upon the cross is for the reconciliation of rebellious humanity to God and to all other people. And the Church—that community of people who have been gathered together by faith and love and obedience about the Crucified One—that body of people is the reconciling and unifying agency of God for the future. How wide the sweep, how high the reach, how propulsive into the future is the great apostle's thought!

There has emerged in the Church in recent years a theology of hope based on the future, not the past, the future of God. What God has ahead for the human family has come to dominate some of the best Christian thinking of our time.

Not only the theologians are becoming pilgrims of the future, but the most exciting, creative philosophers and politicians of our time are also among the pilgrims of the future. They see that future as laying hasty hands on our present and imploring us to follow its tugging.

Coach Lou Holtz of Notre Dame was asked by Volkswagen to write a letter to the next generation. Here's a part of what he wrote:

> During my teenage years, I was of the opinion that the future and security of this country would be dictated by the combat readiness of our military forces. However, as I grew older ..., I became increasingly aware that our greatest enemy is ourselves. I will never forget a cartoon of Pogo that said: "We have met the enemy and they is us." ... The vulnerability of most societies lies within. As long as we remain strong within, I feel our future is secure.
>
> ... I believe our focus of attention should be upon the future.

Norman Cousins, in the lead editorial of the first issue of his new magazine *World,* wrote:

> The compression of the whole of humanity into a single geographic area is the signal event of the contemporary era. The central question of that arena is whether the world will become a community or a wasteland, a single habitat or a single battlefield. More and more, the choice for the world's people is between becoming world warriors or world citizens.
>
> Perhaps the starkest discovery of our time is that our planet [like young Teilhard's curls] is not indestructible and that its ability to sustain life is not limitless. For the first time in history, therefore, the physical condition of the planet Earth forces itself upon human intelligence....
>
> ... Life is now imperiled not because of any failure of the cosmic design but because of human intervention.
>
> ... The banner now commanding the greatest attention [for the future] has human unity stamped upon it.

Now what does all this mean for us—this pressing pilgrimage into the future? Teilhard de Chardin's search for the durable and imperishable and his coming at last to be a pilgrim of the future? Saint Paul's proclamation of the Christian manifesto in terms of a future for mankind and the world in Christ? The reemergence in urgency of a theology of hope in God's future? The growing consciousness among all thoughtful and responsible people, young and old alike, of the heavy hand the future is now laying on us? What does all this mean?

For our personal life and daily work it means that becoming a pilgrim of the future is the way out of our present frustrations, disappointments, and despair. "Michelangelo, so a story goes, was asked once how he went about carving a head of Christ," Sproxton recounts in *Teilhard de Chardin.* "He replied that he saw the head of Christ already existing in the stone and it was a matter of chipping away the unwanted material." If we see our responsibilities in our place of work and study and service and artistic creation in terms of liberating Christ, already enshrined here and ordained from all eternity to emerge and rule, what an inspiring and liberating motivation for all our efforts.

It was once my privilege and joy to work on a church staff with a very remarkable woman. She was the church secretary and had been for twenty-five years before I came to the church as a pastor. She remained in that position for almost twenty years more. How often I wondered how we at the church could keep her, with the modest salary the church was paying, when her professional skills, quick intelligence, impeccable judgment, and personality endowments could demand three times as much in an executive position in the business world. How often I wondered how she kept cheerful and patient and courageous in spite of the ruffled feelings and unreasonable demands and the touchiness she was always running into among all of us with whom she had to deal.

How did she do it? Gradually I learned it was because she was a genuine pilgrim of the future. She really believed that God is sovereign in this world and that Christ is the first, last, and upholding principle of this universe. She believed that the future was in his hands and she would always serve him. Like Michelangelo, she had seen as her task that of removing the unwanted material so Christ could emerge in human lives and human relationships, in church programs and service for both time and eternity.

But see also what becoming a pilgrim of the future means toward our comfort and consolation for the losses we inevitably suffer on this earthly pilgrimage. Teilhard de Chardin spoke often of the "forces of diminishment" that waylay us. We lose by death beloved members of our family and trusted friends. Such losses are irreplaceable. Are we overwhelmed by the devastating diminishment we've suffered in our vulnerable little corner of the world?

Only a true pilgrim of the future can say with P.T. Forsyth as he wrote in *This Life and the Next* of the losses he had sustained: "I know that land beyond. Some of my people live there. Some have gone abroad on secret service there, which does not admit of communications. But I meet from time to time the commanding officer—the one in charge both here and there—and when I mention them to Him, He assures me all is well."

Finally, how rich with meaning is the concept of pilgrims of the future for the whole Church and our responsibility for the Church's emerging character in the future. How sad to read these days that statistics for the churches and denominations of America show that the congregations that are growing fastest are the narrowly dogmatic ones, those deeply rooted in their traditional past, still emphasizing their separateness and their differences from their Christian brethren from other traditions and refusing fellowship; while the congregations declining in numerical strength are those of an ecumenical spirit, open to new ideas and new people, and eager to serve contemporary needs with a relevant message and ministry.

The oldest Christian churches of Greece and Italy and Sicily show a strong Byzantine influence in their architecture and artistic symbolism, one of the most impressive features of which is the bright mosaic head of Christ set in the top of the center apse looking down on the people in worship. This pictorial mosaic in the Greek is called *Christos Pancrator* (Christ, Ruler over All). There before all worshipers, high above their heads, is the face of him through whom and for whom all things are.

In the consciousness of all Christ's disciples, his lordship over all the Church must increase. Divisions that are separating walls between his people must be obliterated. Dogmatic distinctions that perpetuate hostilities and obscure his truth must fall.

Let Christ's Church proclaim his gospel of the future. As Sproxton says of Teilhard's message: "He who stands at the End is with you in the Process. He is Love, and love is the only power which can achieve the convergence and unity of all mankind."

Sursum Corda. "Lift up your hearts!"

The Silence of God

"But he answered her not a word." (Matt. 15:23).

Isn't it puzzling—God's silence? His whole round world in an uproar—people sinning, little children neglected and suffering, evil smelling to high heaven, God's commandments broken, the beauty of his creation desecrated, polluted, wasted, people starving by the thousands, wars raging, even some of God's so-called ministries on television in angry argument with each other, hurling charges and countercharges about who's right and who's wrong—and God keeping a stony silence. Isn't it strange? Little wonder that God's ancient saint should be astonished at this unfathomable mystery and cry, "Why go I mourning because of the oppression of the enemy? ... Keep not thou silence, O God: hold not thy peace, and be not still, O God. For, lo, thine enemies make a tumult: and they that hate thee have lifted up the head."

And isn't it strange—Jesus' silence at the repeated, reverent entreaties of that poor Canaanite woman beseeching the Son of God to heal her sick daughter, "But he answered her not a word"? How unlike the sympathetic, compassionate Christ!

Do you remember that dramatic production of some years ago where the voice of God broke in on the radio every day for a week, jamming all the channels at an appointed time, the voice of God expressing himself, his pleasure and displeasure, with the way his world was being run? Would not a plan like that be much better, infinitely more fitting the power and prestige of the Lord of the universe, than God keeping an uncaring silence?

Now we must admit that it is thoroughly understandable why God would be silent sometimes with some people. When the prodigal son deliberately turns his back on his own home and, renouncing the life at his father's side, loses himself in the riotous living of a far country with never a letter home or a glance in its direction, how can the father speak to him? He's gone. He's out of earshot and spiritual range. There's no meeting of minds—no choice but silence. And the Gospels tell us that Christ was silent before Herod and Pilate. And there is little wonder. "Whence art thou?" asked Pilate. "But Jesus gave him no answer." What could he say to a Herod or a Pilate when the flippancy of the one and the brutal lust for power of the other had so corroded them that there was no true metal left on which his words could ring?

The Expositor's Dictionary of Texts notes:

> The scriptures, which are so responsive to some, are silent to others. Why? The extent to which the Bible is a revelation to any man or woman is conditioned by the moral character and distinctive principles of the person reading it. Among the influences in people which make the Bible a silent book to them is prejudice. If you bring a full pitcher to the spring, you can take no water away from it. If your mind is already made up to reject the Bible, it can give you no answers to your questions. Habitual indulgence in sin will also make the scriptures silent.

Yes, it is understandable that God should be silent sometimes with some people.

But the silence of God with his devoted servants and with us his earnest seekers for him—this is what troubles and baffles us. The broken, yet faithful, heart on whom life has unexpectedly sprung a trapdoor and all that was precious and beautiful is suddenly dropped out of life, and in bewilderment the faithful heart has prayed over and over, "Why, God, why?" and God has answered not a word. And that sufferer who feels his strength slowly slipping away, pleading in trust and resignation with the giver of all life and the sustainer of all health to rescue him, and while help is delayed and he slips farther into the slimy pit, all he gets from heaven above is uncaring silence. And that poor fellow who is fighting for a faith, pummeled by doubts, searching for some assurance of God's reality and of some evidence of God's interest in him as a person, getting for all his pains no clear answer from God, just the silent treatment. This is the silence of God that stymies us. How can we explain this strange silence of God?

Can we not say first of all that God is often silent because we or those about us are not ready for his answer? Take the case of Joseph when he was in prison in Egypt. Joseph prayed that he might be delivered from prison, but it pleased God to keep him there for a time that he might be a comfort to his fellow prisoners. And it may be so with us. God may have his own reasons for not granting you some timely blessing at once. God may be dealing with some other member of your family at the same time. He has not completed his purpose, and the delay should not distress or disturb you.

For Ann Lee, the mother of Robert E. Lee, those were hard years in Alexandria, Virginia, when she was left alone to care for her little family because she had a husband who did not carry well family responsibility. When financial worries pressed, and the cupboard was almost bare, and the whole weight of training and directing her children was on her slender shoulders alone, how often devout Ann Lee must have dropped to her knees and prayed for a merciful Providence to lighten her heavy load. And how the uninterrupted divine silence must have puzzled her! But God was working his purpose out. He was making a Robert E. Lee. Douglas Southall Freeman, in his biography of Lee, shows that across the years all who knew General Lee best traced those peerless qualities that made him great—his self-discipline, his sympathy, his gentleness, his strength under stern adversity—to his noble mother and those bleak Alexandrian years. Yes, sometimes God is silent because we are not ready and those about us are not yet ready for his answer.

And then, there's this: Sometimes God is silent because circumstances have to be rearranged and readjusted to bring greater benefits than we have ever dreamed of. How long was it that Saint Paul prayed for healing of some illness or physical defect, his "thorn in the flesh"? While the apostle prayed, God was silent. God never did answer that prayer save with a silent "no," for all the while God had something better in store for Paul. God was going to give Paul more grace, and when Paul knew that, he said he would rather keep the thorn and have the grace. The same thing is true in the case of the Canaanite woman who came asking Jesus to heal her daughter. The Lord gave her, at first, no encouragement at all, but the delays and hindrances he put in her path only increased her faith and made her more determined to get what she requested of him. She stands out as one of the great figures of all spiritual history. Her faith was being stretched and expanded and made glorious by the silence of God!

And let us not forget this—that God's gift to us of our freedom imposes upon God an obligation of some silence. All parents should understand this. We have our time when we can be vocal with our children and pass on to them something of our ideals and values for life, but the time comes when with the child grown into adult freedom, we parents must keep a discreet silence.

A few years ago some of us enjoyed watching "The Barchester Chronicles," an offering of public television's "Masterpiece Theatre," and some of you may remember what Anthony Trollope said in his novel *Barchester Towers* about that inept clergyman Dr. Stanhope, that though he had never intended not to influence his children's morals, yet he had been so idle about the matter that he had found no time for doing it, until the chance to do it had gone forever.

God gives his word to us in Christ. He sets us in his world where we may be nurtured by his Church, but he will not compel us. In granting us our freedom and complete spiritual autonomy, he has imposed upon himself some obligation of silence.

Also, God's decision to use us for proclaiming his word and influencing the development of his children has imposed an obligation of silence upon him. Suppose God were always shouting down our errors and drowning out our moronic babbling? But God is a God who believes in the principle of delegated responsibility. And one of the reasons for God's silence, says Henry Drummond, the popular Scottish lecturer, in one of his texts, *Spiritual Diagnosis,* is that "God offers men and women the glory and honor of sharing in His work and He wishes human souls to be graven with the marks of other human souls in all their free and infinite variety. No two leaves from a tree are the same, no two sand grains, no two souls. And as the universe would be a poor affair if every leaf were the counterpart of the oak leaf or the birch, so would the spiritual world present but a sorry spectacle if we were all duplicates of John Calvin."

Why is God silent on the great questions of heresy and orthodoxy that disturb the Church? One divine oracle, one thunderclap from heaven could settle any controversy. But no, that is not the divine pleasure. God has set a desire for truth in all his children's hearts, and each must seek it according to the light given him or her. And God's silence should temper us with both toleration and humility.

Years ago, when Drummond came to lecture in our American universities, his liberal theological views, his interest in science and the evolutionary hypothesis stirred some opposition in certain conservative quarters of the church. He was invited by Dwight L. Moody to speak at the conservative conference center in Northfield, Massachusetts. But shortly after his arrival there, a delegation waited on Moody and insisted that he question Drummond on the soundness of his faith before allowing him to speak. Reluctantly, Moody agreed to do it the following morning. The delegation questioned Moody right after breakfast as to his success:

"Did you see him?"

"Yes," said Moody.

"And did you speak to him about his theological views?"

"No," said Moody. "I did not. Within half an hour of his coming down this morning he gave me such proof of being possessed of a higher Christian life than either you or I that I could not say anything to him. You can talk to him yourselves, if you like."

God's momentous decision to use us in proclaiming his word and influencing the development of each immortal soul in its infinite variety has imposed on God an obligation of silence, which in turn points us in the direction of humility and toleration.

But finally—and certainly this is most important of all—silence is God's own chosen, clearest language for communicating with the human soul. We do not know him until we learn to "be still and know that he is God." The prophet Elijah, standing on the mountain, felt the earthquake, saw the raging fire, and heard the roaring wind, but the Lord was not in the earthquake, wind, or fire. Then there came to Elijah the "still small voice," or, as *The Interpreter's Bible* points out the original Hebrew rendering is more accurately translated, "a sound of gentle stillness." God, as defined in the *Westminister Shorter Catechism,* "is a spirit, infinite, eternal, and unchangeable in his being, wisdom, power, holiness, justice, goodness, and truth" and he speaks in the language of silence to the souls of men and women.

In "O Little Town of Bethlehem" we sing:

> *How silently, how silently the wondrous gift is given!*
> *So God imparts to human hearts the blessings of His heaven.*
> *No ear may hear His coming, but in this world of sin,*
> *Where meek souls will receive Him, still the dear Christ enters in.*

And for us the supreme significance of God's silence is that we, too, have need of silence in which he may speak to us.

The Eternal God

"The eternal God is thy refuge, and underneath are the everlasting arms."
(Deut. 33:27).

In his book *The Art of Survival,* Cord Christian Troebst tells about cases where people have been caught in a life or death emergency. The book shows how some survived because they were resourceful enough to make use of readily available supplies. Other did not survive because they were not resourceful enough to lay hold of and use the not-too-obvious, but nevertheless available, life-sustaining necessities.

There was the New York couple whose car was stranded in a snowstorm back in the winter of 1956-57. They found shelter in a roadside shed with plenty of fuel at hand to keep them warm. "The man tried to light a fire in the stove with his sodden matches, but did not succeed. When all his matches were spent, he and his wife wrapped themselves in their coats and some old rags they found there, and lay down to die," Troebst writes. They didn't think of using the car cigarette lighter to light the fire when the matches failed.

On the other hand, there was the American soldier in the jungles of Southeast Asia who kept himself alive for twenty-two days by eating insects, grasshoppers, worms, and butterflies.

Then there was the family touring the Grand Canyon whose car broke down when they turned off the main road onto a side road. But they survived the 124-degree heat, the thirst, and the hunger, and were finally rescued because they were resourceful enough to drink the water in the car radiator, smear their lips and cheeks with lipstick to prevent sun blistering, feed themselves on wax crayons they found in the car and a pot of glue made from milk products, send up a smoke signal by burning an oil-soaked tire, and bury themselves neck deep in sand for protection against the stifling heat. They were rescued just as they were about to give up hope.

Just as there is an art of physical survival in times of emergency, so there is an art of spiritual survival, too. Many people become spiritual casualties when caught in life's emergencies because they have not the resourcefulness to make use of the readily available, but not always too obvious, means of survival.

The Book of Deuteronomy describes the dramatic parting of Moses and the people of Israel. Moses knows that the time has come at last for him to die. He, who had liberated them from slavery in Egypt, led them safely through the wilderness with its dangers and hardships, delivered to them a moral law to order their personal and common lives, he, Moses—liberator, leader, lawgiver—soon will be with them no more. How will they survive? As his last great service to them, Moses gives his people this spiritual staff to lean upon in all life's emergencies: "The eternal God is thy refuge, and underneath are the everlasting arms."

For every conceivable spiritual emergency life-sustaining supplies are available if only we are resourceful enough to find and use them. Resourcefulness in such emergencies is always dependent on three things: (1) an understanding of the divine nature, (2) knowledge of how the Eternal operates in his universe, and (3) making an intelligent response to these available rescue resources.

First, it is necessary that we understand something of the divine nature. "The eternal God is thy refuge." There is a whole lot of meaning, not just words, packed in this declaration of Moses, "The eternal God is thy refuge." The definition of God in the *Shorter Catechism* affirms what Scripture principally teaches about the nature of God, namely, his spirituality: "God is a spirit."

The spirituality of the divine nature is further defined in the classical catechism answer by those three broad, mind-stretching terms: "infinite, eternal, and unchangeable." What do they mean?

"Infinite" means without limit in spatial existence as finite man is limited. Human beings are all limited to existence at one place at a time, to one moment at a time, to one thought in the forefront of consciousness at a time. God is infinite, unlimited in all these categories and ten thousand times ten thousand categories of which we cannot even conceive.

"Eternal" means without beginning or ending. As man has a birth-date and a death-date, so he is temporal; God has neither and is eternal. Isaiah sets this contrast in the familiar lines, "All flesh is grass.... The grass withereth, the flower fadeth.... But the word of our God shall stand for ever."

"Unchangeable" means constant, without change or fickleness or inconsistencies. God is forever constant and dependable. When ninety-year-old Albert Schweitzer was laid to rest in the Lambarene jungle, the African tribesmen gathered to weep and mourn for the passing of the compassionate healer who had given his life for their sakes. But the newspaper reports recorded that when the funeral was over, those momentarily moaning and wailing Africans turned to the river and soon were laughing and slapping one another on the back. As it is the nature of man to be changeable in mood, emotion, and even morality, so is it by complete contrast for the divine nature to remain unchanging.

There are two dangers we all run in our thinking about God. One is the danger, as J.B. Phillips puts it so well in his book *Your God Is Too Small,* that we draw our God "too small." We think of him as one who has nothing better to do than cater to our whims. We treat him like an errand boy or a bellhop: "Get me that job I'm praying for." "Straighten out for me that wayward child."

Or we treat him as a God of battles and ask his blessing on our armies alone.

Or we worship him as the God of a particular race or religion who is concerned with redeeming only those of a given skin pigmentation or who welcomes only those who are baptized a certain way or have been confirmed by the right bishop.

But the other error we tend to make, equally disastrous, is that we worship a God who is so large and latitudinarian that he is lost in the misty swirls of mysticism and syncretism. The words of our *Shorter Catechism* definition tend in that direction: "God is a spirit, infinite, eternal, and unchangeable." The danger is that they leave us with an impression of the divine nature as an oblong blur, a tranquil vacuum, an everlasting law of thermodynamics.

It is at this very point of escaping both the danger of having a God too vague and of having a God too small that the word and work of Jesus are so helpful to us. The fifteenth chapter of Luke's Gospel contains three brief stories like fine-cut jewels: the lost coin, the lost sheep, the lost son. Here we see the infinity, the eternity, the unchangeableness of God, not simply as philosophical propositions, but as these divine qualities impinge on individual human beings at the point of their deepest need.

As a woman who has ten coins and loses one of them or as a shepherd who has one hundred sheep and loses one of them is concerned over the single loss, and is busy searching for the lost, and is happy when the lost is found, so is God with his millions of children concerned when any one of them is separated from him by a rebellious spirit or by neglect. And God's joy is boundless when that child's spirit returns to him. The infinite God is not limited to a concern for a limited few. His infinite nature renders him capable of infinite compassion for an infinite number. Everyone is missed. Not one is surplus to infinite love.

More poignant and revealing still is the story of the prodigal son—the lost boy—who, when he comes to himself in the far country whence he has strayed from his father's house, finds that the father's love, though outraged and sinned against, remains steadfastly unchanged, eternally ready to receive him.

The divine nature of God is such that he is a "spirit, infinite, eternal, and unchangeable," impinging on every human being at every moment of his or her existence with inexhaustible resources for rescue in every emergency. "The eternal God is thy refuge, and underneath are the everlasting arms."

But it is not only necessary for us to understand something of the divine nature in order to avail ourselves of the resources at hand for survival in life's emergencies; we need also to understand something of the divine activity.

Moses told his people that they could have every confidence that in every emergency always there would be "the everlasting arms." What did Moses mean? Was he saying, "It doesn't make any difference what fool thing you do; God will take care of you. That is the way he acts in the world. You never need to bother about what is right or wrong"?

Remember who's talking. It is the stern lawgiver who gave his solemn oath that from God himself he had brought those commandments: Thou shalt not steal. Thou shalt not kill. Thou shalt not commit adultery.Thou shalt not covet. Thou shalt not bear false witness. Thou shalt have no other gods before me. Thou shalt keep the Sabbath day holy.

No! When Moses says, "underneath are the everlasting arms," he means the everlasting arms of the maker and sustainer of this moral universe, who will not act capriciously. He is unchangeable in his moral nature and activity. We can count on that.

Paul Scherer, the Lutheran pastor and teacher, says in *Event in Eternity* that the best way to draw a diagram of the divine activity in human history is to draw a circle and label it "God's will." Then draw another circle about that one and in the space between the concentric circles write "God's judgments." Then draw a third circle and label that area "God's grace."

All this means that at the heart and center of life there is operating the divine moral law. A man may give a glad obedience to this and so order his life to remain within this blessed inner circle. But a man may also rebel and break away from living his life according to the divine will. If he does, inevitably he runs headlong into God's judgments. Some men never get out of that second circle, but, Scherer says, "Beyond there is a third circle, drawn more widely still: the circle of God's grace, which somehow like two great arms includes the rest.... It means that in and through, over and above, the will and the judgment there is a mighty, healing something at work in the world; that when you and I have blundered about and come to the end of our resources, there are still open to us great stores of pardon and reservoirs of power which we cannot even begin to tap till we have despaired of our own."

What God is most active about in history, then, is rescue. And we all are like that poor woman Saint Luke described as having suffered from "a spirit of infirmity eighteen years, and was bowed together, and could in no wise lift up herself." But those everlasting arms are there, and they are able, just as able as we are feeble.

But human survival is dependent on a third factor. We need not only an understanding of the divine nature and divine activity; our survival hinges on our making an intelligent human response. The Scriptures are full of assurances, not only that the eternal purpose of God is rescue, but also assurances of the necessity of meeting God's requirement of repentance. The prodigal son must come to himself and say to his father from his heart, "Father, I have sinned against heaven, and before thee, And am no more worthy to be called thy son: make me as one of thy hired servants."

God is always ready to accept us, writes Bishop James Pike in his book *A Time for Christian Candor,* "to guide, to inspire, to comfort, to accept, to heal, to enrich; such barriers as there are to His thus operating in us, with us, and through us are in each of us and in our respective situations—not in Him."

Pike gives this illustration: The famous cable cars of San Francisco are powered by a cable that is always running under the open middle track. If one car is stopped and another is running, it is just because the grip-man in the running car has let the clutch down to connect with the moving cable. In the case of the stopped car, it is simply that the operator has not linked the car with the moving power.

When the emergencies of life find us struggling for survival, we should never forget that the supplies and powers to sustain us are close at hand: "The eternal God is thy refuge, and underneath are the everlasting arms."

But more often than not, survival depends on resourcefulness, a resourcefulness that must surely include some knowledge of the divine nature, an understanding of the divine activity in human affairs, and an intelligent response from us to our God.

Interpreting the Times

"To every thing there is a season, and a time to every purpose under the heaven: A time to be born, and a time to die" (Eccles. 3:1-2).

We are living in difficult and perplexing times. Martin Malachi says that people feel that "nothing seems to be working as it should." He writes in his book *Three Popes and the Cardinal:* "The judicial system does not work. The prison system does not work.... Control of drugs and pollution (air and ear) does not work.... Congress does not work.... Our cities do not work.... Marriage does not work.... Parenthood does not work.... Nothing, in fact, seems to work, to achieve at least a satisfactory minimum of its intended purpose."

The events of the last few weeks constrain us to add that millions of people in Eastern and central Europe no longer believe that communism works.

What's happening? Who of us understands the way our world is going? How are our times to be interpreted? What is the meaning behind the strange, startling events?

One of the most beloved Advent cantatas is Bach's "For unto Us a Child Is Born." John Mackay, in his book *Heritage and Destiny,* tells us that for "two centuries after the death of Johann Sebastian Bach the meaning of all his chorales remained obscure and enigmatic to the most ardent students of his music. The solution was not found until Albert Schweitzer discovered that the chorales must be interpreted in terms of the Biblical text which had inspired their composition." The most competent students and critics of Bach compositions for 200 years were "puzzled by his excessively abrupt antitheses of feeling." These enigmas were made plain only after Schweitzer matched the music with the Scripture texts that had inspired them.

Mackay, in *Heritage and Destiny,* offers us a clue to interpreting the puzzling events of our time: "The Bible, containing as it does the record of the self-disclosure of God and His will for human life, is the only Text that can explain to us our thoughts and aspirations, our aberrations and our tragedies. When this Text is studied the enigma of life's strange, meaningless music becomes plain, and the nature of our predicament is made clear to us. Modern culture went astray by giving to man the place that belongs to God. Let us therefore heed the prophetic words: 'Cease from man.'"

But how to apply the Scripture to the strange, sad melody of our fitful times? How wring from the Bible an intelligent divine interpretation of our times?

There came to the church office one morning a man who introduced himself as Brother Langford. He told me that he had come to give his testimony, but before he had finished, he also made his touch for some travel funds. He was under deep conviction, he said, that we were living "in the latter days," and he quoted his Scripture texts to prove his point.

Brother Langford said that a prophet of God named Terrell, in Dallas, Texas, had revealed that God was sending a great famine in 1975 because of the exceeding wickedness of the world. Again, he quoted texts at random to prove the point. But God, in his mercy, was establishing three havens in the United States. One was in Alabama, around Fort Payne, twenty-five miles square. Another was in the neighborhood of Brownwood, Texas. And the third place of refuge he mentioned I've forgotten.

The people were already pouring into these places, according to Brother Langford. "God has revealed to my wife, " he said, "that she should go to Fort Payne, and I'm on my way there now to join her and my four daughters. I've been in prison out in California. I lived in sin, but God came to me and changed my life. My mother came to see me in prison. She had on one of those abomination pantsuits. The Bible says it's an abomination for a woman to wear pants. [Again he quoted text for this judgment.] Some people say I'm a 'clothesline preacher.' I can't help it. If it's in the Bible, I preach it. My mother is a good woman, but if she transgresses the word of God, she's going to be damned."

Finally, Brother Langford made his pitch for me or Idlewild Church to finance his travel from Memphis to Fort Payne, Alabama. When I signaled my coolness to his proposition, he handed me a slip of paper on which he had written two Scripture texts describing dire calamities to come and a three-word exhortation: "Repent or perish."

Now, I can't believe that the Scriptures can be used to interpret our times through any such hopscotch method of picking random passages and putting them together to predict coming dire events of the latter days or the next few days. This is to misuse the Bible, to handle it as a guidebook for sorcery.

The basic biblical principle I believe in for interpreting our time and all times is expressed in the Advent doctrine. The Advent doctrine affirms that this is God's world. Both the physical universe—the creatures made in God's image who inhabit the earth—and the historic drama composed of the events of men's lives are God's world.

But God did not make his world and then just tuck it away in a corner of his universe and go off, leaving it to its own devices. He comes in judgment and in salvation. He came in the past; he will come again and again in the future. He is coming now, in our present. This is the Bible story.

But the nature of his Advent, or coming—past, present, and future—is not some mysterious, strange phenomenon, predictable or unpredictable. The nature of his coming is supremely revealed in the birth of the babe in Bethlehem who grew to manhood as Jesus of Nazareth.

The words Jesus spoke about God and the way Jesus treated people and accepted the experiences of his life as told in the gospel story reveal the ultimate principles of God's love, his righteousness, his justice, and his mercy. These, and only these, will always characterize God's coming.

There is no magic, no legerdemain, no soothsaying, no literal reenactment of ancient predictions about God's advents. Though men cannot know the time or the exact nature of God's coming in judgment and salvation, nevertheless always his coming will be as the Scriptures have revealed in an increasing fullness of God's love and righteousness and mercy and justice. God cannot contradict his revealed moral character.

The Scriptures are given us, then, not to foretell events, but that we may know the truth about God and about ourselves, that we may recognize the right and the merciful and love it and do it. As Thomas Carlyle put it: "Our grand business undoubtedly is, not to see what lies dimly at a distance, but to do what lies clearly at hand."

The approach of the comet Kohoutek in the Advent skies stirred up among some people an end-of-the-world panic as astronomical spectacles always have. One man called Dr. Kenneth Franklin, the astronomer, at his office at the Hayden Planetarium in New York, saying he had heard that Kohoutek was going to collide with the earth. "Listen," the man said. "I have a mortgage payment due on my house and the kids' tuition to pay, and if it is all going to be over soon, I'd like to go out and have a good time." Dr. Franklin told the man that he had better pay his bills.

To give up before threatening catastrophe, real or imagined, is surely not the Christian way of life. But neither is the Christian called to overcome evil through joining forces, however temporarily, with greater evil, but to seek to overcome evil with good, in the Christ-like way of love.

The Christophers have a radio program called "The People Who Are Changing the World." The biblical Advent doctrine would change that title slightly to read, "The People through Whom God Is Changing His World."

Are you and I among that company?

The Secret and the Known

"The secret things belong unto the Lord our God: but those things which are revealed belong unto us and to our children for ever, that we may do all the words of this law" (Deut. 29:29).

Have you ever noticed how quickly your interest picks up when someone whispers to you, "Let me tell you a secret"? Just let someone beckon you to hold your ear a bit closer while he speaks softly behind the back of his hand, and your attention stands on tiptoe.

Why are we all so interested in secrets? I'm afraid it is one sign of our Original Sin. We want to know what we are not supposed to know or what others don't know, because, in our own thinking, it exalts us above others. It puffs up our pride to be in the know. But our interest in learning secrets is also an indication of the divinity God has set in our hearts, that spark of eternity that has propelled the questioning soul of man up from the slime of the cosmos to wrest from nature the answer of one secret after another, to think God's thoughts after him. Man's interest in the secret, the unknown, the mysterious, is indicative of both his sublimity and his degradation.

Nowhere has the secret, the unknown, been more intriguing to the mind of man than in the realm of religion. In expressing his religious instinct, man has universally dramatized the secret and mysterious and enshrined it in his religion.

At the very heart of Hebrew temple worship was that *mysterium tremendum,* the holy of holies, a small, secret, darkened room into which no person was permitted to enter save one man, the high priest, and he on only one appointed high day in the year. The ancient Greeks had a religion that taught that the messages of the gods were inscribed in secret code on the veins of oak leaves and only the priest, learned in such secret crafts, could interpret the Olympian pronouncements to mortals. In the old mystery religions so-called divine secrets were revealed in the initiation ceremonies of the neophytes. Only one who had been initiated knew the secret, divine wisdom.

As the Pharisees of Jesus' day kept demanding from him a sign, saying, "Show us a sign from heaven"—a startling, secret revelation—so people today are still demanding of religion that it satisfy their insatiable curiosity about the secret, the mysterious. Witness the sects to which the multitudes flock where the stock in trade is talking in unknown tongues or searching the Scriptures for secret, hidden prophecies of startling events about to take place in the immediate future.

A few years ago I fell into conversation with a chance traveling companion. He was a very intelligent man whose obsession was searching the Scriptures for obscure passages that he pieced together and in some mysterious manner spliced with the dimensions of Egypt's Great Pyramid, coming out with prophecies he said had been fulfilled concerning Adolf Hitler and the Second World War, a clear prediction of the date the Third World War would break out, and, wonder of wonders, the precise moment God had in mind for finishing off this little show of world history! What that fellow had a big dose of we all have in more or less degree. People everywhere have an insatiable curiosity about the secret things of religion.

So Moses' farewell words to the children of Israel, which we read from the book of Deuteronomy, are quite pertinent for us: "The secret things belong unto the Lord our God: but those things which are revealed belong unto us and to our children for ever, that we may do all the words of this law." When Moses—the man who had seen God face to face, who had put off his shoes on the holy ground before the burning bush, who had communed with God in the smoking, shaking mountain, and whose face had shone from the glory of that experience—came to the end of his life and bid goodbye to the people whom he had loved and liberated, he gave them as his final advice: "The secret things belong unto the Lord our God: but those things which are revealed belong unto us and to our children for ever, that we may do all the words of this law."

In our religion there are two elements: the secret and the revealed, the known and the unknown. Moses' word to us is that we concentrate on what has been revealed, rather than bothering too much about the secret and unknown. Mark Twain said that he had never been too bothered about those portions of the Bible he could not understand; it was the part he could understand that gave him the most trouble!

Well, what is the revealed and not secret in our religion? First there is the moral law. This is what Moses was talking about specifically. "Don't trouble yourself about the deep secrets of God, which you can't understand," Moses is saying. "The ten commandments he gave us should occupy all your religious interest and zeal. Just major in keeping them. Worship the one, true God. Don't make any idols or images to use in worship, for this leads to wrong impressions, for God is a spirit. Be reverent before him in word, thought, and deed. Remember the Sabbath day, one day out of seven, to keep it holy. Honor and respect your parents. Never lie; never steal; never commit adultery; be faithful to the life partner God has given you. Never take the life of another human being. Be content with your lot in life and guard your heart from covetousness.

"Let this law that God has revealed to you be the principal concern in your religion, rather than speculating on why he gave this law and not another, or how God's righteous judgments will ultimately be worked out."

What else is revealed and not secret in our religion? That the way to come to God is through Jesus Christ, his divine Son. Did not Jesus say, "I am the way, the truth, and the life: no man cometh unto the Father, but by me?" He is the Alpha and the Omega, the beginning and the end of all human striving, and he holds the keys of life and death.

The deep secret of how the great Creator could be the created, of how divinity could become humanity, of how the Eternal could enter into time God has not revealed. Nor has he made known the great mystery of just how the Savior's sacrificial death could atone for the whole sinful race or by what secret process his broken body was raised from the tomb and given glory. These are secret things that belong to God, but the revelation of Christ's heavenly beauty and his saving power for lost sinners God has made known and given to us.

What else is revealed and not secret in our religion? That the way God comes to us is by his Holy Spirit. "Nothing is more certain," said Herbert Spencer, the English philosopher, "than that we are ever in the presence of an infinite energy from which all things proceed." Who could doubt this who has lived through a springtime and watched while suddenly, miraculously, the stripped and barren trees slip over their uplifted arms glorious green garments of ten thousand times ten thousand leaves and the flowering shrubs burst forth in all the rainbow's hues? How that resurrection power of the springtime operates is a deep mystery well-nigh incomprehensible to us, but that it does is revealed and known by all.

The Gospels reveal the fact of the Incarnation, the coming of the Son of God in human form, and the Book of Acts reveals the fact of the coming of the Holy Spirit with power into the human lives of those disciples as they waited in Jerusalem.

"Wait for the promise of the Father," said Jesus. "Ye shall receive power, after that the Holy Ghost is come upon you: and ye shall be witnesses unto me both in Jerusalem, and in all Judea, and in Samaria, and unto the uttermost part of the earth." They waited—that is, they trusted and believed and prayed and stayed in the fellowship—and the promised power came. By the Spirit of the living God they became the few mighty ones who turned the world upside down.

It is not revealed to us by what mysterious, unseen avenues and agents the Almighty operates—whether by guardian angels or other heavenly messengers. But what is revealed and known to us is that prayer, worship, study of God's word, trustful waiting on the Lord, relying upon him rather than self, and remaining in the fellowship of the saints—these are the channels through which the power of God comes into our lives, transforming our weakness into strength and blessing us with personal power, peace, and poise. This is the testimony of all the saints of all the ages.

Furthermore, our text reminds us that these revealed things of God—the moral law, the Redemption through Christ, the channels for the indwelling of the Spirit—are not only the known and revealed things of God, but they are what he has committed to us, what he has made our own, what he has given to us and to our children for our inheritance, forever. "The secret things belong unto the Lord our God: but those things which are revealed belong unto us and to our children for ever."

And yet we won't claim our inheritance. We had rather consult astrologers or spiritualists or fortunetellers or delve into occult, mysterious speculations than take the plain path of religion revealed to us. For me the greatest tragedy of our present time is the repudiation of our great traditions. How many of us will now sincerely pray with John Baillie, as put forth in *A Diary of Private Prayer,* "Grant, O Father, that I may go about this day's business with an ever-present remembrance of the great traditions wherein I stand and the great cloud of witnesses which at all times surround me, that thereby I may be kept from evil ways and inspired to high endeavour"?

"The secret things belong unto the Lord our God: but those things which are revealed belong unto us and to our children for ever, that we may do all the words of this law." Here is the purpose of the revealed things of God that he has made known to us and given us and our children for our inheritance: that we may do all the words of the divine proclamation.

Joseph Parker writes in *The People's Bible:*

> A word is to become a deed: a thought is to be embodied in expressive action.... The architect draws his plans not that they may be exhibited as pictures but that they may be built up into visible and useful edifices. If the builder has taken the architect's plans, framed them in gold, and hung them up in the best room of his house, he has not honoured the plans but dishonoured them.... Have we not framed the law of God and made a picture of it and worshipped the letter with a species of idolatry? What have we done with the Bible? We have published it in letters of gold; we have bound it in richest morocco; ... but where is the mansion of a noble, holy, and useful life? We received the law that we might "do" it; if we have failed in the doing our admiration is hypocrisy and our loudest applause is but our loudest lie.

The Lord of Glory, Jesus Christ, has come, and we have professed our faith in him as our divine Lord and personal Savior, but have we made real our profession by doing what he commands?

Jesus said, "Not every one that saith unto me, Lord, Lord, shall enter into the kingdom of heaven; but he that doeth the will of my Father which is in heaven."

Let the word of the Lord prevail!

Your Portrait of God

"And Moses prayed, 'Show me thy glory'" (Exod. 33:18).

I was visiting with a friend who showed me a number of water color paintings he had done. They were all beautiful. As I stood silently admiring each picture, my friend talked of how he had painted them. "Our class," he said, "would go on cross-country jaunts to find subjects. When we had selected some scene or landscape to paint, all of us would go to work, each one painting the same thing. But when we got through, no two pictures would be alike. Sometimes there would be the greatest difference between the finished water colors, and yet each was a recognizable likeness of the subject."

Now, why the difference? Because each person, however skilled he or she might be, was short of perfection. No one could make an exact copy of the subject. And then each student brought a varying degree of talent and learning in water color painting to bear on the task, so that some pictures were more striking likenesses than others. And though each painted the same subject, each had a slightly different point of view. Each saw it from a little different angle. This was true of each student, not only objectively, but subjectively. Because of varying temperament and experience, what one could and would see, another could not or would not see. And so great differences are always apparent in the finished pictures of the most competent artists, even if they paint the same subject.

What a parallel there is here for us in our religious life! How varying are our separate views of God! No two of us worship the same God in the sense that no two of us have exactly the same conception of his nature, the same knowledge of his person, the same convictions of who he is and what he demands of us. To put it bluntly, but really and graphically, all of us have our own, separate portraits of God, painted on the canvas of our souls, and that God, as each of us knows him and understands him, that God is the God each worships, serves, and obeys.

If this were not so, how could we account for such a wide variety of behavior and conduct on the part of sincere Christians? One Christian worships a God who will not let him enjoy his Sunday dinner until he has shared it with a hungry brother, while another Christian, a member of the same congregation, sits placidly in worship Sunday after Sunday and then indulges herself in all sorts of extravagances the rest of the week, refusing to lift a finger as all about her men, women, and children suffer from malnutrition and disease.

None of us believes in worshiping idols. The second commandment forbids the worship of God by means of or through any graven image—of man, beast, or celestial creature. Our Protestant sensitivities are outraged by images and statues put in churches. We don't even believe in the icons of our Greek Orthodox Christian brethren, those sacred pictures used in their worship. For us "God is a Spirit: and they that worship him must worship him in spirit and in truth."

And yet, as John Calvin himself said: "The mind of man is ... a perpetual manufactory of idols.... The mind of man, being full of pride and temerity, dares to conceive of God according to its own standard; and being sunk in its own stupidity, and immersed in profound ignorance, imagines a vain and ridiculous phantom instead of God.... The mind then begets the idol, and the hand brings it forth."

Therefore, though we may restrain our hands from bringing forth an idol, we cannot get away from forming some mental image of God. We each paint some portrait of the God we worship in the sanctuary of our souls, and no matter how vague, sketchy, or misshapen an image of deity that spiritual portrait may be, to us it is our God.

And how important it is for each of us that this personal portrait of God be a reasonably true likeness of the Eternal God. They can't all be identical, but each portrait should be a faithful likeness. Of course, we do not make or unmake God by our soul's picture of him, any more than the actual beauty of a lovely woman is marred or enhanced by whether or not her portrait painter does a good job. God remains eternally the same, but oh, the subtle, the persuasive influence of our soul's portrait of God on our own lives!

Oscar Wilde's fanciful work *The Picture of Dorian Gray* tells of the remarkable affinity between a beautiful portrait and the handsome young man depicted in the portrait at the zenith of his youthful strength and beauty and charm. The amazing affinity between portrait and subject is this: Instead of the portrait's remaining unchanged through the years as all normal portraits should while the man himself is marked and broken by his experiences and the toll of time, the strange portrait of Dorian Gray changes year by year while the man continues in the full flush of youth and beauty. When Dorian Gray spurns the pure and unselfish love of a young actress and breaks her heart, the portrait shows a hard line developing about the mouth, but the man remains unchanged. When Dorian Gray cheats and steals and lies and debauches himself and others, the portrait acquires a greedy look, a deceiver's eye, a dissipated countenance, but Dorian Gray looks as young and pure and innocent as ever. Whatever Dorian Gray does, thinks, becomes in his own soul is immediately registered on that fateful portrait hung and shrouded in the attic of his house.

Now this fanciful story reminds us of this fact of human experience: There abides a deep and unerring affinity between the portrait of God that hangs in a person's soul and that person's character. Each one of us is molded, made, subtly changed by his personal picture of God. Whatever lines and color of faith, of conviction, of knowledge of God are painted into our soul's portrait of the deity we worship fashion our character and our conduct.

Look at Saul of Tarsus, that haughty Pharisee who had no time or taste for gentile dogs. Behold that cruel and relentless persecutor of the new sect of Christians. Suddenly we see him leave off persecuting and begin preaching to the gentiles that Christian gospel of salvation. What happened? Why, there came a sudden change in the portrait of God in Paul's soul.

How important it is for each one of us that this personal portrait of God be a reasonable likeness of the Eternal God. Our character, our conduct, our very dispositions are subtly changed and wrought out by those personal portraits of God.

"If your conception of God is radically false," writes Archbishop William Temple in *Readings in St. John's Gospel,* "then the more devout you are the worse it will be for you. You had much better be an atheist. It is just as much idolatry to worship God according to a false mental image as by means of a false metal image."

How are we going to perfect those portraits of God that hang in the chapels of our souls and on which so much depends? By a closer study of the subject, of course. By a more ardent application of ourselves to the divine artistry.

First, we need to go to Moses and get his help. That incident from Moses' life we read in our Scripture lesson should be highly helpful to us. Moses says to God, "Show me thy glory." Here is the desire of every person who is the least bit inclined to see God: "Show me thy glory." So one of the disciples of Jesus, Philip, says to Jesus, "Shew us the Father, and it sufficeth us."

But for Moses as a religious leader the problem was doubly pressing. Had he not just come from that disheartening and disgusting experience of seeing his own people bow themselves before the golden calf they had made with their own hands out of their melted-down golden trinkets? Moses knew his own people's weakness, their need for tangible evidence of the God they worshiped. Moses knew the time had already come once, and would come again, when he would be like that minister routed out of bed at midnight by a desperately disturbed parishioner who beat on the minister's front door, grabbed the half-waked man by the shoulders, and fiercely demanded, "Tell me something about God, not what you have read, not what you have heard somebody else say, not what you think, but tell me something you know about God."

"Show me thy glory," cries Moses out of a consciousness of his own and his people's need. He needed to know. We all do.

What is God's response to Moses' earnest demand, "Show me thy glory"? Is it a theophany in gorgeous colors and celestial forms? No. The Lord causes his servant to hear the name of the Lord proclaimed. "And the Lord passed by before him, and proclaimed, The Lord, The Lord God, merciful and gracious, longsuffering, and abundant in goodness and truth, Keeping mercy for thousands, forgiving iniquity and transgression and sin, and that will by no means clear the guilty; visiting the iniquity of the fathers upon the children, and upon the children's children, unto the third and to the fourth generation."

When Moses says, "Show me thy glory," God's response is to impress the soul of his servant with the moral and ethical excellence of God's character. And Moses, his face shining, brought back from the Mount for his people, not an image in stone or metal, but a moral code of righteousness, justice, and mercy that they might know God and see his glory.

So for us, God will be perceived, not in magical incantations, not in gorgeous rituals of worship, not in ecstatic visions, but in moral and ethical uprightness. The pure in heart, the righteous in purpose are the ones who see God.

And then we need to come to Jesus, to God incarnate, to perfect the painting of those portraits of God that hang in the chapels of our souls, and we must stay ever close to that Master. Moses helps us to see that only the person who knows God morally knows God truly. Jesus shows us the merciful, forgiving heart of that righteous Father. The best news mortal tongue can tell is that God is like Jesus Christ. Saint Paul said that we behold "the light of the knowledge of the glory of God in the face of Jesus Christ."

To perfect our personal portraits of God, we must become close students of the Christ of the Gospels. Too long has the Bible been for us what Saint Augustine said it was for the Jews, when that church father called the Jews "the librarians of the Christian church because they furnished us with a book of which they themselves made no use." Far too many of us have been librarians, keepers of the book, rather than students of it.

But we must be more than students of the Christ of the Gospels. We must become disciples of the living Christ today. Knowledge is perfected only through action. It's by doing God's will as revealed in Christ that we really know him. Though we memorize all four Gospels word for word and yet do not step forth in true discipleship to follow Christ, we can never know in our own souls the God he came to reveal. It's by putting to the test of experiment and experience the moral and ethical truths revealed by God's word, comprehended by the mind, accepted by the will, and done by the individual, that we really know him as he is. "Truth is in order to Goodness."

The Eternal God—who can know him? Who can search out all his goodness or exhaust the excellence of his ways? Is it an impossible task for all human striving? Has not Job said, "Canst thou by searching find out God? canst thou find out the Almighty unto perfection? It is as high as heaven; what canst thou do?"

But it has pleased God to give us some glimpses of his glory. And there is that secret artist in the soul of each one of us who's always at work at his portrait of the Almighty. Those portraits, true or false, crude or masterly done, have a profound influence on our character, our conduct, our disposition, even our eternal destiny.

So, whoever we are—the farmer in the field, the student at her desk, the salesperson behind the counter, the mother in the home, the pioneer away out on the frontiers of civilization—each in his or her own way can and should always be searching for new truth and new knowledge of him whose glory we would paint on the canvas of our souls.